THE LAST LIGHT OF DAY

THE JAMIE JOHANSSON FILES

BOOK 1

MORGAN GREENE

Book Cover Design by EbookLaunch.com

ALSO BY MORGAN GREENE

Bare Skin (DS Jamie Johansson 1)
Fresh Meat (DS Jamie Johansson 2)
Idle Hands (DS Jamie Johansson 3)

Angel Maker (DI Jamie Johansson 1)
Rising Tide (DI Jamie Johansson 2)
Old Blood (DI Jamie Johansson 3)
Death Chorus (DI Jamie Johansson 4)
Quiet Wolf (DI Jamie Johansson 5)
Ice Queen (DI Jamie Johansson 6)
Black Heart (DI Jamie Johansson 7)

The Last Light Of Day (The Jamie Johansson Files 1)
The Mark Of The Dead (The Jamie Johansson Files 2)

THE LAST LIGHT OF DAY

CHAPTER
ONE

The girl was just fourteen, but she had already killed.

She could even still taste the blood on her lips. Dried now, crusting on her skin, but still fresh enough that she could feel the spray if she closed her eyes tight.

She steadied her breathing, seeing nothing through the hood they had over her head. All she knew was that she was in the back of a vehicle. A van, she thought, considering the cold floor under her bare hamstrings. The cotton dress they'd put her in was freshly washed and itchy, stiff and barely clean from the sweat and blood washed out of it.

Where they were taking her, she didn't know. She didn't know anything except that the men with her were going to kill her, or worse. And then, a thought seized her. How hard would she have to slam her head into the steel between her naked feet to end it all right now? Did she have the strength? The time?

Her hands were bound behind her back, and she was weak. So weak.

But she knew she had to act soon, do something, or her fate would be sealed. Another girl, disappeared into the night, never to be seen again.

'Water,' she croaked.

The man behind her – she could smell his cheap aftershave, overpowering and pungent, the kind that lays on your senses like a wet, putrid blanket – grunted a little. 'Hungh?'

'Water, please,' the girl said again, voice strained and hoarse.

The man laughed a little. Amused.

The girl sagged, lolling forward and then to the side.

She felt a heavy hand on the back of her neck, pulling her back into a sitting position.

But she was limp now, falling whichever way the bouncing of the van pushed her.

She coughed, muted at first, and then harder, more violently. A hacking, wheezing, throat stinging cough.

The man swore, grabbing the hood and roughly tearing it from her scalp, taking hair with it.

She pushed through the pain, coughing still, eyes swivelling in her head as she fell sideways once more.

The guy, fat and hairy, panted as he got to one knee, holding her upright by the side of her face while he fumbled the cap from a bottle of water.

His thumb pinched her ear, his pudgy, clammy fingers sinking into the flesh around her jaw and throat.

She felt the hard rim of a water bottle pressed to her lips and drank greedily, slurping it down.

The guy told her to go slowly, she'd have to piss herself otherwise. But the water didn't matter. It was something else she wanted.

A quick twist of the head pulled her cracked lips from the bottle and one of those clammy fingers slid into her mouth.

Before he knew what was happening, she bit down, hard, her teeth grazing the cool, smooth metal of a ring as she did.

His scream threatened to burst her eardrums, his other hand flinging the bottle away and taking a fistful of her hair, pulling hard.

But before her teeth came free, they met in the middle with a hard click and she felt his blood explode into her mouth, pour down her chin.

He wailed and fell backwards and the van swerved a little, the driver shocked and yelling over his shoulder.

This was her chance. Her only chance.

The girl got to her knees and then sprang to her feet, leaping out of reach of the fat man's grabbing hand.

There, ahead of her, the handle for the back doors of the van. She'd only get one chance at this, and turned so her back was to it, reaching up behind her with her bound hands, taking hold of it.

She saw the man's eyes widen in the darkness of the

interior, his blood splashed around his knees, glinting black. And then she pulled.

The mechanism clicked and a rush of cold air hit her in the back.

A creak of metal.

The doors swinging wide.

She tried to turn, to see, but she couldn't, the motion of the vehicle pulling her clear of it.

For a moment, she was flying, free in the cold night air, drinking it in, grinning through the blood.

And then she hit the ground, the rough tarmac tearing at her exposed skin.

She let out a sharp scream through gritted teeth, rolled, rolled, rolled to a stop. She raked in a painful breath knowing something, maybe everything, was broken, and looked up through one eye. The tail lights of the van flared as it began to slow, but then quelled suddenly as the van seemed to accelerate again, driving away into the night.

Was it leaving her? Was she free?

She struggled to one knee, trying to get up. Run. She had to run. Had to run now, before they came back, before they—

But she never got to finish the thought.

Headlights flooded the ground around her, the screech of tyres filling her ears a moment before the impact flung her up over the bonnet and sent her careening through the air.

She caught one final glimpse of the night sky above,

studded with stars, tiny pinpricks of light stretching in all directions. Beautiful, she thought. So beautiful. She'd forgotten how beautiful it was, the night sky. She'd not seen it in so long.

A smile spread across her lips, her eyes filling with tears of joy.

And then she hit the ground, and the darkness came all at once.

CHAPTER
TWO

The man was about forty-five. He was lying face down in the middle of a field north of Stockholm and there was a beetle crawling across his pasty naked bottom. Its carapace was shining black in the weak summer sunlight, the days now waning into autumn with the end of August in sight.

Överinspektör Jamie Johansson of the National Operations Department of Sweden watched the bug as it meandered its way towards the shadiest spot it could find, wondering if this man, too, would be castrated, as the last ones had been.

'What do you think, *chef?*' Behnsson asked. He was one of her konstapels, young and hungry and full of ideas. Most of them rash and not thought through. She was training him, but it was proving difficult.

Jamie sighed and pushed upwards from her crouched position, looking around the field. 'I think he's dead,' she replied, trying not to be too curt. It'd been a year since she'd been in this job, but she still didn't much like being in charge of a team. Well, that wasn't true. She didn't much like being the person everyone asked their stupid questions to. Being in charge of a team wasn't all bad. Definitely meant less paperwork, which was just fine with her.

'Good observation,' Behnsson replied, pushing his wavy hair out of his eyes. It was fluttering a little in the breeze.

'Don't be glib,' Jamie said coolly.

'I wasn't.'

She didn't feel like arguing.

'So, fourth body,' Behnsson mused, hands on hips. 'What are you thinking?'

Jamie looked at him, wondering why the fuck she brought him, exactly. Oh, that's right, because her other konstapel, Margo, was even worse. And Jamie's arse was still sore from the last brown-nosing she provided.

'What do you think?' Jamie asked instead. 'You always seem to have a theory.'

He drew a slow breath, as though to build up to a grand reveal. 'The castration strikes me as an act of anger, of real malice. This is a true act of violence. The killer targeted these men specifically, wanted them to suffer.'

'You gathered that from the fact that someone hacked their balls off with a saw? God, you're astute. Whose nephew are you again?'

'Nephew?' Behnsson asked, shaking his head. 'I don't ... my uncle's name is Ulrik?'

Jamie sighed, her phone thankfully buzzing in her pocket. *'Ja?'* she said, answering it.

'Chef,' her other konstapel, Margo, said. 'Got a minute?'

'What's up?' Jamie asked, watching as her team of crime scene technicians finally made their trek across the field from the road towards them, white overalls pulled down to their waists, aluminium flight cases in hands, cameras around their necks.

'There's a lady on the phone,' Margo said. 'She keeps asking for you. Called five times already this morning.'

'Tell her I'm busy.'

'She said it's urgent. Said she absolutely *has* to speak to you. Says you'll want to take the call.'

Jamie's brow furrowed. Out of the corner of her eye, Behnsson was getting down on his hands and knees, either to try to get a better look at the castration, or try and find that beetle. 'What's her name?' Jamie asked.

'She wouldn't tell me.'

Jamie sighed. 'Tell her if she wants to talk to me, she can leave a message and—'

'She's not going to stop. She said that.'

Jamie ground her teeth, waving the CSTs over. They continued to dawdle, laughing as they approached. 'Fine, fine. She on the line now? Can you connect her?'

Before Jamie even finished saying it, the line clicked and then there was a little bit of static.

'*Hej, det här är Överinspektör Jamie Johansson,*' Jamie said.

'Jamie? Is that you?'

That voice. The use of her name. Her skin erupted in gooseflesh, her voice catching in her throat. 'Mum?'

'Jamie ... it's been ... um ... sorry ... Hi, how are you?'

Jamie stepped away from the body and the CSTs. They knew what they were doing. 'I'm ... I'm fine. What's ... what ...' She resisted the urge to ask, "What do you want?" So instead, she said, 'Is everything alright?'

'Does a mother need an excuse to call her daughter?'

Yes, Jamie thought. You probably do. 'No, no. I just ... It's been a few years, and ...'

'I know. I tried to call, but your number didn't work anymore.'

'I moved to Sweden.'

'Well, I know that now. Didn't think to tell your mother?'

Jamie bit her lip. 'Must have slipped my mind.'

'You're so like your father,' she laughed a little.

Jamie bristled, clearing her throat. 'Look, I'm right in the middle of something. Can I call you back later, or—'

'I need your help.'

There it is. 'Oh,' was all Jamie said. 'Not sure what I can do, being in a different country and everything.'

'You're not going to ask what's wrong?'

'You're not going to ask how I am?'

There was silence from her mother. Then, 'I don't want to fight.'

'Then maybe you shouldn't have called.' Damn, even Jamie thought that was cold.

Her mother drew a rattling breath. 'I wouldn't ask if I wasn't desperate. And ... there's no one else. No one we'd trust. It's important, okay?'

'We? Who's we?' Jamie asked.

More silence.

'Mum?'

'Me and my husband.'

Jamie blinked in astonishment. 'Did you just say your husband? When did you get married?'

'Two years ago.'

'I didn't even know you were seeing someone,' Jamie said, still shocked.

'You would have if you'd bothered to ask.'

Jamie set her teeth. 'Nice catching up. Don't wait so long next time—'

'No, wait, Jamie ... I'm sorry, I'm sorry, okay?' She exhaled as though it physically pained her to apologise.

Jamie was fairly sure it did.

'Richard. It's Richard, alright? He's in trouble.'

'Your husband? He's in trouble ... and you want me to do what, exactly? Bail him out of jail with a magic phone call? Jesus, Mum, we don't speak in four years and then, suddenly, you call me up, and—'

'He's not in jail,' she cut in bitterly. 'He's Chief Superintendent for Dyfed-Powys Police.'

Jamie took a second to process that, then scoffed. 'You married a police officer? Jesus, Mum, talk about falling into old patterns.'

'He's *nothing* like your father.'

'Yeah,' Jamie said, sighing. 'Well, whatever's going on, I don't know what hole you expect me to dig him out of that he can't fix himself. Especially considering I'm in Sweden right now, in the middle of a case.' She glanced over her shoulder at the naked man in the field, at Behnsson, directing the CSTs with his chest puffed out.

'Richard is overseeing a horrid case. Two women found, buried in the middle of nowhere. It's been all over the news, you haven't seen it?'

'No, Mum,' Jamie sighed. 'I haven't. We get different news here.'

'Right,' she said, sounding disappointed, 'well, the police are working with the NCA. Do you know who they are?'

'The National Crime Agency,' Jamie said, trying to ignore the air of condescension.

'That's right. Anyway, they think it's to do with human trafficking. Maybe modern slavery. That's why the NCA are involved. Am I going too fast?'

Jamie shook her head, closing her eyes. 'No, no, I think I'm keeping up. Just about.'

'There was some hullaballoo about evidence — Richard can't tell me all the details, of course.'

'He shouldn't be telling you *any* of the details.'

'The evidence got contaminated, and other samples they had got lost or destroyed. And now they think Richard is involved.'

'Oh.' Jamie didn't even bother to sound interested.

'They've suspended him, Jamie. Put him on leave. Do you understand?'

'I understand.'

'I don't think you do.'

Jamie sighed, loudly. 'Right, so explain it to me then. Talking louder, more slowly, and more patronisingly might help.'

'God, you are your father's daughter.'

That was three swipes at her father now. Another one, and she'd just hang up. She felt like doing it right now. 'So, your new husband is dirty. Wouldn't be the first police officer to be on the take.'

'He's not your father—'

'Bye Mum.' She hung up then, swift and decisive, pushed the phone into her back pocket, and returned to her scene.

Behnsson stopped ordering the CSTs about and clammed up.

Jamie cast an eye around, letting them work, ignoring her phone buzzing in her back pocket.

The CST next to her lowered his camera. 'Your arse is ringing.'

'I know,' Jamie said, ignoring it.

'You gonna answer it?'

The look she fired him was enough to make him circle to the other side of the body. But her phone was unrelenting. And she knew it wouldn't stop unless she changed her number. If there's one thing her mother was – other than spiteful and opinionated – it was relentless.

Jamie hung her head, then stepped away, grabbing her phone. 'What?' she snapped.

'Did you just hang up on me?'

'Went through a tunnel,' she growled.

'Richard says the NCA are corrupt,' her mother said quickly. 'He says that they tampered with the evidence. That they're freezing him out of the investigation and trying to sabotage it.'

'So, call the IOPC.'

'The who?'

'The Independent Office for Police Conduct. It's *exactly* the kind of thing they exist for.'

She laughed, as though that were a joke. 'You think we'd be talking to you if that was an option?'

'Oh, so I'm the last resort. Gotcha. Look, Mum, this has been nice and all, but—'

'Jamie, Jamie, Jamie, no,' her mother interjected. 'You're not brushing me off. I've been trying for a straight week to find you, and I'm asking for your help. I've never asked you for anything. Ever. But now I'm asking.'

'Fine,' Jamie said. 'I'll, uh, make a call, or—'

'No. That won't work. You have to come here.'

'I have to come *there*? Where? Where are you even living? Wales? Why?'

'Because ... because Richard says that he needs help, and there's no one he can trust. Not the NCA, not his own team. This could ruin his career, our lives. You're the only person we could call.'

I doubt that, Jamie thought. She licked her lips. 'And what is it *exactly* that Richard thinks I'm going to do?'

'He read up about you. And he says if you can help find out who actually tampered with the evidence, then he can take that to the ICOP and make something happen.'

'The IOPC.'

'That's what I said.'

'No, you ... you know what. Never mind. I just don't think—'

'Is it about money? If it's about money, then—'

'It's not about money,' Jamie said. 'Fuck.' She pinched the bridge of her nose. Her mother wasn't going to let this go. The options flashed in Jamie's mind. Either she was right, her new husband was being framed, in which case he'd likely go to prison. Or she was wrong, and her new husband was actually dirty. Either way, the case didn't have much hope of getting solved if someone was trying to intentionally tank it. Her mind cast back to her days at the London Met. Her second big case. That had been a dead girl too. A mother-to-be. That had been a long, hard road, leading to a trafficking ring. Young women, abused and sold like meat. How many more would have died if it wasn't for her? That's what her mother said. Trafficking. Modern slavery. And someone out there wanted it to go on.

She had the mind to call the IOPC herself. Just let them handle it ... Fuck. Fuck! Why did she have to call? Why did she have to drag Jamie into this? She was free. Things were finally easy.

'Jamie? Are you there?' her mother asked.

She swallowed. 'Yeah. I'm here.'

'So, will you come?'

She looked out across the green fields, Stockholm's skyline rising out of the haze in the distance. 'Yeah,' she said, closing her eyes. 'I'll come.'

CHAPTER
THREE

The second Jamie touched down at Cardiff Airport, she turned her phone back on.

It lit up with half a dozen missed calls, all from her SO, Dahlvig. Ivar Dahlvig was a polisöverintendent for the Swedish NOD, and Jamie's boss. Since she'd begun working for him twelve months ago, she'd solved five cases. Big ones. He wasn't really on her back about anything, but she guessed skipping the country without warning in the middle of a murder investigation hadn't really made him feel all warm and fuzzy inside.

So it was a good thing that Jamie'd spent the entire time she'd been travelling doing research. She did her best work under pressure, after all.

She called Dahlvig, and he answered on the second ring.

'You better have a damn good explanation for—'

'Greta Berglund,' Jamie cut in.

'What was that?'

'Greta Berglund,' Jamie repeated.

He sighed. 'Am I supposed to know who that is?'

'That's the Uppland Chopper. Our murderer.'

'You know I don't like that name,' Dahlvig replied. 'Where the hell are you?'

'Wales.'

'You're on a boat?'

'No, not whales, *Wales,* the country. The UK.'

'I hope because Greta Berglund has fled the country and you're there to find her?'

'Not quite,' Jamie said, joining the queue for passport control. 'But I put Behnsson and Margo on it. They should have her in custody by now. I made sure that they had uniforms with them. Behnsson's going to update me once they've made the arrest.'

'And exactly *how* did you come to suspect this person? It's the first I'm hearing of her.'

'I did some digging,' Jamie replied casually. 'She was the wife of the first victim.'

'Sven Forssberg.'

'Steffan Karlsson,' Jamie corrected him. 'He died in 2011. Body was found on the roadside, ruled a hit-and-run, killer never found. But when he was discovered, he was in a bathrobe, and had a large cut on the side of his testicular sack. It wasn't cause of death, so didn't show up in our initial sweep. Turns out that Greta Berglund falsified her alibi, then went back to her maiden name following his death. Her husband cheated on her, and that's why she killed him. But guess who her neighbour was before she moved away?'

'Sven Forssberg.'

'Right,' Jamie said, ambling forward in the line. 'And her best friend was Forssberg's wife. I bet Sven Forssberg was also cheating, so his wife went to Berglund and told her. Greta-the-knife—'

'Don't like that name either.'

'Takes care of him, too, then gets a taste for dishing out justice to men who mistreat their wives.'

Dahlvig sighed again. 'And you found all that out on the plane?'

Jamie laughed. 'God, no. I started thinking that last night after I booked my ticket, and then proved it this morning while I waited at the gate. I gave the team the details just before I boarded.'

'Thought you deserved a holiday to unwind, then?'

'Not exactly. Attending to a personal matter. Family matter. Nothing serious, don't worry.' Jamie stepped up to the passport control window and handed over her British passport, and showed her Swedish police badge, lowering the phone so the guy behind the glass could get a good look at her. He waved her through and she put the phone against her ear again.

'Jesus, Jamie, if you can solve cases in a day when you want to, what the fuck am I paying you full time for?'

She laughed, hiking her duffle a little higher on

her shoulder. 'Because if I solved them all in a day, what the hell would I do the rest of the time? There's not enough serial killers in Sweden to keep me *that* busy.'

He chuckled a little. 'Suppose not. Well, look, I trust you, but Behnsson and Margo don't seem to have two brain cells between them.'

'They're learning to share, which is helping.'

'Aha, well, look, if you're wrong, I expect you to get your ass back to Stockholm, alright?'

'Sure. If I'm wrong.' Jamie paused, looking for the exit sign.

'You're not infallible, Jamie.'

'I'm not,' she replied. 'But I'm rarely wrong. It's why you hired me, remember?'

'Mmm,' he said. 'I'll call you if I need you. Don't take too long.'

'I won't.'

'And Jamie?'

'Yeah?'

'Have you spoken to Thorsen lately?'

Jamie was at the exit, the doors open in front of her, the bright afternoon sunshine streaming into the arrivals building.

She stopped dead, her heart beating a little harder. 'I, uh … no, not lately. Last time we spoke, it was … it wasn't good.'

'You should call him, he's doing better,' Dahlvig said. 'His PT says he's walking better every day, and his speech is really improving. They think he'll be walking without a stick by Christmas.'

'That's good,' Jamie said, her voice choked. She lifted her free hand to her face and ran her knuckles across her cheeks. 'That's really good. I'm really glad.'

'You should go see him, Jamie. Don't put it off. I'm not telling you as your boss. I'm telling you as your friend.'

She cleared her throat. 'I will. When I get back. I promise.'

He didn't say anything more about it. 'Stay safe, Jamie. Let me know if you need anything.'

'Thanks,' she said. 'I will.'

And then she hung up, and stepped into another world, and another world of shit.

OUTSIDE, THE SUN WAS BLAZING – WHICH IN itself felt wrong. This was Wales after all, and every time Jamie had been here, it'd been raining. She even recalled driving past Bristol once and it being sunny, and then as soon as they got to the end of the Severn Bridge and saw that Welcome to Wales sign ... rain.

'Jamie?' Her name echoed across the curb in front of the building and she turned her attention to look at the source.

A man, mid-sixties and tall, with a long face and wispy hair came gliding towards her, hand raised, grinning. 'Richard Rees,' he said, holding his hand out for

Jamie to shake. 'Chief Superintendent, Dyfed-Powys Police.'

Jamie took it, shaking firmly. 'You're my mother's new husband?'

He smiled warmly. 'Not so new anymore. We'll be two years, soon.'

Jamie let out a low whistle. 'My sympathies.'

He chuckled nervously, as though it were a joke, and then gestured towards his car, a black BMW 5 Series.

Jamie didn't move. 'So, Chief Superintendent, tell me, do you always travel with an entourage?' She lifted her chin at the car parked about fifty feet behind his, an Audi A6 estate that was trying to look inconspicuous. 'Or am I supposed to feel special?'

He showed his teeth nervously. 'That would be the NCA. They've taken to following me everywhere in the last two weeks.'

'Because they think you tampered with evidence for this big trafficking case?' Jamie read the mild shock on his face. 'My mother has a big mouth.'

He adjusted his shirt and regained some composure. 'Because they *wrongly* think that, yes. Please, come with me, I'll explain more in the car. Your mother is waiting for us.'

Jamie sighed. She was already here, she might as well hear the whole story.

The car was roomy and modern, the leather interior cool, though the smell was ancient and familiar. The same perfume her mother always wore, now bedded into the headliner and carpets in here, lingering.

Richard Rees pulled away from the curb and one quick glance in the wing mirror told her the A6 was hot on their tail.

'Okay, tell me,' Jamie said. 'Tell me everything. Tell me why I'm here. My mother said you felt that I was the only one who could help, so explain it to me – before we get too far from the airport.'

He shifted in his seat, checking the rear-view to watch as the A6 overtook a car to get directly behind them. 'About a month ago, the body of a woman was unearthed along the northern edge of the Brecon Beacons. Some amateur detectorists stumbled across it, getting a hit off some metal pins the woman had in her wrist, if you can believe that. When we got there, sniffer dogs alerted at a second grave nearby. Both women were young – one late teens, the other early twenties. Both of them bore marks that pointed to torture – stab wounds, scratches, clumps of hair missing. Bruises, broken noses and missing teeth, black eyes. They'd been through the wringer. Both died within the last few months too. Decomposition was in the early stages.'

'And the NCA were brought in?'

He nodded. 'Yes, the women couldn't be easily identified, and didn't match any missing persons' reports. The older woman was of North African descent, and the younger woman appeared East European.'

'Trafficking,' Jamie said. 'My mother mentioned it. That'd definitely get the NCA's back up.'

'By the time they arrived, we'd already gone through the scene, removed the bodies, and sent them for post-mortems. Some tissue and blood was removed from beneath the fingernails of the younger woman congruent with defensive action. Standard practices said to run it for DNA, in case it belonged to the attacker, presumably the person that killed and buried her.'

'What was cause of death?'

'Strangulation, as far as we could tell. The older woman died of a stab wound to the abdomen and massive bleeding.'

Jamie kept herself even, listening carefully. She needed to stay objective, pragmatic. She had no intention of stepping on the toes of the NCA, even if it was her party trick, seemingly. She was trying to make positive changes, though. Keep herself to herself, her head down. So far, it wasn't going so well.

'Just as the test was about to be submitted, the NCA arrived and stuck their fingers into everything. The whole team was scrambling to get them up to speed. The bodies and samples taken were all examined, rearranged, relabelled ... and then, the DNA results came back as contaminated. Who knows? These things happen, right? So, when the NCA tried to find the samples to resubmit the test ...'

'They were gone?'

'Supposedly mislabelled and lost, or accidentally destroyed.'

'And they pointed the finger at you?'

'And my team. But it seemed to be me they targeted personally, and then accused of God knows what. Being crooked? Corrupt?' He scoffed. 'I know it was them. Either an accidental fuck up, or an intentional one. And I don't know which is worse.' He sighed, his weathered hands tightening on the leather steering wheel.

'An intentional fuck up is worse,' Jamie replied. 'But it's also a very serious allegation against the most serious and stringent law enforcement agency in the UK.'

'Hence your presence.' He glanced over at Jamie. 'I read up on your career. I must say, I'm impressed.'

'We can skip the platitudes,' Jamie said, noting Richard's quick glances in the rear-view, the slight sheen of sweat on his temples.

'They aren't platitudes,' he said. 'Your mother told me you were a detective, but I never suspected that you'd have been so accomplished at your age.'

'I fell into some heavy cases. I seem to have a knack for it.'

'You've got a knack for solving them I'd say. And I'm hoping you can do the same here. Look, I know what I'm asking isn't easy. But I'd just like you to take a look, make some calls, ask some questions, see what you think. If I am to go to the IOPC, then I'd at least like to have someone else who thinks it's the right call.'

'I'm not looking to get swept up in any scandals here,' Jamie said firmly.

'And you won't be. You have my word. I just want to make sure I'm not acting rashly before I try to pitch the idea of the NCA being on the take and trying to blow up a trafficking operation.'

Jamie drew a slow breath. 'Then maybe they're not, and it is just good old fashioned ineptitude.'

He laughed a little. 'Sure, it's possible. But I've been a police officer for near forty years now, and my experience has taught me that if it walks, swims, and quacks like a duck ...' He took another look in the rear-view, narrowed his eyes, and then looked ahead, scanning the junction they were approaching. 'All I'm saying is that two bodies turned up, and the NCA just materialised. We didn't even call them. They rushed in, disrupted and held up our investigation, seized control of the case and, on their watch, what might have been crucial evidence just disappeared. And then they put me firmly in their crosshairs, and are now following me day and night. That doesn't seem suspicious to you?'

It does, Jamie thought. But the fact that they feel the need to tail you raises some other questions, too.

Before she could verbalise any of her thoughts, though, Richard stamped down on the accelerator, swerving around the car in front that was stopping for a red light, and understeered through a junction, speeding down an adjacent street.

Jamie threw her hand against the dashboard to

steady herself and swore, car horns blaring around them as they nearly took the wing mirror off a transit.

Richard checked the rear-view, not slowing, and grinned a little, the A6 stuck in the queue and traffic now flowing across its path.

'Want to tell me what the hell that was about?' Jamie asked, gripping the handle above the door as he drove like a madman, violently steering down a residential street, much to the dismay of the tyres.

He let off the accelerator finally and seemed to relax a little, still keeping one eye on the rear-view. 'You'll see,' he said. 'We're almost there.'

CHAPTER
FOUR

Richard pulled off the main road, swinging quickly into The Heath Hospital in Cardiff. The car jostled over the red speedbumps and clanked through the metal plates leading into the multi-storey car park.

He drove quickly, stopping so that the car faced the road, and that he and Jamie could see where any cars might pull in after them.

She didn't need to ask what he was looking for. But there was no sign of the A6.

When he finally seemed to soften, wiping the sweat from his forehead, Jamie spoke. 'You wanna tell me what the hell we're doing here?'

He opened the door and stepped out. 'Best if I show you. Come on, we'll go in the back way.'

Jamie reserved judgement, instead following in silence as Richard led her across level 2, down the stairs, and around the back of the main hospital building, entering through one of the sliding doors there. A few nurses stood around outside, grabbing a few breaths of fresh air, texting and chatting, making the most of the afternoon sun before they plunged back into their work. They cast Jamie and Richard – an odd pairing, she had no doubt – a few looks, but said nothing.

Jamie never much liked the smell of hospitals but, luckily, Richard was carrying pace, seemingly wanting to get this over and done with.

He slowed at a lift and called for it, looking over his shoulders.

'We're not being followed,' Jamie said.

He just sighed a little, clenching his shaking hands. 'Can never be too careful.'

'I'm curious as to why we needed to lose our friends at the NCA for this,' Jamie said. 'And especially why you felt the need to almost kill us in the process.'

She felt like his silence had a *you'll see soon enough* implication. So instead of answering, he just stepped through the opening doors of the lift and pressed the button for the fourth floor.

A quick glance at the plan on the wall told Jamie it was the paediatric ward. A creeping feeling of dread began to seat itself in the pit of her stomach.

They rode up without a word and Richard stepped onto the fourth floor knowing where he was going.

They walked past room after room of people laid up

in beds with ventilators, bandaged and in casts, in traction and slings.

Richard stopped without warning and Jamie nearly ran into him. 'In here,' he said, keeping his voice hushed, glancing around again.

He pressed the handle and opened the door enough for Jamie to squeeze in, guiding her by the arm.

She shrugged him off and he slipped in after her, closing the door. His nerves seemed to have returned and she couldn't help but wonder if she was somehow being an accessory to something she shouldn't be.

Though those worries fell away when she saw whose room they'd entered.

Lying on the hospital bed was a girl – maybe fourteen, but no older. She had a youthful face beneath the cuts and bruises, long, curly brown hair and a tanned complexion that told Jamie she was Middle Eastern, Israeli perhaps, or Syrian. Iraqi or Iranian even. It wasn't easy to tell through the swelling and the tube down her throat.

'Jesus,' Jamie muttered, stepping a little closer. The girl was unconscious.

'She was brought in a week ago,' Richard said, his voice barely above a whisper. He hung back by the door, but the room was quiet, his eyes fixed on her.

'Who is she?' Jamie asked, circling the bed to get a better gauge of her injuries. She could see through the collar in her gown that her body was bandaged, her left arm in a sling and cast from above the elbow. She had a medical pad over her left eye, too, scrapes across the side of her head and ear, across her cheek.

'We don't know,' Richard replied. 'No ID, nothing.'

'What happened to her?'

'She was hit by a car.'

Jamie looked up at him.

'After she jumped from the back of a moving van on a B-road through the Brecon Beacons.'

Jamie's brow furrowed.

'The guy who hit her said that he was driving behind a van for a while – a transit, he thinks. It went over a crest and he saw the back doors fly open. Then, as he came over the top, she was there in the middle of the road. He tried to brake, but it was too late by the time he saw her. Her head hit the windscreen and she was thrown into the air. She landed twenty-five feet away.'

'Fucking hell,' Jamie muttered, looking at the girl again.

'Detached retina, dislocated shoulder, broken tibia, fractured wrist. Three broken ribs. Punctured lung. And that was just from the crash.'

Jamie approached the bedside slowly.

'The doctors who examined her said she also showed signs of malnutrition, chronic dehydration, scurvy. And there were ligature marks on her hands and wrists. She also had two fingernails snapped off at the bed, a broken knuckle, a split lip, black eye, swelling around her face from being struck, as well as bruising on her throat and body, and scratches and bite marks in various places.'

All the information spun in Jamie's head.

'They said that the ligature marks and malnutrition weren't recent. She'd been bound for a long time. The scratches and bruising were more recent, though. Sustained at the same time, they said.'

Jamie just shook her head. 'She's just a child.'

'Yes, she is,' Richard replied, his voice shaking a little. 'But she's a fighter.' He swallowed, clearing his throat. 'The doctor said she's strong. She's recovering well. She has a will to survive. His words.'

'And the NCA don't know she's here?'

'No,' he said. 'I suspect, based on the similarity of her injuries in comparison to the other bodies we found, along with the proximity to where they were discovered …'

'That she's linked to the case.'

'I don't think her leaping from a moving van was part of their plan.'

'She escaped.'

'Before they killed her, is my guess.'

'Brave girl,' Jamie said, looking down at her, resisting the urge to reach out and move a strand of hair from her face.

'She started coming around yesterday, became agitated quickly, tried to tear out her IV and breathing tube. She had to be restrained, sedated, because of her injuries. Though we can't keep her like this forever.' His voice was tender, caring even. Either he was being sincere, or this was one hell of an act. 'If the NCA get wind of her being here, and things are as I suspect ... she doesn't have much of a chance.'

'You think they'd kill her?' Jamie cast him a cautious look.

He shrugged. 'I don't know. But I'm not willing to take the risk. Whether it's the NCA or whoever did this to her to begin with – the fucking *animals* – they're not coming within a mile of her.' He stepped closer to the bed now, resting his hands on the bottom rail. 'I wanted you to see this. We don't know who she is or where she came from. No one is looking for her. And we know she's not the first, and definitely not the last. There are people out there doing evil things to women and girls like her. And it has to stop.'

Jamie didn't need to reply. He brought her here to see what was at stake. Who was at stake. And it worked. Seeing her like this ... it was enough to make her blood boil, hot and painful in her veins.

When she looked across at Richard, he was holding out a lanyard.

She took it.

'This will get you access to the station, the case files. I already granted you access. I can't go near it, but you can, and I briefed my team already. I told them an independent investigator would be assisting with the case and they'll be on hand to help you, whatever you need. Just don't tell them your relationship to me, please.'

'That'll be easy,' Jamie said. 'We don't have a rela-tionship.' She sighed and turned away from the bed, giving him a nod and stowing the lanyard in her jeans pocket. 'I'll make some calls, see what I can find out. Until then, just sit tight. I'll look over the case, shake some trees. But I can't make any promises.'

He smiled a little. 'Thank you.' He lifted a hand, as though to beckon her out. 'We'd better go. I told your mother we'd be an hour, and she's cooking dinner. She said it's your favourite.'

'What is it?' Jamie asked, stepping towards the door.

'I don't know,' Richard replied. 'She said you'd know right away if I said that.'

Jamie paused at the threshold and looked back. 'Honestly, I don't.'

'I suppose it's been a while.'

She walked from the room, heading for the exit. 'Yeah, you could say that.'

CHAPTER
FIVE

J amie couldn't really remember where her mother had been living when she left the UK, but she had to admit that where she was living now was pretty nice. Richard Rees had been with Dyfed-Powys Police for a lot of years, and that was reflected in the size and scope of his house.

It was about twenty minutes outside Llandeilo, with a wonderful view of the western edge of the Beacons.

The house itself was traditional, with ivy climbing the two-foot-thick stone walls, small windows, and a wide frontage awash with wildflowers and mature trees. From what she remembered, her mother hadn't ever had a green thumb, so it must be yet another string to Richard's bow.

Right now her mother was in the kitchen, finishing off preparations of something that smelled like gone-off fish. Jamie still didn't have a handle on what her favourite meal was supposed to be. But considering she didn't think her mother had cooked her a meal since she was about twelve and they lived in Sweden, she doubted that it was going to be either good, or her 'favourite'.

She had work to do, thankfully, to take her mind off the smell. She'd not dialled this number in three years but, thankfully, it still worked.

The call connected, then rang a few times. And then he answered. 'Hello?' came the somewhat cautious voice.

Jamie figured that any call from a Swedish number would be met with a little bit of suspicion, especially when the person being called was a DCI with the London Met.

'Detective Chief Inspector Smith,' Jamie said, allowing herself to smile.

'Holy hell,' he replied. 'Jamie Johansson?'

'You can tell by my voice?'

'It still haunts me, considering everything you put me through.'

Jamie laughed. 'Was I really that bad?'

'Worst best detective I ever had the trouble of trying to keep control of.'

'I'll take that as a … compliment?'

He chuckled. 'Probably best to. Jesus, I didn't think I'd ever hear from you again. How are you?'

'I'm well, thanks.'

'Last I heard, you'd shacked up with the Stockholm Police. You still working there?'

'Yeah ... sort of. I've been around,' Jamie said, not really wanting to relay the entirety of her career of the last few years.

He waited for her to expound, but when she didn't, asked, 'So, is this where you ask me for your job back? Think we've probably got room for another DC.'

'Aha,' Jamie chuckled. 'Not quite. I do need a favour though.'

'Oh, alright. Colour me curious. What can I do for you inspector?'

'*Överinspektör,*' Jamie corrected him.

He laughed. 'So?'

'Do you know anyone at the NCA?'

He seemed to think on it for a moment. 'I know several people at the NCA. Why?'

'I'm in Wales, assisting Dyfed-Powys Police with a case they're working, and the NCA are running a joint op. I need to reach out, get a grasp on the situation before I go any further.'

'And you can't go directly to the NCA?'

'It's ... delicate.'

'Right ...' He sighed. 'Well, firstly – on a note of professional courtesy – don't stick your nose in another agency's investigation.'

'Noted.'

'And ignored, I bet.'

Jamie said nothing.

'And secondly ... you're in luck. Nasir Hassan. Remember him?'

'Of course. He basically saved my life.'

'I think he probably remembers it as you getting him shot,' Smith laughed.

'He made a full recovery,' Jamie replied quickly. 'And it was sort of one of the hazards of the job.'

'Well, after he transitioned to DI here, the NCA scooped him up. He's working as an investigator for them now. I'd say reaching out to him is your best bet. Who knows, maybe he's forgiven you by now.'

'Fingers crossed.'

'It's good to hear from you,' Smith said. 'You sound well. I was worried about you when you left the Met. I'm glad you're back working. You were always a good detective. If not a little headstrong.'

'I don't believe that's the word you used in my last performance evaluation.'

He laughed, loudly. 'No, probably not. I'll send Hassan's number across to you. Reach out if you need anything else. And Jamie?'

'Yeah?'

'Good luck. And tread lightly. The NCA don't like being poked.'

'Wouldn't dream of it.'

The line clicked dead and Jamie lowered the phone, the smell of fish once more filling her nostrils.

Her mother's voice echoed up the stairs then. 'Jamie, dinner!'

She was twelve again, anxious and scared, wondering what version of her parents awaited her in the kitchen.

As she began to walk, her phone buzzed in her pocket. Smith. A text. 'Hassan's number. Good luck.'

Good luck, she thought.

For once, I hope I won't need it.

DINNER WAS FISH PIE. JAMIE HAD ALWAYS HATED it. But it had been her father's favourite meal.

Jamie deigned not to mention that part. And after some light conversation, mostly comprised of snipes from her mother about her: hair, fingernails, skin, lack of makeup, lack of 'women's clothes', lack of a husband, lack of children, and lack of plans to pursue those things with any sort of intention ... she slipped from the house and onto the stone patio.

The sun was hanging lower in the sky, the splinters of light streaming through the leaves of the silver birch that was growing alongside it warm on her skin. Martins circled above, and house sparrows chirped on the branches.

She highlighted Nasir Hassan's number on the text and called it. They'd parted on good terms. The last time she saw him was in a defunct tube station in London when they'd collared a deranged killer and his accomplice who were terrorising London. That was the first time Jamie had killed someone. Shot the girl, right in the chest.

The image filled her mind, the flash from the muzzle popping in her brain, making her blink each time, the light still seared onto the inside of her eyelids. Pop. Pop. Pop. The girl's face, twisted in pain as she fell backwards. The sound of her hitting the ground. A dull crunch into the stones between the rails.

'Hello? Hello?'

Shit. 'Uh, hi,' Jamie said suddenly, shaking off the memory and regaining herself.

'Who is this? How did you get this number?'

'Hassan?'

He paused for a moment, then, more evenly, 'Who is this?'

'It's Jamie,' Jamie said, still trying to get her bearings. 'Jamie Johansson.'

'Jamie Johansson?' The surprise was clear in his voice. 'Fucking hell. Ghost of the past. How the hell'd you get this number?'

'DCI Henley Smith.'

'Ah fuck,' he said, sighing.

'Ah fuck? No *hi, how are you? Good to hear from you?*'

'I would, except I expect you're about to ask me for something. And I doubt I'm going to like it very much.'

Jamie's brow creased. 'Is that what you think of me?'

'So you're not about to ask me for something?'

'No, I am,' Jamie laughed. 'But still, it hurts a little …'

He laughed too. 'Shit, it's good to hear from you. How are you? Where are you? You never came back to the Met. Thought we were a good team.'

'We were,' Jamie had to admit. 'Really good, but, you know …'

'Yeah, I do. That shit weighs on you. So, what's up? What's new?'

'What's new is that I'm in Wales. And I'm working. NCA are handling a case – trafficking. Two bodies in the Brecon Beacons. Some trouble with the local police, some issues with chain of custody, some contaminated evidence—'

'Woah, lemme stop you right there,' Hassan said. He shifted a little, as though getting up out of a seat. 'One, how do you know about this case? And two, what are you asking me? Because it's going to determine if I hang up the phone in the next five seconds or not.'

Jamie looked back in through the patio doors at her mother – dyed hair, bright pink lips. She was sucking on the rim of an oversized wine glass, and her husband was grinning at her over the top of his own.

'My mother married Richard Rees.'

'Chief Superintendent Richard Rees? You're fucking kidding.'

'No, I'm not. I'm guessing you know the guy?'

'Know him? Yeah, I know him. And I know he's

dirty too. Stay clear of the guy, Jamie. Stay clear of the whole thing.'

'Too late,' she replied, sighing. 'You know what's going on with this case?'

'I should hope so. I'm working it. Fuck. Jamie, you've gotta be careful. If the police find out you're probing into this, who knows what they'll do.'

Jamie turned to look at her mother and Richard Rees – caring husband, upstanding citizen, dirty fucking policeman? 'Weird that they'd ask me to look into it then.' She knew she should back out right now, just run. Call a taxi. Get back to the airport, on a plane, back to her life. Her real life.

Her mind went to the girl in the hospital then, on the ventilator. The scars she already had and the ones she'd be forced to carry for the rest of her life. Both inside and out.

Jamie had some of those. Enough to know that they only get worse when no one else is fighting for you. She thought of her leaping from that moving van, wondered what kind of fate she was so desperate to escape. And whether she'd be resigned to it if Jamie turned her back on her. 'Look, someone's fucking with the investigation,' Jamie said, hardening. 'You say it's them, they're saying it's you. Why not let me take a look anyway? For my own peace of mind.'

'Why are you so interested?'

'Personal favour. To my mother. Family, you know?'

Jamie lied. 'We'd do anything for our family. Speaking of which – how's the wife, the kids?'

'They're ... they're fine,' he said quickly. 'But seriously, I can't let you into this thing.'

'That's something someone trying to cover their ass might say.'

'I'll pretend you didn't just say that,' he said coldly.

'I'm not trying to imply anything. But I need to look at both sides of this. And you can believe the first person going under the microscope is Richard Rees. But things are rarely as they seem, and I want to make sure that I'm looking at all sides. I'll share whatever I find, and once we know who's really dirty, I'll hand it over to you, and you can take it from there. Whether it's their side, or yours.'

Hassan was quiet for a second. 'Can I ask you a question first? And I want you to answer. Truthfully.'

'Shoot.'

'Have you changed?'

'Have I changed?' Jamie didn't really know what to make of that.

'Are you still as obsessive, stubborn, hard-headed, single-minded, and stubborn as you were the last time we worked together?'

'I think you missed "stubborn".'

'Jamie.'

She sighed. 'Truthfully? Yeah. Worse. I'm probably worse.'

He laughed a little. 'Well, you know what they say.

Admitting you have a problem is the first step to recovery. So you're really not going to let this go then … Shit. I guess I'll pick you up in the morning.'

'You don't have to do that.'

'Oh, I do. I'm not having you trample all over my investigation without a chaperone.'

She smiled. 'Alright then. It'll be good to work together again.'

'Humph, if you say so. Take it easy, Jamie. And try not to get into any trouble before the morning, alright?'

'You know me,' Jamie said, closing her eyes, allowing the fading rays of sunlight to warm her skin.

'That's why I said it.'

CHAPTER
SIX

The morning was colder than Jamie expected.

As she stood on the road outside of Richard's house, the sky already bright and clear above, she shivered. No cars rolled by, and the only sounds echoing through the air were the tweets of birds and the occasional call of some distant sheep, bleating away for no reason at all.

The burble of an engine signalled Hassan's arrival and he pulled to a stop in front of Jamie in another big, shining Audi. This one was a sedan, and had the over-sized wheels and slight idling judder of a vehicle with a powerful engine and the speed to match.

Jamie opened the door and slid down into the leather seat. 'NCA pays better than the Met, then?'

'It's an agency car. And good morning to you, too, by the way,' he said, handing her a coffee. 'Americano, skimmed milk, no sugar?'

'Sweet enough already,' Jamie said, taking it from him. 'You remembered my order?'

'Ha! Don't flatter yourself, Jamie. I've just got an excellent memory.' He grinned at her, still looking the same as the last time she saw him. He was big, just over six feet, and wide-set. Shoulders that carried arms like tree trunks. She was always reminded of a rugby player when she saw him. His beard had thickened some, and covered the lower half of his face in a manicured layer of black stubble. He still styled his hair the same – shaved short on the sides, with the top slicked back. His teeth were still pearly white too, on show most of the time thanks to his perpetual cheeky grin.

'Thanks,' Jamie said, raising the coffee and taking a sip. It was good. Hot, and bitter. Just what she needed. 'Where to?'

He shifted into drive and put his foot down. The wide tyres bit the tarmac and pulled them forward smoothly, the speedometer flying through the numbers.

'Coroner's office,' he said. 'But we're late. Why the hell are you staying in Llandeilo?'

'My mother's husband lives here.'

'Richard Rees, right. You seen through his bullshit yet?' Hassan asked, glancing right at a roundabout and then flying through it without braking.

Jamie said nothing. And she certainly had no intention of mentioning the girl in the hospital.

'That evidence you were talking about yesterday? The DNA sample that got destroyed? I looked into it again after we got off the phone. Between the time it was catalogued and the time it was discovered to be missing, no one from the NCA even went into the lab. Only police personnel. That enough for you?' He looked over at her.

'It's enough to tell me that if it was the police messing with it, that they were pretty stupid not to cover their tracks.' She sighed. 'And who's to say it wasn't damaged before it was logged? Rees told me that the samples were all reorganised and relabelled by the NCA. Seems like a far better time to fuck with something.'

Hassan sucked on his teeth. 'I don't buy it.'

'Didn't expect you to. I'm just not jumping to conclusions. Sort of comes with being an independent observer, right?'

He took a slow breath. 'Right. So, after we get to the coroner's office, we gotta swing by HQ. Someone wants to meet you.'

'Who?'

'Catherine Mallory. Intel officer overseeing the investigation.'

'Your boss?'

He laughed, easing the car up to a cool eighty miles an hour. He weaved around a slow-moving Vauxhall Corsa and pushed onwards towards the coroner's office. 'You sound surprised. You thought I'd keep this from her?'

'I didn't think much at all, really. I was hoping not to become too entrenched in any of this.'

'Well, I called her the second you hung up. And she wants to meet you.'

'How did she sound?'

'You mean, was she pissed off that you were here?'

Jamie waited for him to answer his own question.

'Guess you'll have to wait and see.'

THEY PARKED UP AND HEADED ON INSIDE THE coroner's office, a sizeable brick building that was greying with age. It's one thing she already missed about Stockholm - the colourfulness of the city.

Despite the myriad of greens and the life that seemed to burst from every hedgerow and field ... Jamie guessed she was just getting a little homesick. Which was weird, because she'd spent more time living in the UK than she had in Sweden.

Maybe it was a sign. Cut your losses. Forget about the girl. Go home. Before it's too late.

Hassan opened the door for Jamie and she slipped inside.

He approached the desk, holding out his NCA credentials, and leaned languidly on the front desk. There was a young woman behind it, and within seconds he had her laughing and throwing her head back. He was handsome, sure. Strong jawline, thick head of hair, clean skin, well-kempt. A real 'man', you might say.

Jamie recalled that women always seemed to respond to his boyish charm, his toe-the-line humour, his naturally flirtatious aura. She was immune it seemed. Either that, or he knocked it down a few notches for her. She didn't care either way. When she was working, she was working. That was how it had to be now. She wasn't going back to how it was before. She couldn't.

The woman behind the counter buzzed them through the security doors and Hassan strode down the corridor like a prized stallion, cutting right into cold storage.

A bank of refrigerated lockers stared out at them and Hassan gave the labels a quick scan. He'd already been in here, so he knew what he was looking for.

'Ah,' he said, grabbing a handle and pulling on it. The seal hissed and released and a six-foot drawer slid smoothly into the space between them, revealing the pale corpse of a woman. The cold flooded out and Jamie felt it wash around her feet.

The woman had a sheet drawn up over her torso, folded down at the collarbones. Jamie recalled that Richard Rees had told her that of the two bodies, one was strangled, the other stabbed. This was clearly the woman who'd been strangled. That much was apparent by the deep purple welting on her throat.

'Both bodies have been in cold storage since they

were found. The coroner thinks they were buried just a few days apart. A week at most.'

'A week?' Jamie looked up at him from under her eyebrows.

He nodded. 'Yeah, we scoured the area but didn't find any more. They hadn't been in the ground long. Decomp had obviously started kicking in, but they managed to arrest it during the autopsy, embalming, storage.' Hassan sighed. 'Trying to keep it that way in case more turn up. See if we can't link a pattern together.'

He made to push the drawer back in, but Jamie motioned for him to keep it open, leaning in and inspecting the woman's face more closely.

Hassan went on. 'We have all the paperwork from the reports – both crime scene and coroner's, including photographs, if you want to look them over.'

'I will,' Jamie said slowly, moving along the woman's body. She reached out and drew the sheet down, exposing her torso and the Y-incision.

Hassan let his eyes rise to the ceiling. Either to preserve what little dignity the woman deserved, or simply because he'd spent too long looking at her already.

'Interestingly, despite both bodies being in differing stages of decomp, they were buried at the same time.'

Jamie paused now and looked up. 'They died a week apart but were buried at the same time? Why?'

He shrugged. 'I don't know. The first victim had

some injuries sustained post-mortem. The coroner said they were congruent with being manhandled, thrown around after she died.'

Jamie drew the sheet down further, briefly checking the woman's legs, before she covered her up again and nodded for Hassan to push her back in.

'So whoever buried them had a different plan origi-nally,' Jamie mused. 'A different way of disposing of them. But then changed tack when they had another body, and decided to bury them instead. Maybe they thought their original method of disposing of them was about to be discovered.'

Hassan locked the drawer and sighed. 'Or maybe it was just full.'

Jamie grimaced at the thought. The case already had all the hallmarks of a trafficking ring. Non-native women, no active missing persons. Malnutrition, liga-ture marks ... these women were brought to the UK for something. And it wasn't a better life. There was one thing though that was a positive, though it was a surprise. 'There didn't appear to be any sign of sexual assault,' Jamie offered. 'No bruising on the inner thighs. Usually the giveaway.'

'Every cloud,' Hassan replied. 'Coroner noted that too.'

'Strange for a case like this, right?'

Hassan shrugged. 'In most cases, there is a sexual element to trafficking, especially when the victim type is female and there's evidence of bondage and imprisonment. It just means that whatever they wanted these women for, it wasn't the sex trade.'

'Slavery?'

'Maybe. But we already kicked that around – two bodies in the same place, and their wounds suggest violence, but not the kind you get from a beating from those kinds of dynamics.'

'You're an expert,' Jamie said, with as much sincerity as she could muster in the situation.

'Not by choice. But it's the job, you know? I've seen some shit. Armed response was one thing. Used to sleep like a baby, even after a hard day. Now? I toss and turn all night. See it when I close my eyes.'

Jamie let out a long breath. 'Join the club.'

Hassan motioned her towards the door and she started walking. 'So it's not sexual, likely not slavery. But there's violence, that much isn't in dispute.' Jamie stopped, looked back. 'What about snuff films?'

He raised his shoulders a touch, closing the door behind him. He seemed to loosen a little now they were outside. 'We came to that conclusion too. But the injuries don't correlate with how that pans out normally.'

Jamie nodded, thinking, as they walked. 'Yeah, and the fact that she was strangled by another woman.'

'What?' Hassan stopped.

'Or a child,' Jamie said, turning and looking at him. 'Coroner didn't note that?' Jamie read the surprise on his face. 'He must have put in the report that the way the strangle pattern overlaps was suggestive of someone with small hands?'

He continued to look surprised.

Jamie sighed. 'When a man strangles a woman,' she said, putting her hands up, 'unless they're a pro, they'll put the web of skin between the forefinger and thumb under the soft palate.' She demonstrated on herself. 'And then put the other hand underneath it. Their dominant hand is on top – the right, usually, and the left hand is nested underneath. A pro will usually put their thumbs right on the trachea to cut off the air supply and crush the windpipe more effectively.' She moved her thumbs so they pressed right in the middle of her throat. 'But a woman, or someone with smaller hands, especially if they're inexperienced, will try to cover the whole neck, and will end up with their thumbs crossed, like this.' Jamie held her hands up like a butterfly, with her knuckles showing to Hassan, and her thumbs entwined. 'It's a signifier of a female-on-female crime, and the bruising on that victim's neck was characteristic of that. Though it's not easy to tell, as there are multiple marks from several attempts. I'd assume that it was a prolonged fight of some kind, and the person who strangled her was pushed off, at first, and took some time to really get into a strong position. The bruising on the outer edges of her breasts and on her ribs is sugges-tive of someone straddling her. Though there's no bruising on the inside of her biceps, so I'd think her arms were free. That's another signifier it was another woman – men most often pin the arms down. The damage to the victim's nails support this too. Some of them are snapped off, where she was likely clawing at the person strangling her.'

Hassan blinked, his surprise turned to astonishment. 'You only looked at her for two fucking minutes,' he said. 'Jesus, where'd you learn that trick?'

'The NOD don't deal with mundane cases,' Jamie replied. 'And I've been sort of throwing myself into my work of late.'

He laughed now, putting his arm around her and squeezing hard as he walked her towards the exit. 'Holy shit,' he said. 'Mallory's gonna love you.'

CHAPTER
SEVEN

Jamie half expected the NCA to have set up at the Carmarthen Police HQ. But she supposed, considering the friction, it wasn't surprising that they weren't there.

They'd taken over the floor of an office building in Brecon and, in true NCA style, no one seemed to know they'd moved in. The NCA weren't some clandestine organisation, but they worked quickly, they worked quietly, and they got things done. Jamie appreciated that. She'd been with the NOD for a year and had learned the beauty of focusing on the task at hand. And from the way Hassan was harping on about Catherine Mallory, the intelligence officer running this investigation, Jamie thought she probably embodied that ethos to a tee.

The way he described her, though, was making Jamie a little curious. One, as to how she handled a case like this. And two, how she was going to handle Jamie already being knee deep in it.

Jamie did think it was odd that Hassan had taken her to the coroner's office to see one of the bodies first, rather than coming straight to Mallory. But Jamie suspected there was some sort of plan in play here. Hassan wouldn't have the inclination to drive Jamie all the way out there on his own, so Jamie betted he was under orders to do so.

She just wondered exactly what this Mallory person wanted to get out of the exercise. Though she figured her question would be answered soon enough.

They pulled into the small car park at the side of the office building and exited, walking through the shade towards the side door.

Hassan let himself in with a key fob and strode across the small lobby area. There was no reception desk, just a pair of lifts with a plaque between them that said who was on what floor. There was an accountancy firm, a solicitors, and then just some random company called 'Intrajet'. Jamie wondered if it was aviation or office printers, but she guessed the latter considering this was Brecon. Either way, she kept her observations to herself as they rode to the 'vacant' third floor and got off.

There was a short corridor, an unmanned reception desk, and another door that led into the main office space. The floor looked like every other she'd ever walked. White walls, speckled ceiling tiles, dark blue carpet tiles under foot. Even down to the fake ficus in the corner. The small window on the door had been covered over with brown paper to stop anyone seeing in. Standard practice, really. Something that most wouldn't notice, but a dead giveaway for anyone in the know.

Hassan flashed himself through the door with his key fob again and stepped inside.

Jamie didn't know whether it would be a big operation or not. But the reality was 'not'. Of the dozen desks in the space, only three were occupied. Two by women, one by a man. They glanced up, nodded to Hassan, and then went back to work. Or, two of them, at least. The guy looked to be in his fifties, the bookish sort. Intelligence officer, Jamie thought. Not the field type. But the type that knew everything, and if he didn't, he would soon. The woman was younger, tough-looking, with short hair. She was scowling, and made no effort to look their way or exude any air of friendliness. Jamie wondered if she'd stepped on her toes here. Was this Hassan's partner? They usually had investigators working in twos, she thought she remembered. Had Jamie just relegated her to the back seat of this op?

The second woman was already out of her chair and walking towards them. She was probably in her late forties, pretty tall for a woman, but then again, she was wearing heeled boots. She had a pair of office slacks on that hugged her legs, and a white shirt rolled to the elbows. Her hair was tied back into a curly bun, and her dark features and thick eyebrows made her appearance all the more striking.

She extended a hand to Jamie. 'Catherine Mallory,' she said, before Jamie even shook. 'Nasir has told me a lot about you.'

'I hope not,' Jamie said. The standard polite-yet-self-deprecating response to that.

Mallory smiled a wide smile through closed lips. 'Well, what he didn't tell I didn't find it hard to look up. You've quite the coloured history in law enforcement. At least for the last few years.'

Jamie just sort of shrugged. 'It's been challenging.'

Mallory put her hands on her hips and looked Jamie up and down, tongue between her teeth, appraising her as a deft racehorse trainer might a prize mare. 'Well, I'd like to hear about those challenges first hand. But for now, you're here, and we'll take what help we can get.'

Jamie appraised Mallory in return. Take what help they could get? 'Is the NCA not taking two dead bodies with links to trafficking seriously anymore?'

Mallory smiled a little. 'Oh, it's quite serious. But like all law enforcement, we're spread thin. More people are getting out of the police than getting into it, and it's where we get most of our people from. Mental health concerns and stresses, reduced working hours, IOCP investigations and suspensions, poor pay scaling, general stress and increased danger on the job, and declining public opinion of governmental and civil services as a whole are all contributing to us being shorthanded, underfunded, and, of course, overworked. We'd love to have twenty people here working on this, but it's not the only trafficking case on the map and, sadly, not the worst. Just last week the NCA broke a slavery and grooming ring in Birmingham. Nineteen boys between the ages of nine and thirteen identified and rescued. Three found dead. And triple that number still unaccounted for. Four men and two women arrested, and warrants out for several others. And that's not even the biggest one. Not by a long shot.' Mallory ground her teeth, a genuine look of disgust seizing her face. 'We do all we can, but it's never enough. And with our budgets and resources being throttled ... well, when someone with your reputation steps in to lend a hand ... Ha, you know what they say about gift horses, right?'

Maybe she was a horse expert after all.

Jamie just nodded.

'Like I said, we'll take all the help we can get. Hassan spoke highly of you, as did your SO – Dahlvig.' Mallory turned on her heel and began walking back towards her desk.

'You spoke to Dahlvig?' Jamie asked, following her.

'Mhm,' she nodded over her shoulder, then flashed Jamie a disarming grin. 'He was very complimentary of you, and when I outlined the case in brief, he seemed amenable to you assisting us. Providing we didn't try to poach you after it.' That same grin again. 'He was insistent on having you back. I told him what will be will be.'

'And I suspect he took that well?'

'Ha, what do you think?'

'I think he probably told you where to go.'

She sat at her desk. 'There was some intimation that he'd come here and drag you back to Sweden if it came to it. Must be nice to be so in demand.'

Jamie smiled, then sighed. 'Something like that. But it's not really a professional curiosity that brought me here. More like ...'

'A personal favour?' Mallory offered.

'I was going to say emotional blackmail.'

'Aha, Hassan did say that your mother twisted your arm. Wanted you to look into hubby. Richard Rees,' she said, allowing his name to roll off her tongue like the Welsh would say it. Her accent was distinctly neutral. Jamie suspected north of London somewhere, south of the Midlands. But Mallory disguised it well, and Jamie's ear had been tuned to Swedish regionality recently.

'Dirty as they come,' Mallory added, leaning in and typing something on her computer. 'No way he didn't fuck with our evidence. You know he was intentionally dragging his feet with those DNA tests, right?' She looked up at Jamie so suddenly she almost jumped. 'He had the DNA for nearly a week before we got there, and seemingly had no intention of putting it in for testing. When we found that out ... didn't sit right. He was cagey about it too. Not the most pleasant conversation. Honestly, with how limited we are here it seemed only sensible to let DP lead, and we'd assist however we could.'

'DP?' Jamie asked, struggling to keep up. Mallory had a sharp mind, and was speaking at what seemed like double speed.

'Dyfed-Powys. Police.'

'Right.'

'I offered our services in full support, said that we needed to integrate with their team there, utilise our resources and skills, paired with their local knowledge and network, to tackle this together. Though, once the tests came back inconclusive and the other samples were miraculously contaminated, well, that was all the encouragement I needed to take this thing by the reins.'

'So that's what you did.'

'Yeah, I mean we'd already begun to try to help them by sorting out the evidence they already had into some sort of coherent system. You know they still use paper filing over there? Writing reports on the computer, then printing and filing them, with electronic as a backup. I mean, talk about arse backwards. But, I suppose it provides cover when they want to fuck with evidence.' Mallory let out a long breath, lacing her hands across her stomach and rocking back on her chair. 'Anyway, once we realised that they'd intentionally messed with the investigation, we pulled out of there. Stupid fast.'

'So you went to the IOPC?' Jamie asked, trying to get a gauge of what was going on here.

'Not yet. A lack of evidence against is not the same as evidence for, despite what some may think. But I have enough weight to throw around when I need to. I don't have the authority to suspend myself, but a quick call to Richard Rees' SO, explaining the situation and my intention to look at all the facts and present a case once the investigation was over – and in the meantime I'm not going to the IOPC or the media – was enough to whip Rees with a suspension in the meanwhile. I don't need him involved while we work, and DP don't need any more time in the news for misconduct. You follow UK news much in Sweden? Been keeping up with any of the police scandals?'

Jamie just shook her head, not feeling much like talking – or even feeling like she was capable of doing so in her company. It was like Mallory was vibrating on a different frequency altogether. One that was making Jamie's head spin.

'No matter,' Mallory went on. 'Water under the bridge for the moment. Or at least we need to consider it that way. For now, I want your attention on the case, not on Rees. Let's see how this plays out, alright? You can see how we work and what we're working on, and once we catch the bastards behind this, you'll be able to confidently say that we're all above board here. And by process of elimination ...'

'That the police are not?' Jamie offered, seeing the expectation in Mallory's eyes.

'Glad we're on the same page here.' She cleared her throat and then nodded to her screen. 'Albanians.'

Jamie looked at it, at a set of mugshots there. Three guys with pronounced cheekbones and mean looks.

'Interpol's been tracking a ring of Albanian smugglers with ties to human trafficking out of the Middle East, especially Turkey, Syria, and Lebanon. They've mostly been working into Europe – France and Germany have seen the brunt of it, but we know these three are in the UK – and we just discovered they're actually in Wales – a travellers' camp about thirty miles from here. Coincidence?' She shrugged. 'We'll find out. Anyway, the Albanians have been making waves in mainland Europe with some bodies cropping up here and there, and we had the heads-up that they may have expanded operations. Interpol tracked some money changing hands that points to them purchasing a fleet of old fishing boats from a company in Algeria. They were registered to a shell company in Montenegro, but the address there is a warehouse that burned down a decade ago, and the port they were supposed to be docked at has no record of them ever being there. So ... We don't know. We don't know where these ships are, but they're the right size and type to smuggle both goods and people, and they're rugged enough to tackle the open sea and a lengthy journey. So if they're looking at the UK as destination number one, it's not out of the question that they're bringing these women out of the Middle East, going through the Strait of Gibraltar, and circling up the Atlantic coast. It gives them more inroads into Europe, as well as opening up the UK. It's a natural step for any expanding operation, and that's what they are. Ambitious, ruthless, and ballsy. And now they're here. And they're not above selling, torturing, and murdering women. We know that. So, yeah. Fuck 'em. Animals,' Mallory said.

Jamie was out of breath just listening to her. And she'd said all that without glancing at a single note. Though Jamie figured that it was the exact reason she was an intelligence officer, and running her own team. Because if there were two things that Jamie already knew about Mallory it was that she was both intelligent and more than capable of being in charge.

Hassan took the brief moment of silence to interject, looking directly at Mallory, but speaking for what seemed like it might have been for Jamie's benefit. 'I went by there, did some initial recon. They've set up on an old colliery site. There are about ten caravans, a few campers, several pickups and other vehicles. There's also a good number of tents and other non-permanent dwellings there. I counted at least two dozen adults, predominantly males, and at least a dozen children. Though I expect those numbers to be pretty conservative. Aerial shots via the drone, when compared with similar size sites, usually mean around thirty or more adults, so it wouldn't be out of the realm of the possible here.'

Mallory was nodding, looking back at Hassan.

He went on. 'From my initial sweep there, I did see evidence of both cock fights and dog fighting as well as farming.'

'Farming?' Jamie asked, picturing turnips for a moment.

'Puppy farming,' Mallory offered.

'Ah,' Jamie said sadly.

Hassan kept talking. 'Local police and a quick ask around in the surrounding villages suggest that pet disappearances and thefts are on the rise too. Not uncommon for groups like this to steal local pets – the ones capable of breeding are kept for breeding. The ones who aren't ...'

Jamie grimaced. 'Animals,' she muttered.

'Fucking right,' Mallory echoed. 'Signs of human imprisonment?'

Hassan shook his head. 'No, but dogs and chickens are one thing to keep locked up where you lay your head. They may be scum, but they're not stupid. The ligature marks on the bodies of the female victims suggest imprisonment, and the coroner's report suggested that their complexions were congruent with a lack of sun exposure. So it's fair to assume they're being kept inside, wherever they are.'

Mallory knocked her fist gently on her desk. 'So they're keeping them somewhere. Probably not far away. I'll have Jerry and Ash look into potential sites nearby.'

Jamie glanced over at the man and woman sitting at their desks. Both looked up, so Jamie guessed they were Jerry and Ash respectively.

'Think it's time to shake some trees. Nasir?'

Hassan gave a firm nod and grinned. 'Been waiting for you to say that. But first, Jamie had an interesting thought about the strangled victim.'

'Oh?' Mallory said, looking at Jamie.

'Go on,' Hassan urged her. 'Tell her about the marks on the neck. The thing you did.' He mimed choking himself.

Jamie raised her eyebrows. She didn't like being put on the spot. 'Uh,' she said, formulating her thoughts quickly. 'It was just that the strangle patterns might be suggestive of smaller hands, potentially a female assailant.'

Mallory's brow creased and she pursed her lips. 'Interesting.' She shrugged then. 'Guess we shouldn't be too surprised that a small-town coroner didn't catch that.' She looked at Jamie directly. 'No point spending hours discussing it. Can you write it up for me? Quick report, references and comparisons to previous cases if possible. Nasir can give you the relevant images you need from the coroner. Just broad strokes to get everyone up to speed here?'

'Uh, yeah, sure.'

'Great,' Mallory said, smiling. 'I look forward to reading your thoughts. Good work.'

Jamie tried not to blush a little. She didn't like being complimented - it made her squirm.

'Nasir?' Mallory said then, the tone clear.

'Right, going,' he said, touching Jamie's elbow.

'Good luck.'

And then Hassan was moving, and a second later he was out of the door, buzzing with energy.

And, as much as she didn't want to admit it, so was Jamie.

She liked Mallory.

And for Jamie ... that was saying a lot.

CHAPTER
EIGHT

Hassan drove quickly, zipping down through the Beacons, putting the Audi through its paces.

Jamie didn't deign to tell him that just because he was working *for* the law, that didn't mean he could disregard the law. She just kept stoic and let him drive. He was good at it, and she knew he'd done advanced courses as part of his training. She remembered when they were partners that for all his boyish qualities and humour, he was an extremely deft partner. Both physically and mentally. His years of experience as a captain in armed response had made him battle-hardened and cool, and his time as a detective had obviously showcased his intelligence too. She didn't think there was a more potent combination.

Though last time they'd worked together, he'd talked a lot about his family. Wife, two kids.

'How are the girls?' Jamie asked.

'They're good,' he replied, keeping his eyes front.

'Where are you living now?'

'Here and there. I go where they tell me.'

Cryptic. 'You're staying in Wales?'

'Renting a house with Ash in Brecon while we're here.'

'Ash?' She was surprised. 'The woman?'

He nodded.

'How does the wife feel about that?'

He sighed a little. 'Wouldn't know.'

Ah. 'Sorry to hear that.'

'How it goes,' he said, shrugging.

'The job?' Jamie asked. A story as old as time.

'My job definitely gave her plenty of time to fall in love with another man.'

'She cheated?'

'No,' he said, with a prolonged exhale. 'She had too much respect for me to do that, she said. She just told me it wasn't working anymore, she'd found someone else who 'sees her'.'

Jamie swallowed. Brutal. 'So you and Ash?'

'Strictly professional,' he replied. 'She's my partner. Or was, I guess.' He glanced at Jamie. 'She's new on the job. Supposed to be taking her under my wing or some bullshit. Hell, I'm new at this myself. A lot of pressure, honestly. Glad to have a more seasoned hand by my side in all honesty. I expect this to get a little messy, and I know you can handle yourself.'

'Messy?' Jamie asked.

'Albanian human traffickers and dog-fighters aren't known to be the most welcoming sort.'

'God, I wish I had my gun,' Jamie said, watching the barren and beautiful countryside sweep by.

'Me too,' Hassan said dejectedly. 'Me too.'

Jamie spotted the stacks of the colliery poking above the canopy of trees and Hassan slowed, pulling them off the road and into a layby about five-hundred metres from the site.

'Okay?' he asked.

She nodded.

'Nervous?'

She shook her head.

'Good. Let's do it.'

'We just walking right in the front door?'

'Let's see if we can get up close, look around. And then we'll knock. Give them a chance to go quietly.'

'You expect they will?'

'I doubt it. But I never say never.'

Jamie smirked, getting out of the car. 'Never pegged you for a Justin Bieber fan?'

'Bieber?' Hassan looked shocked. 'Please. Back Street Boys for life.'

'Dancing around your bedroom as a teenager, singing into a hairbrush?'

'A can of Lynx Africa, actually. But that's about the sum of it.'

Jamie laughed.

'Everybody ...' He pointed to her.

She raised her eyebrows. 'Not a chance.'

'Yeah-eh. Rock your body.' He pointed to her again.

She could only laugh.

'Come on, you know the words.'

'I do, but I'm not going to sing them.'

'Chicken shit,' he said as they began walking.

Jamie had to admit he was good at lightening the mood. And if he hadn't been, the reality of what they were about to do might have already set in.

She might even have realised how fucking stupid it was.

But as she and Hassan walked, with him reciting every word, inflection and all, to his favourite Back Street Boys tracks, she didn't.

And then they were at the gate.

And it was already happening.

CHAPTER
NINE

T he colliery was a large brick structure surrounded by an old chain link fence. There was barbed wire on the top, and tarps had been hung up along most of the perimeter. They were old and beaten up, browned with dirt and time, left there by the company that owned the land to prevent onlookers from getting a glimpse of the redevelopment. Except, like so many other old sites, that never happened. The costs outweighed the profit potential, or maybe the land was just too poisoned by the chemicals that had leeched into the earth over the centuries. Either way, this place was abandoned, and as they got closer their boots began to crunch on the shards of slag and coal left behind.

Above the fence they could see the stacks and the remaining walls. Through the holes in the tarps, they could see the great concrete foundations and plinths, stretching in all directions. Piles of rubble and steel littered the place, and trash was strewn everywhere. Tents were visible past the first building – some smaller structure lacking a roof. They were clustered together in what would have been the car park when the place was functioning. Smoke was rising from between them and voices carried distantly, dogs barking.

Jamie and Hassan looked at each other, and then started walking the perimeter of the fence, keeping silent and moving quick.

They didn't expect the women to be just locked up in cages outside, but they were hoping to see something more illegal than trespassing. At least then they could avoid any confrontation, and just skip straight to putting people in cuffs. But right now there wasn't all that much to observe, and there was no way a few local unis were going to answer a call to come and round up forty Albanians with a reputation for violence and lawbreaking. No, they needed something substantial. And as Jamie neared a fence post leaning away from the chain link, the bottom ties severed, she knew there was only one way to find it.

Before she even reached out for the bottom, Hassan's hand took hold of her elbow. He shook his head. 'Don't.'

'If we go around the front they're just going to turn us away. We have to get a look at what they're doing, at least.'

His lips bunched. He knew she was right, that just

walking around out here would achieve nothing. And going in the front and asking if they were keeping women prisoner and murdering them was going to achieve even less.

'Fine,' he said, fishing his phone from his pocket and pulling up a stopwatch. 'Two minutes. If we don't find anything, we pull out. And we *definitely* don't get seen. We stick to the perimeter, get a better look. Then we're out. Got it?'

The cold flash in his eyes and his tightening grip on her arm signified he wasn't joking and nor was he going to ask twice.

'I got it,' Jamie said. 'I've got no intention of getting my head caved in by some Albanian dog-fighters.'

She lifted the fence and ducked inside, and Hassan followed.

The ground in front of them was overgrown with weeds and long grass that led to the start of the concrete.

A path was already cut through it, as though this back entrance was being used to slip in unnoticed when required. Or possibly for fast escapes. Either way, they didn't have to wade through nettles, and that was something.

Jamie stepped up onto the concrete and Hassan followed, eyes roving back and forth.

They were shielded from the camp by the main building, but it was the low-slung secondary structure that was attracting Jamie. Mostly because despite it not having a roof, it still had a door, and there was a padlock on it. A new one.

She approached from behind, looking for a window, but didn't find one.

Hassan came behind her and tapped her on the shoulder, clearly understanding what she was wanting to do. He already had his hands cupped together, ready for her foot, and nodded to confirm.

His instincts were on point.

Jamie stepped up with his help, her hands cresting the craggy stone wall and bearing her weight.

Hassan lifted her without issue until her head was over the top and she could see inside.

No women, but this was where they were keeping the dogs. A row of small cages lined each wall, and inside half of them, dogs were lying, dirty and thin, in their own waste.

Jamie's stomach turned over, a dozen sets of sad and helpless eyes looking up at her, half in fear, half in hope.

She couldn't stop looking, a cold and ugly rage building inside her.

Hassan was still holding her foot, and when he lowered his hands, she couldn't help but go back down too.

'Anything?' he asked as she touched down.

'Dogs,' she said. 'A lot of them.'

He read the expression on her face. 'Stay cool, Jamie.'

'We have to do something.'

'And we will but, right now, busting through that door and letting them run free is only going to piss these guys off. Remember, we're just looking.' He held up his phone. 'And we're already inside a minute. Come on, let's check the other building.'

Jamie glanced back up at the wall above her, trying to think of a way she could get over and get the door open without making a sound.

Though as Hassan led the way to the next building, she couldn't come up with one.

'Fuck,' she muttered, following him, staying low. She was coming back for them. She promised herself.

Hassan reached the main colliery and pressed himself to the wall. This one had windows, and he peeked in one, eyes sweeping the interior.

The building itself was massive, and at one point would have processed the raw coal mined from the hills nearby. He didn't know a whole lot about the process, but he knew that it was crushed, sifted, sorted, and charred or cooked to refine it into usable material.

Jamie took a quick glance inside too, under Hassan's arm, and still saw the metal structures that would have housed the hoppers, as well as the old defunct conveyor belts to transport it to the sifters and into the back of trucks and other bins. Mountains of rough material lay around, jet black and filthy. The walls inside were stained black with the soot and ash kicked out by the huge furnaces now lying dormant and cold.

Jamie ducked backward and Hassan did too, holding up his phone. 'Ten seconds. We're out,' he whispered.

'Ten seconds, *then* we're out,' Jamie answered, scrambling around him and scurrying along the length of the building.

Hassan remained planted as Jamie peeked in again, this time seeing the room from a different angle, along with something a little more interesting.

She waved to Hassan and motioned him over.

He shook his head.

She motioned him again and, begrudgingly, with a shake of the head, he snuck towards her.

When he arrived, she pointed through the window at something below. A row of what might have been crates or boxes covered by a thick green tarp.

'What do you think?' Jamie asked, voice hushed.

'I think we're out of time. Let's go,' Hassan insisted.

'That green,' Jamie said, still staring at it. 'Looks military.'

'Military?' He seemed doubtful.

Jamie lifted her head. 'There's a big army base near here, isn't there? Outside Brecon somewhere?'

Hassan sighed. 'Yeah, there is. But I doubt there'd be surplus here.'

'Maybe it's stolen.'

'Nicking dogs out of back yards is different to lifting military surplus from an army base. It could be nothing.'

'Or it could be what we need.' Jamie took another

look inside, seeing the building completely empty. 'Help me down, I just want to take a quick look.'

'That's not what we're here for.'

'It's exactly what we're here for,' Jamie replied. 'These people are fucking *scum*. What if these are the crates they use to smuggle women? Full of DNA and evidence enough to put these guys away? If we go and ask them, they'll just rush in and destroy them. Hell, there could be women in there right now. Six feet from us. And you want to walk away from that?'

'Jesus, Jamie,' Hassan hissed. 'You'll be the fucking death of me.'

'Just shut up and take my hand,' she replied, getting up onto the sill and turning to face him. She reached out, offering her hand to him, looking past her hip into the building. The outside floor level was raised, and it was a good drop onto the boxes below them. Enough that it'd make a loud bang if she landed heavily.

Hassan stared at her outstretched fingers, and relented. 'Fucking hell,' he whispered to himself, getting a good grip and bracing himself on the sill. 'Just don't fall and break your leg or something.'

Jamie stepped backwards keeping her balance, and then edged over, finding a foothold on the rough brick.

Hassan leaned forward and Jamie let herself down as gently as she could until she was hovering over the crate. She looked up, Hassan holding her entire weight, her feet dangling. He was straining a little, a vein bulging in his forehead.

She opened her hand and he did the same, dropping Jamie the last foot or so.

A dull thunk rang out, the crate below her flexing as she touched down, crouching to try to minimise the sound. It wasn't loud, and she hoped it'd be swallowed up by the din still emanating from beyond the building.

She and Hassan both froze, waiting. But nothing stirred.

He made a cycling motion with his hand above her. 'Hurry up.'

Jamie got down onto the stony ground and grabbed the bottom of the tarp, pulling it up. At the bottom, there were big wooden boxes with holes drilled in the sides of them. The smell of shit was wafting out, but when Jamie pulled her phone out and shone a torch through one of the openings, the thing was empty. And she'd smelled human shit before. This wasn't it. Dog shit, definitely. Though there were no dogs inside. Hassan had said they were puppy farming – there was big money in it if you got the right designer breeds. They were using these to ship the animals out, she figured.

Jamie reached up, about to lower the tarp when she stopped, pulling it back a little further instead. The top box wasn't a dog crate, and nor was it empty. She knew the size and shape, and what looked like Russian characters spray painted on the side was a giveaway. She flipped the lock and opened it, seeing the sort of straw that they used to pack and protect ... guns.

She stared down into the box, a clump of the straw in her fingers, the black snub nose of a Russian standard issue Makarov pistol looking out at her.

Jamie glanced up at Hassan, who could see it too. He set his teeth, jaw flexing, then motioned her to come back up.

She closed the box and threw the tarp back over it, making to climb back up when she paused, pricking her ears.

Crunching.

Footsteps.

Fuck.

She waved Hassan back and he disappeared from view.

Jamie turned, then quickly dropped to a bear crawl and scrambled behind one of the mounds of old coal, hiding herself just as a man appeared with a dog on a leash.

Jamie listened to him approach, moving slowly around to the other side of the pile, matching her footsteps with his so she didn't alert him.

He was whistling a tune she didn't recognise, then bent and said something to the dog in a language she didn't recognise, but had to assume was Albanian.

She peeked out, watching a chunky British Bulldog being led towards the crates.

The guy reached down and threw back the tarp Jamie had just moved herself, ready to load the dog inside.

She breathed steadily, watching the guy. He wasn't that big. That was her first thought. Her second was that she could pick up the chunk of rubble next to her right heel and brain him with it.

But the only reason she didn't was because he reached into his pocket and pulled out a ring of keys. They jangled as he searched for the right one, kneeling and unlocking the padlock on the crate.

The dog turned to look at her, sad-faced with a huge underbite, drool coming from its jowls. It didn't seem distressed, but she knew what fate awaited it.

In that moment, her mind went back to her own dog. Hati. Jamie had never been a dog person, but she'd rescued him because someone had chosen to be cruel to him, too, and that was the thing she despised the most. Cruel people. Those who sought to do bad things to those who couldn't defend themselves. Dogs. Women. Children. Human fucking filthy scum who put their hands on people and took what they wanted. Who inflicted violence and pain, and who enjoyed doing it.

Her dog was safe now, with someone who would care for him. Better than she could. He was lucky. But this dog, stolen from its home and family, being traded and shoved into a box, ready to be used like a piece of meat ... didn't have that luxury. It didn't have anything except horror waiting for it. Innocent and unsuspecting as it was.

And she could intervene. Do something to protect it. To protect something that couldn't protect itself. It's why she did this job, wasn't it? To make a difference? To tip the scales? To make sure that the people who committed these vile acts got what they deserved?

And just like that, the chunk of brick and concrete was in Jamie's hands and she was advancing on the guy, slowly raising it above her head.

Hassan's face loomed above. He shook his head, eyes screaming at her. Don't do it!

But she didn't care. Was this piece of shit going to sue her? No. Was he going to cry to the police? Fuck no. This was justice in the only language guys like him understood. And if she'd had her gun, she would have banged him over the head with that. But she didn't. She just had a rock. And she was going to try not to crack his skull with it ... probably.

Five steps. That's all it was.

The rock was up, her breathing tight, sweat beading at her temples.

And then the dog barked.

An awkward, strained, bark that more resembled a grunt.

Jamie stared down at it, snorting and snoring while awake.

The guy on his knees froze, suddenly aware of what was behind him, and turned, standing quickly. His surprise quickly turned to anger as he saw Jamie and the rock above her head.

Fuck.

The guy dropped the dog leash and came forward quickly, hands rising.

She'd have to make this count. She wound up, ready to throw the rock, but before she even could, Hassan was flying through the air.

He led with his knee, crunching into the guy's shoulder and sending him into the ground with so much force Jamie was shocked that his spine didn't snap in two.

The Albanian landed face first, yelling out, and slid through the soot coating the ground.

The dog scarpered, leash trailing, barking and grunting.

Hassan didn't let up, taking the guy by the arm and rolling him onto his back.

He made to swing at Hassan, but he was too fast and too experienced to let it land, allowing the guy's fist to sail in front of his chin.

Hassan returned the favour with a swift right cross, plunging it into the guy's cheek with enough impetus that his head bounced off the ground and his eyes lolled in his head.

Hassan's eyes shot up to Jamie then. 'He came at you, I had no choice,' he said firmly. But it wasn't an explanation, more an affirmation. As in, when we have to stand in front of Mallory and explain it, that's what happened.

Jamie nodded. Yes. Of course.

'Drop the rock. We have to go.'

Jamie did so, and by the time it landed, Hassan was already ten feet away and hurtling towards the door.

She started after him then paused, hesitating, and looked back at the guy on the floor, now groaning and clutching his face.

'Shit,' she hissed, doubling back and stepping over him.

She grabbed his bunch of keys from the padlock on the crate and then hurdled once more towards the door.

Hassan was beckoning her frantically. And then they were in the sunshine and running for the back fence, a commotion already starting behind them, with shouts and threats erupting from the camp. The scream, the dog running around with a trailing leash, and the two strangers making a break for the back fence were probably enough of a giveaway that the camp had been invaded in some form.

'Come on!' Hassan called, leaping off the concrete foundation and back into the weeds. But when he looked back, Jamie wasn't following.

She ran right past towards the first building they'd checked out, already fumbling with the keys.

She reached the door, panting, and jammed the first key into the padlock. No good! The second. No. Third? Fuck!

More yells from behind them now, footsteps. Lots of them.

Jamie risked a look, saw eight or nine men running towards them.

Then the lock clicked and she looked down, seeing it open, a key sticking from the bottom.

She ripped it from the door and threw the thing open, dashing inside, rushing to the first cage, pulling the bolts across to release the doors.

A noise behind her.

She glanced over her shoulder, readying for a fight.

But it was Hassan.

'Jesus Christ, Jamie!' he yelled. But instead of dragging her out of there, he dived in to help, starting on the other side.

Each door that opened set a dog free and running. They barked and howled, leaping to freedom and scattering through the camp.

Just a few to go.

They met at the back of the building, closing in on each other, meeting at the final cage. A pit bull, blue-furred and battle-scarred looked up at them, terrified and snarling, all teeth and muscle.

Jamie's hand reached out, but Hassan was faster and snatched it from the air. 'No,' he said. 'Look at that thing! It'll fucking rip you apart!'

Jamie swallowed, looking at the poor animal, ears back, teeth bared and gnashing.

She exhaled, looking over her shoulder at the doorway. The first Albanian reached it, sagging onto the frame, out of breath and sweating. He stared at them, furious, calling out threats.

'It's not me that it wants,' Jamie said, shrugging Hassan off and closing her hand around the bolt.

The Albanian advanced towards them, hurling harsh words.

But the second Jamie pulled the pin and Hassan dragged the door open, he froze in his tracks.

There was a moment of stillness, a low growl echoing through the sudden silence.

And then the dog launched from the cage like a cruise missile, tearing across the room and hurling itself at the Albanian.

His arm came up, but the pit bull didn't care. Flesh was flesh and all it wanted to do was wreak havoc.

As the Albanian's blood-curdling screams rose in the summer air, Jamie and Hassan stood straight and looked away. Hassan pointed over the wall, through the missing roof.

They climbed onto the cages and he hoisted himself up. Jamie stopped for just a second, spotting something lying on a bloodied rag on a shelf to her right.

She grabbed it and then followed, rolling over the stony top and dropping to the ground outside. She staggered sideways, Hassan steadying her, and they made for the back fence, a couple of the dogs already scrambling under it.

They reached it and Hassan ducked through, holding it up for Jamie.

She crouched to get under it, but they weren't alone,

and before she got through, a fist closed around her belt and yanked her back.

Jamie was sent onto her backside and rolled sideways just in time to avoid a heavy kick to the chest.

The guy was big, bald, mean-looking, with a scarred face and tattooed arms. But he was slow, and Jamie was armed.

Being the vicious bunch they were, they sought to control the dogs with fear and pain. And the perfect tool for that was now in Jamie's hands.

The guy's eyes widened when he realised what it was. But before he could react or dodge, Jamie rammed the sharp end of the cattle prod into the soft patch of flesh under his chin and pulled the trigger.

A bolt of electricity surged into his head, his teeth chattering violently, hands forming themselves into misshapen claws as his muscles seized.

His legs gave out and buckled, a dark wet patch forming on his jeans as he pissed himself, spitting flecks of saliva over the weeds.

Jamie released the button and pulled the prod away.

He gasped, filling his lungs just in time to watch Jamie twist onto her left leg, wind up, and then unleash a fierce crescent kick, right into his jaw.

The guy spun to the ground, face down in a clump of stinging nettles, missing a few teeth.

And that was all the invitation Jamie needed to get the hell out of there.

Hassan was still holding the fence as she all but

dived through it, the camp denizens yelling in panic and terror behind them as the dogs took their sweet revenge and Jamie and Hassan made their escape.

'Still been keeping up with the Tae Kwon Do, then?' he panted, hurrying her back through the trees towards the car.

'Found a sweet little gym in Stockholm,' Jamie replied, hurling the cattle prod deep into the undergrowth.

'Bet the fat fuck regrets grabbing your belt now!' Hassan laughed as they neared the layby and what seemed like safety.

Jamie slowed to catch her breath. 'What can I say? I guess he *wanted it that way …*' she said, singing the last part.

Hassan grinned at her. 'That's good – but I'm still really pissed off at you.'

She shrugged, pushing through the last branches and emerging next to Hassan's Audi. 'They had it coming. And then some.'

'They did,' he said, pulling out his phone and dialling Mallory. 'But we might well have just kicked the hornets' nest.'

Jamie looked back, listening to their distant howls echo through the trees. Three words came to mind as she drew a slow, steadying breath.

'Let them come.'

CHAPTER
TEN

By the time the commotion died down and everyone was rounded up, the sun was already going down.

Some escaped, slipped away. A few of the caravans and motorhomes, cars ... they managed to hit the road before the first flashing lights arrived and barred the exits. But for the most part, it was a success.

Mallory arrived shortly after, and took charge of the uniformed officers like a Roman commander, ordering them here and there with precision and callous efficiency. As such, eleven adult males were placed under arrest, along with three females – who decided they didn't want to play nicely with the police. The rest were placed in custody but not arrested while their belongings were searched.

Thankfully, the dogs that were set loose were all

rounded up too, the RSPCA arriving with a large van and a chip scanner, their owners called.

While the sun set, there was a lot of face licking and tearful children. Though the biggest score was the haul of weapons.

Jamie and Hassan watched from the roadside as uniformed officers carried the crate of guns to a police van and loaded it in the back.

And then, suddenly, the cars were pulling away, the blue lights fading into the distance, and silence was falling over the countryside.

The colliery was still private land, and the remaining unarrested denizens had packed up what they could carry and had already shipped out, looking for greener pastures. All that was left behind was trash. Broken tents and forgotten clothing. The odd shoe. A strange, dress-less doll with glinting eyes, peering skyward, life-less and eerie.

Mallory walked over, shaking Hassan's hand, then Jamie's. 'You two okay?' she asked, standing with them at the roadside, her Mercedes sitting just in front of their Audi.

They both nodded.

'I'm not going to ask what happened. I know things go sideways fast. And if you hadn't intervened like you had, who knows where those guns would have ended up. Or what they'd be used for.' She sighed, staring into the thick canopy over the road. It rustled gently. 'One of the guys was pretty badly torn up by a dog – serves him right – he'll be in the hospital for weeks. And he'll never look the same. Not that he was a looker before, mind you. Reckon that's just cosmic justice at work.' She smiled briefly at them. 'Not much to worry about there. Though there were two others, said that they were assaulted. Screamed it, actually. One with a cracked cheekbone and a nasty cut on his scalp. The other one pissed himself and then got a face full of stinging nettles?' She looked from one to the other. 'Anything I need to be prepared for?'

Jamie and Hassan looked at each other. Then Jamie spoke. 'The one with the head wound. He came at me. Nasir had no choice. He would have killed me,' Jamie said firmly, hearing Hassan breathe a quiet sigh of relief next to her to hear his own words parroted back.

He quickly chimed in. 'The one that pissed himself – he tried to take Jamie's head off. Forced her to use a cattle prod on him.'

'A cattle prod?' Mallory raised her eyebrows.

'They were using it to torture the dogs,' Jamie said coldly.

'Hope you stuck him somewhere where it hurt,' Mallory replied.

'I did.'

She curled a small smile. 'And the boot print on his face? That self-defence, too?'

'That one might have been just for me,' Jamie answered dryly.

Mallory's smile widened. Then she nodded. 'Alright, just so I know what's coming. If there's nothing else ...?'

'There isn't,' Hassan confirmed. 'We went in to take a look, found their stockpile of illegal weapons and the stolen animals, and then we were set upon by the camp, forcing us to flee – and fight – for our lives.'

'Good,' Mallory said. 'And the women?'

He shook his head. 'But as we said, we didn't think they'd be kept on site. Hopefully something will come out during questioning.'

Mallory turned to Jamie, waiting for her to chime in.

'I ... don't think it's them,' she said then.

'Elaborate?'

'Stealing and breeding dogs? A few handguns from the 80s?' She stared back through the open gates into the colliery. 'These people ... they may be scum, but they're just trying to make ends meet. They might be connected with trafficking, but I'd bet it's their own people, escaping worse situations than this one. What the hell do they want with women? And where would they even think to keep them?'

Mallory bit her lip.

'I'm not ruling them out,' Jamie added. 'I've been wrong before. But ...'

'It's a feeling,' Mallory finished for her. 'Okay. Well, either way, we did a good thing here, probably saved some human lives. Definitely saved some dogs. The chickens ... I can't speak for ...' she said, shooing a hen away with her foot that had wandered between them. It clucked and then paced quickly towards the other birds that were pecking around near the gate. 'It does leave us with a problem, though. If not the Albanians, then who?'

Neither Jamie nor Hassan had an answer for that.

'A question for tomorrow. You two should get back, I'm sure you're both tired.'

Hassan yawned right on cue and nodded. 'It's been a long day.'

'Drive safe, Nasir. And thanks again.'

He gave her a courteous dip of the head and circled the Audi towards the driver's seat.

Jamie made to get in the passenger side, but Mallory put a hand on her shoulder. 'What are your plans for this evening?' she asked.

'Plans?' Jamie repeated back, a little thrown. 'I don't know. Go back to my mother's house and hear about how a little eyeliner might do me wonders for attracting a decent man?'

Mallory smirked a little. 'Sounds tantalising. Here's another option: Thai green curry.'

'Dinner?' Jamie was a little surprised. 'I'm sorry, I'm not ... I mean, I don't ...'

Mallory's eyebrows raised. 'I'm not asking you on a date, Jamie,' she laughed. 'I'm asking if you'd be interested in coming to dinner. I'd like to hear more about your experiences, your story. You came up through the Met, made DS, made a big splash with a few tough cases, left the Met, threw in with Stockholm Polis, cracked an international corruption ring. Left Stockholm for the wilds of northern Sweden, got sucked into a trafficking investigation, barely got out alive, and then eighteen months later you're running your own investigatory team for the Swedish National Operations Department? And all by forty?' Mallory looked genuinely amazed as she recited it.

Jamie looked away instead. 'I'm forty-one. And I don't know if there's much to tell. Sounds like you already know everything about me.'

She put an arm around Jamie without invitation. 'Oh, I don't think I've even scratched the surface.'

HASSAN SET OFF. JAMIE GOT IN MALLORY'S Mercedes. And the sun set.

Mallory drove quickly and in silence, which seemed a little odd to Jamie considering she'd invited Jamie with the express purpose of getting to know her.

Whether there was a job offer coming, Jamie wasn't sure. She didn't want to be presumptuous, but nor did she want to give Mallory the impression she had any intention of staying in the UK. Things were finally good back in Stockholm. Stable. She had a nice apartment, a car, a stable job ... she was happy. Or at least as happy as she'd been in years, she thought. Except for Thorsen. She felt so guilty. Not that it was her fault, this time. She'd not got him shot. He'd wanted that last investigation, that last case on Gotland. He'd brought her back.

And said he would have gone anyway. She didn't want to. She was retired. Was glad about that. But he wouldn't let it go. He was determined to return to work ... and now, he was the one doing hours of physical therapy every day, relearning to walk, to talk, even. A shadow of his former self. A shade of the man he once was, the man that Jamie ... loved. No, fucking hell Jamie. You piece of shit. Don't say that. You haven't stopped loving him just because he got hurt. Don't do that. Don't be a fucking bitch about it. He gave you everything. He wanted to give you everything. You were just too scared to give it back. And now ... and now you're going to lose him unless you grow a spine and face him. Face your life and the consequences it comes with, instead of just running away at every sign of things getting difficult, or complicated.

'Jesus Christ,' Mallory said then. 'I can hear you thinking. Those gears churning hard over there,' she joked, glancing at Jamie as they whipped through a hedge-lined B-road somewhere near Brecon.

'Sorry,' Jamie said. 'Just ... a lot on my mind.'

'You hungry? We're almost there.'

'I could eat.'

'Me too.' She flashed Jamie a smile, the headlights catching the white of a sign: *Croeso i Brecon.*

And suddenly, Jamie felt very far away from Stockholm.

. . .

Mallory let them into a home she was renting for the duration of the investigation. It was a modest stone cottage on the outskirts of town with a bright interior and a back garden that had a deck surrounded by flowers and plants and had fairy lights suspended above it.

'Go out,' Mallory said to her. 'Take a seat.'

Jamie glanced back from her position in front of the French doors, and then exited into the warm night air. 'Do you need a hand making dinner?'

Mallory shook her head. 'No, it's fine, honestly,' she laughed. 'I made this two days ago and I've just got so much of it.' She fished in the fridge and pulled out two big Tupperware boxes, one with rice and the other with the curry. 'It's going right in the microwave.'

As Jamie sat at the patio table and stared up at the stars, Mallory kept talking. 'I tend to prep my meals for the week at the weekend and then eat them throughout, but I don't think I can do curry four times this week and I definitely miscalculated the portion size.'

'You weren't expecting company?' Jamie asked.

She laughed. 'Uh, no. No, I wasn't. I don't do that when I work.'

'Only when you don't?' Jamie replied, looking in at Mallory, who was already getting plates ready, the microwave humming away on the countertop.

'I'm never not working,' Mallory called. 'Take that to mean what you will.'

'That relationships are more trouble than they're worth,' Jamie answered.

Mallory was leaning on the door then, head outside. 'For people like us, probably.' She flashed Jamie a grin.

'People like us?' Jamie squirmed a little, well aware that she wasn't exactly neuro-typical ... especially when it came to relationships, either platonic or otherwise. Luckily, she'd managed to keep that part of herself fairly well hidden. Her career depended on it. Though the job itself did provide some smokescreen. People often didn't question 'quirky-yet-astute' detectives. Or at least didn't give them much of a second look. Though Mallory appeared to be looking a little harder than most. Jamie would have to tread carefully. And bear in mind that, despite Mallory's warmth and sincerity, just a day earlier, Richard Rees – the man Mallory was sure was corrupt - appeared the same way. Could Mallory be trusted? Jamie didn't know, and she needed to remind herself of that fact.

'Yeah,' Mallory said. 'Work-focused, driven, responsibility-taking people who refuse to roll over. Even when it's detrimental to ourselves.'

Jamie risked a smile.

'Something to drink?' Mallory added, ducking back inside as the microwave beeped. 'I don't have any wine or anything.'

'I don't drink.'

Mallory popped back to the door. 'Me neither,' she said, grinning with straight white teeth. 'It's *why* I don't have any wine.' Her gaze lingered on Jamie for a second more, then she disappeared and quickly returned with two bowls filled with steaming curry.

She put one down in front of Jamie, and the other opposite, doubled back for two glasses of water, and then sat, eyeing her dinner guest as she began mixing her food.

'So,' she said, chewing her first bite, thoughtfully. 'Where do you want to start?'

'I don't know,' Jamie said, looking at her food. It smelled delicious.

'We've got all night, and I want to hear the whole story. So how about at the beginning?' Mallory said.

Jamie took a bite, swallowing nervously. If there was one thing Jamie hated, it was talking about herself.

'Why don't you … tell me about your father?'

Jamie glanced up at her, at her sharp, narrowed eyes, her unflinching stare that disarmed and charmed Jamie all at once. That calmed her and made her heart beat a little harder at the same time.

'Your childhood. What was it like growing up in Stockholm?' She waggled her fork at Jamie, chewing on another bite. 'And then … I want to hear about the Angel Maker. And don't skimp on the details.'

CHAPTER
ELEVEN

What started as a chronology of Jamie's life quickly devolved into a comparison of mothers, with each of them one-upping the other for whose was worse. Jamie won though, when she told the story of how her father came home drunk one night, her mother tried to throw an iron at him, but it was plugged in, hit the end of the cord, bounced back and broke her nose ... Her father, and Jamie, howled with laughter at it. So, Jamie's mother called the police and said that her father had struck her.

That wasn't a fun night in the end.

Mallory blinked in astonishment at that one.

And Jamie realised she'd never told that story to another person before.

Still, it was good to talk to someone Jamie felt understood her, somewhat. Mallory had grown up in a good family in the south-east of England, had worked with Kent Police for a time, then transitioned to work with the NCA back when it was the National Criminal Intelligence Service. She had always been more interested in intelligence than field work, and her eye for detail served her well, she said. Then it became SOCA, the Serious Organised Crime Agency, and finally, the National Crime Agency. She was promoted to intelligence officer when that happened, and was given command of her own team, small as they were.

She and Jamie had totally different journeys, but the destination felt somewhat the same. Forty and work-obsessed, with little to show for it personally. Though neither seemed that hell-bent on finding the 'personally' side. It was a game of snap for the big things. Never married. Snap. No kids. Snap. Don't think I want them. Snap. Don't think I'd know what I'd do if I switched jobs. Snap. Don't know where I want to live after. Snap. Though Jamie did tell Mallory about her six-month jaunt in Greece with Thorsen – though she seemed to leave Thorsen out of the story. And they both agreed that it wasn't the worst place to end up.

Mallory seemed especially interested in the Angel Maker case, which wasn't surprising. It was an interesting story. Jamie had to admit that. What came after seemed like a rollercoaster upon reflection, and it dawned on Jamie just how close she'd come, time and time again, to dying. They all seemed to meld together in her mind. So much so that when Jamie was listing them all off, Mallory had to interject and ask, 'Wait, didn't you also get shot at some point?'

To which Jamie replied, 'Oh, yeah,' and laughed, pulling up the hem of her shirt to display the bullet scar.

Mallory thought that was hilarious, branded Jamie a certified badass, told Jamie that she'd spent most of her adult life at a desk, and that she regretted not getting out from behind it more.

'It's not all it's cracked up to be,' Jamie said evenly. 'And a lot of people haven't been so lucky. Because, most of the time, that's what it is. Luck. Lucky the air lift arrived so quickly. Lucky that bullet missed my liver. Lucky that the guy taking a swing for you is just that little bit slow to land the punch. Lucky that a million things happen to keep you alive.'

'Sounds like you must have someone watching over you.'

Jamie turned her head then and saw her father sitting in the empty chair next to Mallory, big as he was, in that huge peacoat he always wore. His blue eyes sparkled in the light of the bulbs overhead, a wide smile on his even wider face. Just like he always was when she saw him.

'Don't give them an inch, Jamie,' he said. The words so burned into her memory that she would never forget them. Could never forget them.

She tried to swallow the lump of hot iron in the back

of her throat, then looked away so Mallory wouldn't see the tears.

'I'll get the plates,' Mallory said then, standing and taking Jamie's, heading inside.

It was exactly what Jamie needed, and she appreciated it.

When she looked back at the chair, her father was gone again.

He visited her less and less these days.

And one day he'd be gone forever, she thought.

Though she really hoped she was wrong.

When her phone buzzed on the table next to her, she nearly fell off her chair.

Jamie roughly wiped her eyes and grabbed it, recognising the number right away.

'Hey,' she said, keeping her voice low and standing up from the table. She made a beeline towards the end of the garden, realising only now how late it was.

'Jamie,' came the reply. Richard Rees. Her mother's husband. Chief Superintendent of the Dyfed-Powys Police. And by Mallory's account, a corrupt piece of shit. 'Where are you?' he asked.

'Working.' Jamie stopped, standing next to a stone bench tucked beneath an oak tree as far from the house as she could get. 'What's up?'

Mallory was already watching her through the patio doors, slowly washing their dishes.

'It's the girl,' Rees said, sounding agitated.

'The girl from the hospital?' Jamie asked, trying to

keep her expression neutral. 'The one that jumped from the moving van?'

'Yeah, *that* girl,' Rees sighed.

'What's wrong? Is she okay?'

'Yeah,' he said, sounding breathless now, as though he was hurrying somewhere. 'She's awake.'

CHAPTER
TWELVE

She had to play it carefully.

When Jamie returned to the kitchen, Mallory asked, 'Everything okay?'

'Yeah,' Jamie said with a sigh, deciding that lying was the worst option. 'Richard Rees.' She held her phone up and wiggled it a little. 'Wondering if I was coming back to the house tonight.'

'And are you?' Mallory asked, making slow circles on a bowl with a sponge. Jamie was fairly sure the bowl was clean five minutes ago.

'I love to run, but I think thirty kilometres on the side of the road in my boots is probably a little much after consuming my body weight in Thai Green curry,' Jamie said. And it was the truth.

'I could take you,' Mallory offered. 'Or you're welcome to take the guest room. It's not been slept in.'

She held up her wrist, fingers dripping with dish soap, and checked the time. 'It's almost eleven.'

The way she was looking at Jamie told her that Mallory was testing her. She was an intelligence officer. Her job was information. Gather data. Analyse data. Extrapolate data. Form hypothesis. Test hypothesis. Confirm hypothesis.

This was data gathering. Was Jamie lying? Did she need to get home? What for? Was it important? Was Jamie not telling her things? What things? What was Richard Rees hiding? Where would he hide it?

Mallory hadn't mentioned that Rees had picked Jamie up from the airport, that he'd been tailed by the NCA, that Rees had lost them and he and Jamie had disappeared somewhere. That Jamie hadn't come forward with that information. Mallory knew Jamie knew something she didn't. Knew that Rees knew something she didn't. But asking wasn't her job. Information was her job. And she would get it, sooner or later.

So Jamie did the only reasonable thing she could, and said, 'It's been a long day, I'll stay here.'

Mallory's eyes twitched almost imperceptibly as she made her calculations. Then her countenance softened and she went back to scrubbing, finally finishing the bowl. 'Okay, great,' she said. 'There's soap and everything in the shower, fresh towels in the cupboard inside the door. Oh, and there's a spare toothbrush in my wet bag on the side of the sink.' She flashed Jamie a smile. 'Unused, don't worry.'

Jamie returned it and nodded. 'Thank you.'

'Sure,' Mallory said. 'My pleasure.'

Jamie lingered for a moment more, then hooked a thumb over her shoulder. 'I, uh ... I think I'll grab that shower.'

Mallory just nodded. 'See you in the morning. I'll be up early for a run. So feel free to fix yourself some coffee or whatever. I'll be back.'

'Don't suppose you have some extra running shoes?'

'Ha,' Mallory said, nodding. 'Actually, I do.' She looked at Jamie's feet. 'Though I don't know if they'll fit. I'm a five.'

'Six and a half,' Jamie answered with a sigh. 'It's all good.'

'Next time.'

Next time? That rolled over in Jamie's head for a moment. She said nothing about it, just nodded, and then turned away.

Next time ...

THE SHOWER WAS HOT, THE TOOTHBRUSH unused, and the bed comfy. Though she didn't sleep very well. She never did, really, but this night was worse than others. Light and uncomfortable, she tossed and turned, thinking about the girl. About her injuries, and about what she'd been through. About how Jamie should have been more concerned with her wellbeing and what would drive her to leap from a moving van. But instead, she'd been focused on playing mental chess with Mallory.

When the sun rose and Mallory roused, padding around quietly next door, getting ready for her run, Jamie rose also, and dressed, coming down the stairs as Mallory was lacing up her runners.

'Hey, early bird,' she said, smiling. She looked tired, too. But who wasn't at six in the morning?

'Morning,' Jamie replied, smiling.

'Sleep okay?'

'Okay.' Jamie pushed her hands into the pockets of her jeans. 'Not to disrupt your morning schedule or anything, but you think I could get a ride before your run?'

'Everything okay?' Mallory asked, eyes twitching again as all the possibilities reeled in her mind.

'Yeah,' Jamie said. 'I just ... Up all night thinking. Thinking how I'm looking at this from just one side. I came here to help Rees find the truth, and I don't feel like I'm doing that. In fact, I've done nothing to help discover who tampered with the evidence.'

Mallory stood straight and put her hands on her hips.

'I know you'll say that Rees is the one who did that, that spending more time with him will just muddy the waters. And it might. But I've not spoken to a single colleague of his, anyone on his team. And with you and Hassan telling me he's dirty, well, I might just start believing you unless I see for myself.'

Mallory stuck out her bottom lip, then nodded. 'Alright.'

'Alright?'

'I'd do the same thing. I appreciate the honesty. Hell, you don't know if I'm the one who snuck into the police station and destroyed those samples. And if I were in your shoes … the friendly welcome, coming for dinner, staying the night. It could all be easily misconstrued as trying to butter you up so you're blinded to my duplicity.'

'Is that what you're doing?'

Mallory just smiled. 'If I were me, and I was hiding something, and you – Detective Jamie Johansson – just showed up on my doorstep, unaffiliated and determined as you are, well, it'd be in my best interest to befriend you, wouldn't it? Try to shield myself?'

'It would …' Jamie said slowly.

'So let's go. I'll drop you off wherever you want. You do your due diligence, get to the bottom of this, and then let me know.'

'Let you know what?'

'Whatever you want.' Mallory shrugged. 'We're just going to keep doing our job. Keep searching for the truth. Keep hunting the bad guys. And you do your thing.' She stepped forward, touched Jamie on the top of the arm, and then stepped past. 'I'll get my keys.'

And Jamie just stood there, watching the sun rise over Brecon through the front door of Mallory's cottage.

CHAPTER
THIRTEEN

Mallory was pleasant on the drive, but the conversation was superficial. Either she'd just completely flipped on Jamie and decided that she didn't want to be friends anymore, or she was really playing into the whole Switzerland thing and doing her best not to give Jamie anything more to think about. Except, it was giving Jamie *even more* to consider. Or maybe that was the point and it was all mind games. She was an intelligence officer, and the clue was in the name. Intelligent. More so than Jamie could give her credit for, she thought. Not someone who could be outwitted or outplayed. Which made her very dangerous. At least, to whoever was on the opposing side.

She dropped Jamie at the curb outside Rees' house and looked past her into the driveway. 'No Rees?'

Jamie shrugged. 'I'm not his keeper. Don't you have a tail on him anyway?'

'Sometimes,' Mallory said, grinning. 'Ash didn't seem to have a very good grip on the term "covert surveillance".'

'Right ...' Jamie said. 'She was the one following Rees when he picked me up from the airport?'

Mallory nodded. 'She was the one that lost you.'

Jamie waited for the next question, but it didn't come.

'Anyway, I pulled her. An expenditure of resources with no seeming payoff. I mean, what chief superintendent is going to go about his nefarious and deviant doings if he's being followed?'

Jamie looked out at his frankly beautiful and somewhat lavish house. 'Don't you mean "What chief superintendent is going to go about his nefarious and deviant doings if he *knows* he's being followed?"'

Mallory chuckled through closed lips, then reached across Jamie's lap and opened the door for her. 'See ya, Detective Johansson. Daylight's burning.'

Jamie got out, but before she could even properly close the door, Mallory was pulling away.

Jamie managed to throw it shut as the Mercedes peeled from the curb and disappeared into the distance. She let out a long breath, and then turned towards the house. It wasn't even seven yet, and Rees wasn't in work, that much she knew. So where was he?

She got to the door and jiggled the handle. Locked. Fuck. She knocked. No answer.

Knocked again. 'Mum?' she called. 'Mum?'

Nothing.

'I know you're home, your car is here,' Jamie yelled, having a weird flashback to her childhood. Where she'd be at home *with* her mum, and her father would come home late. He'd find the door locked, her keys in the back of it so he couldn't even open the damn thing. He'd jiggle it, nothing. Knock. Call. Nothing.

Jamie would be on the sofa next to her mum, the TV muted, the curtains drawn. Just listening. When Jamie would get up to go and open it, her mother would grab her arm. 'Don't,' she'd say. 'I told him I'd lock it if he came home late.'

Her grip would be like iron, hard enough to bruise Jamie's pale young skin.

Her father would bang and yell. But her mother wouldn't move a muscle, just sit there with her other hand clutched around the stem of a wine glass filled with cheap red.

Her father would eventually have to clamber over the side gate, come around the back, try the back door, find it also locked, and swearing and huffing, would open his office window and crawl in – no easy feat for the six foot four man he was. And the only reason that would be open was because the door was locked from the outside. It was the only place he could go to escape Jamie's mother. At least, when they were together.

Jamie shook off the memory, and the bitterness, and knocked again. 'Mum, please,' she said. 'It's important. Richard needs me to help, and I can't—'

And suddenly, she was there at the mention of his name, swimming from the darkness of the living room in her pink robe. 'Yes, yes,' she said, coming through the kitchen. 'I'm coming as fast as I can.'

She unlocked the door.

'Jesus, some of us actually sleep, Jamie, you know that, don't you?'

Jamie tried not to ball her fists too obviously. Instead, she took a breath, counted to three. As she always did when she spoke to her mother, trying not to fixate on the fact that; a) she came from the living room, not the stairs, and b) she had clearly been awake for some time judging by the coffee on her breath and the pot on the counter that said the coffee had been warming for nearly sixty minutes.

'I do, and I'm sorry,' Jamie said quickly. 'But I need to speak to Richard—'

'Well, he's not here. Did you try calling him?'

'No,' Jamie said through gritted teeth, feeling a little like she was being barred from entering.

'That would be best, don't you think, if you're trying to find him? Not that you'd be here to spend time with your own mother.' She sighed theatrically.

'You're the one that begged me to come here to help him,' Jamie said defiantly.

Her mother scoffed. 'Beg? I did no such thing. I

simply asked for a favour from my only daughter. Is that so heinous a crime?'

'Look, I don't want to fight.'

'Oh, no? That's a surprise. Everything's always been a fight with you. Just like your—'

'Don't,' Jamie said coldly. And whether it was the tone or the flash of anger in her eyes, she didn't know. But either way, her mother paled a shade and shrank into the doorway a little.

She cleared her throat. 'Richard left early this morning. Around four. He took a phone call, got up, dressed, and then left in a hurry.'

'Who from?'

'Hmm?' she asked, seemingly not interested by the conversation or the fact that her husband ran out of the house at four in the morning without telling her why.

'The phone call,' Jamie said through gritted teeth. 'Who was it from?'

'How should I know?' She tutted.

Jamie swallowed her growing frustration. It had to be the hospital. 'I need to change,' Jamie said, pushing in past her mother.

'Yes, you do. And shower!' her mother called after her. 'You smell like a homeless person.'

Jamie paused on the stairs and turned back. 'I *smell* like I raided a camp full of Albanian scumbags that fight dogs and smuggle guns!'

'I wouldn't know what that smells like.'

'It smells like ... It smells ...!' Jamie's hands rose to

the sides of her head, and then shook violently. 'Rrrrgh!' she yelled, then turned away and stomped up the stairs.

'And don't use all the hot water!'

JAMIE DID NOT SHOWER. SHE SHOWERED THE night before, after all. But when changing, she did spend more time than she would have liked to admit smelling her own armpits.

Once she had clean clothes on and a fresh layer of deodorant, she slipped down the stairs and into the kitchen, stopping briefly at the counter to fix herself a coffee.

'Don't drink it all! I didn't make enough for two,' came her mother's shrill call over the sound of the TV.

Fuck, she should go.

Her eyes came to rest on the key hook next to the door, and then drifted through the glass to her mother's shining BMW Z4 sitting on the driveway.

A second later, she'd dumped the remainder of the coffee pot into the sink, grabbed the keys, and pulled the door shut behind her.

Whether it was the sloshing of liquid, the bang of the door, or the starting of the engine, Jamie wasn't sure. But either way, as she shoved the car into first and sprayed the barn sitting behind Richard Rees' driveway with gravel with the back tyres, her mother was on the porch yelling at her, waving her arms madly.

For a second, she felt guilty. But then, as the wind

caught her hair and the car sling-shotted itself towards the rolling hills of the Brecon Beacons, it faded.

And then, as she drove, she felt free.

Though, despite not knowing it then, the feeling would be momentary.

Things were about to change.

And fast.

CHAPTER
FOURTEEN

Jamie got to the hospital and pulled into the same parking structure as she had before. And in almost the exact same spot as last time, she found Richard Rees' car.

She parked next to it, killed the engine, and then jogged down to the entrance. She rode the same lift to the same floor and got off, walking quickly towards the girl's room.

As her hand hit the door handle, she stole a quick glance around. Nothing out of place. Okay, good. But what awaited her inside?

Would the girl even still be here?

Jamie pushed through and Richard Rees stood up so quickly from the chair in the corner of the room it made her jump a little.

'Jamie,' he said, a look of relief flooding his tired face. 'I didn't know if you'd come. I thought you'd be here last night, so I assumed ...'

'I couldn't get away. I was with Catherine Mallory.'

His brow crumpled, but he didn't press the issue. 'Well, you're here now.' He looked at the open door behind her. 'Alone, I hope?'

'I am,' Jamie said, shutting the door, turning her eyes to the girl in the bed. She was indeed now awake, her quiet, fierce eyes fixed on Jamie. Her arm was still in plaster, the paper stitches on her cheek and around her eye looking fresher than last time, and fewer in number. It'd only been two days, but the girl seemed to be recovering quickly. 'Why is she restrained?' Jamie asked, gesturing to the padded cuffs around her wrists, fixed to the rails on the bed.

'Because when she woke up last night, she tried to escape. And injured two hospital staff in the process,' Rees said sternly, looking at the girl.

She was still staring at Jamie.

'Jesus, what happened?'

'When the nurse was removing her IV, she grabbed a pair of forceps off her tray and stabbed her in the leg with them. And when the other nurse tried to restrain her, she bit him on the arm, then jumped from the bed and tried to make a run for it. She made it to the door before she fainted.' Rees glanced at her again. 'No food in your stomach for a week will do that to you, won't it?'

She didn't answer, just kept looking at Jamie, who was looking back.

'She speak English?' Jamie asked.

'Don't know, hasn't said a word,' Rees replied. 'This all happened last night, which is when they called me – I'm listed as her emergency contact. They told me they can't keep her here if she's violent. Not unsupervised. And they can't do a psychological evaluation if she doesn't speak English.'

'She's not violent,' Jamie said, looking at her. 'She's just terrified.'

'Either way, it puts us in a difficult position. Yesterday, your friend Mallory requisitioned copies of our case files from the last three years. Random ones, it seems like. But she's digging for *something*. More shit to pin on me? I don't know. But you know what *does* look bad?'

'Hiding the fact that you have a material witness in an open investigation you're actively hiding from the government agency that has already suspended you for breaking chain of custody and who is investigating you for misconduct?'

Rees scowled. 'Exactly that.'

'So, what do you want me to do? You're not exactly putting me in an easy position here. I should hand this over to Mallory. See what she does with it. That's the simplest, safest, and the best thing to do. Tell me why it's not?'

He seemed to hesitate. 'Because ... the girl isn't all.'

'What do you mean?'

'There's something else. Another piece of evidence.'

Jamie grabbed his arm and pulled him to the corner

of the room. 'What the hell are you talking about?' she asked, voice hushed and harsh.

Rees looked nervous. 'It's the girl, she ...'

'She what? You've got to tell me *everything*. Right now. I'm not about to get slapped with a charge for perverting the course of justice here, alright? I've got my own career to worry about. I'm here as a *favour*. No official capacity. But I can't ignore evidence that you *are* trying to fuck this investigation up.'

'I'm not, I'm not!' he said quickly. 'Jesus Christ.' He put his head in his hands. 'Look, when the samples were tampered with, I had suspicions. When I was suspended, they deepened. So, when the girl came in and the hospital told us what they found ... I didn't know what the hell to do! I wasn't just going to log it as evidence and wait for it to go missing. I don't know!'

'Right. Who else knows about this? About the girl?' Jamie insisted.

'Just you, me, and my DCI. Aled Parry.'

'And where's Parry now?'

'Holding down the fort at the station. Keeping things running smoothly.'

'You trust him?'

'With my life,' Rees said firmly.

Jamie wondered how much that was worth. 'Alright, fine. What is it, this piece of evidence? A piece of clothing? Some papers? What?'

'A finger.'

Jamie did a double take. 'Like a *human* finger?'

Rees nodded.

'What the fuck? Where the hell did she get a finger?' Jamie asked.

He shifted from foot to foot. 'When the paramedics arrived at the side of the road and checked her over, they found it ... in her mouth. Her chin all covered with blood. They thought the blood was hers, maybe she had a few teeth knocked out. But ...'

'She bit it off?' Jamie looked over at the girl, who was still staring at her, corners of her eyes lined as her gaze burned a hole through Jamie. 'Fucking hell.' It was all she could say.

'It came from a man. That much we can tell. And it had a ring on it.'

'A ring?'

Rees nodded. 'Yeah, a gold thing, with an insignia of some kind. We've been trying to look into it, but we've not logged the thing in evidence, so we haven't been able to make much progress.'

'Do I even want to know where this finger is now?'

'It's in the freezer.'

'At the police station?'

He grimaced a little, showing his teeth.

'Don't tell me it's at your house.'

He swallowed and looked down.

Jamie was the one who buried her head in her hands now. 'You've got a severed human finger that's likely an instrumental piece of evidence in a human trafficking case in your fucking freezer next to a box of fish fingers?' she hissed. 'Are you fucking insane? Do you know how fucked you are?' Jamie could only laugh. 'God, Mallory's going to have a field day. You know there's no coming back from this, don't you?'

He was on his phone then, flicking through photographs. 'Here, this is it.' He turned the screen towards her, the photograph showing a sandwich bag which contained a grubby, chubby finger. There was blood congealed at the severed end, and a gold ring, its insignia pressed to the plastic. 'Do you recognise it?'

Jamie stared down at the image. 'No. But it's exactly the kind of thing the NCA would be well equipped to deal with.'

'And we'll hand it over, we will. But first ... find out what it means. You do some digging, identify the symbol. Then we'll give it to Mallory, and see what she says. If they don't come up with the same answers. We'll know.'

'We'll know,' Jamie laughed. 'We'll know it's the NCA that is corrupt. Right. Well, has anyone considered the *remote* fucking possibility that losing the evidence was just human error, and in fact there isn't a big conspiracy going on, and we should all be figuring out who kidnapped and imprisoned this little fucking girl!' Jamie almost shouted it, pointing at the kid in the bed, who recoiled at the sound and gesture.

Jamie noticed, regained herself, and lowered her hand.

'I have considered that fact. But when it's the life of

a child in the balance I don't take chances. Look, I'll send you this photo, and—'

'Not a chance,' Jamie said. 'I'm not going to be sent a photo of something that'll cost me my job. No. I'll look into it, but ... fuck!' She pulled her own phone out, enlarged the image on Rees' phone so she couldn't see the finger, just the ring, and snapped a photo of it with her own camera. 'I don't know what that is,' she reiterated to him, pointing at his phone. 'I never saw it. You never showed it to me. And it's definitely not in your fucking freezer, alright?'

He nodded. 'You'll let me know if you find out what it is?'

'I will,' Jamie said, looking back at the girl. 'And what about her?'

Rees looked over at her too. 'I don't know ... If she doesn't say something soon and she keeps trying to escape ... the hospital will call Children's Services. It's all they can do. She's stable now, ready to be released. They can't keep her here.'

'Shit. Alright, alright,' Jamie said. 'Let's ... let's just cross that bridge when we come to it. Speak to the hospital, get them to hold her as long as possible. I'll get working on this and let you know, alright?'

'Thank you, Jamie,' Rees said, softening a little. 'I really appreciate you being here.'

'Yeah, yeah,' Jamie said, wondering once again how she'd got herself into another situation like this.

'Did you go home? See your mother?'

'I did,' Jamie said, turning to look at the girl once more, inspecting her slight frame, her injuries, her bruised and bloodied face. And the inextinguishable fire in her eyes.

'How was she? Are you two getting on?'

Jamie bit her lip. 'No, I suppose not,' she said, looking up at Richard Rees.

'What happened?'

Jamie sighed and then folded her arms. 'I stole her car.'

CHAPTER
FIFTEEN

I t was the first time Jamie had ever been to the Dyfed-Powys Police HQ.

The building was a sprawling red brick thing with little windows and about as much charm as a gigantic shoe box.

God, Jamie did miss Swedish architecture, even if this part of the world did have a certain irresistible charm. The world seemed to move a little slower here. And the ever-present chirping of birds and bleating of nearby sheep was somehow calming.

Still, Jamie wasn't thrilled with the idea of meeting Aled Parry, Richard Rees' DCI, the one holding down the fort, the one in charge of the investigation before the NCA swept in, the one responsible for chain of evidence. It did strike Jamie as strange that it was Rees who got slapped with the suspension and Parry went on without hindrance.

As such, she was going into this with her eyes open.

Parry hadn't sounded thrilled when Rees had called him from the hospital and said Jamie would be coming over there to get up to speed on what exactly had happened, and discuss how exactly they were going to loop the NCA in on things without all getting arrested for withholding evidence.

Jamie was surprised to see Parry standing outside the front door, waiting for her. She didn't recognise him – in fact she had no idea what he looked like.

But he called out when she was still twenty yards away and said, 'You the detective Rees was on about?'

The guy was probably six feet and three inches, but thin, with a narrow face and wide-set eyes.

'I am probably the detective Rees was *onnabout,* yeah,' Jamie replied, reading the half-sneer on his face.

'Fantastic. Just what we need is someone else sticking their nose in here.'

'Nice to meet you too,' Jamie sighed, reaching him. 'Trust me, I don't want to be here.'

'So why are you?'

'Because you and Rees were dumb enough to hide evidence from the NCA. And neither of you seem capable of getting yourselves out of this mess without ending up behind bars.'

Parry sucked on his teeth. 'Not our fault that NCA bitch is crooked.'

'Which NCA bitch would that be?'

'Catherine Mallory.'

'And what makes you think that?'

'Her pinning that fucked-with-evidence bullshit on the SI not enough for you?'

'No, it's not. And it shouldn't be for you, either.'

'Well, it is,' Parry scoffed. 'Evidence was nice and safe before they arrived. Then, suddenly, it's moved, relabelled, and contaminated. What does that tell you?'

'Nothing definitive.'

He scoffed again. 'You're naïve, aren't you.' Not even a question.

'Yep, just fresh off the boat,' Jamie said. 'So, what are we going to do here? Rees wanted me to meet you, said you wanted some help identifying the insignia on the ring. So, shall we get to it? See if we can't salvage this?' She tried to walk past towards the door, but he barred her way.

'What ring?' he asked, raising his eyebrows.

'The ring on the finger in Rees' freezer,' Jamie said, voice lowered.

He stuck out his bottom lip, shook his head. 'Don't know what you're on about.'

Ah. She understood then. 'You don't know anything about it?'

Another shake of the head. 'The girl, either?'

'Which one? One of the two dead ones we found? Don't know anything about any other girls.'

Jamie bunched her lips. 'Right. So, me coming down here was a gigantic waste of fucking time then?'

'Seems like. Dunno what you want me to say really? Rees called you in, but he's suspended, right, so I don't know what he's got to do with this investigation anymore. I don't even have anything to do with it really. NCA's doing the heavy lifting. We're more like ... support staff, right.'

Jamie laughed to herself, and then nodded. 'Okay, I get it. Fine. You don't want my help, you're on your own.'

'Perfect.'

'Fine.'

'Okay. Drive safe.' He gave her a smarmy grin, then turned away and walked back through the doors into the building.

'Asshole,' Jamie muttered, flipping him the finger as his shadow disappeared into the interior. She sighed then. 'What a waste of time.' She checked her watch. 'Yep, over an hour from the hospital. Fuck!' What had Rees really expected? Parry was just trying to cover his own arse, and she supposed playing dumb was the best way to do that.

Did this mean she just needed to go right to the NCA then? She'd have to drop Rees in it even deeper. Unless she could sell Mallory the story that she didn't know about the girl and the ring ... though she didn't think that was going to be very doable either. Though if she kept it from Mallory, she was only harming herself ... What if Jamie found out what the insignia on the ring meant? What it led to? If she had some actionable intelligence, then she might buy herself some favour. But it all hinged on one question, one she still didn't know the answer to.

Could Catherine Mallory be trusted? Right now, Richard Rees had an accusation lodged against him, but he was protecting the girl. Or was he? Was protecting her from the NCA helping the girl, or shielding the people that put her in the hospital in the first place? Was Rees just getting Jamie to help keep him out of the NCA's crosshairs?

Her head spun with it all. The NCA on one side, Dyfed-Powys Police on the other. And here she was, trapped in the middle with nothing to show for it and no idea who she could trust.

She supposed she only had two options here. She could turn around and run back to Stockholm, forget all this ever happened.

Or, she could find out what the insignia meant, find the people behind all this, and figure out who the hell was on the take.

If she didn't, what would happen to the girl and all those like her? To the ones tied up somewhere dark, with fates worse than death ahead of them.

Jamie's fists curled at her sides. 'God damn it,' she muttered to herself. 'Fine. I'll do it,' she said aloud. 'But this is the last time!' she promised herself, holding one finger aloft, walking back towards her mother's car.

Though she knew she was lying.

Because the last time was never the last time.

Jamie Johansson refused to turn her back on those who needed her. Whether it was the right decision or not.

And it rarely was.

She had the bullet scars to prove it.

CHAPTER
SIXTEEN

The insignia on the ring was something Jamie hadn't seen before. A lot of the elements were familiar to her though.

In the centre was a mitre, the tall hat that popes and other strict Catholic clergymen would wear. The one in the insignia had a cross on it, so Jamie deduced from those two things alone that this was a religious insignia.

The mitre also sat on a stole, the 'scarf' or shawl-looking vestment that Catholic and Christian priests also wore. Two crossed staffs, one with a crucifix atop it and the other with a shepherd's hook, formed an 'X' in the centre of the whole thing. Which meant that Jamie had no doubt that this was a religious insignia of some kind. But whose?

She quickly googled churches in the area and headed for St Peter's, an old and rather grand church with a lofty bell tower.

Jamie pulled into the car park and headed inside, the door open. The interior was vaulted and smelled like only churches could, with a towering organ replete with golden tubes, and a majestic stained glass window at the back.

She walked slowly between the pews, running her hands across the worn, vanished wood, listening to her heels clip on the stone floor.

The place was empty but, weirdly, as she always did when she entered a church, Jamie felt like she was being watched.

She tried not to read too much in to it.

She stopped at the third row, not wanting to get too close to the altar … no, pulpit? Yeah, altar seemed a little too sacrificial. 'Hello?' she called, mindful of her voice.

'Good morning,' came a reply, an older man in a dog collar appearing from behind a velvet curtain as though he'd been hiding in wait for some unsuspecting pilgrim to wander in.

Jamie resisted the urge to make a quip about the Wizard of Oz. She nodded politely. 'Good morning.'

'What can I do for you?' He came forward, smiling at her.

'I, uh, I was wondering if you could help me.'

His smile widened. 'I believe you've come to the right place if you're looking for help.' He took up position next to the front row pew and leaned on it. 'What can I do for you?'

'Oh,' Jamie said, 'It's nothing like that.' She put her hand on her chest instinctively. 'I'm not religious.'

He chuckled a little. 'Whatever you say. Do you need directions then?'

'No,' Jamie replied, smiling back. 'I'm not lost.'

'We're all lost in one sense or another.'

'Right ...' She cleared her throat. 'I'm working with Dyfed-Powys Police and have come across an insignia I can't identify. I was wondering if you recognised this?' She held her phone up, the image zoomed in on the ring.

The vicar came forward, pulling a pair of reading glasses from the top pocket of his black short-sleeved shirt and pushed them up his long nose.

'Hum,' he said, inspecting it. Then he reached out as though to pinch-and-zoom to get a better look.

Jamie pulled it away and laughed. 'Don't do that.'

'I just wanted to get a better look.'

'I don't think you want to see what else is in the picture,' she answered.

His brow furrowed but he didn't question it. Just sighed and then squinted. 'Well, it definitely looks like a church insignia. It's familiar to me, but I don't recognise it as such.'

'Right, sorry to have bothered you,' Jamie said, turning away.

'Wait a moment,' he called after her. 'Let me give someone a call. I have a friend who'll likely have the answer for you. A history professor at Swansea

University – but he has a keen interest in theological study.'

'And you'd be willing to call him?'

'Of course,' the vicar said. 'It's sort of what we do here.'

Jamie just smiled politely, waiting for him to call.

He drew his phone from his pocket and dialled. It was answered quickly, and after a few pleasantries the vicar beckoned Jamie's phone towards him. 'Phil,' he said, 'I've got a challenge for you. A lovely young lady is here, and she needs some help identifying some religious iconography.'

A lovely young lady? Jamie didn't know if she'd been called any of those three things in a decade or more, and definitely not all in the same sentence.

The vicar laughed a little. 'Good man, I knew you'd be up for the challenge. Alright. Ready?' He nodded to himself as 'Phil' confirmed he was indeed ready to be tested.

'It's a mitre with a crucifix, sitting on a stole, two crossed staves: one is a ferula, and the other is a shepherd's hook.'

There was a period of silence as the vicar listened. Then, he answered, 'Yes, small crucifix atop the mitre. Uh-huh. A diamond hanging beneath, with three tassels. That's right. Oh. Hmm. Right. Okay. Thank you. No, thanks. All the best. Yep, yep, okay. Bye, bye.' He hung up then and let out a long breath.

'No luck?' Jamie asked, losing faith.

'Hmm? Oh, no, he said it's the symbol for the Armenian Apostolic Church. Quite distinctive actually.'

Jamie was surprised. 'That's ... that's great. Thank you. Armenian Apostolic Church,' she confirmed.

He nodded. 'Can I ask what this is in relation to?'

'An active investigation,' Jamie said, diplomatically. 'I really can't say more.'

He considered that for a moment. 'Have people been hurt?' he asked then.

'Uh ...' Jamie hedged, thrown. 'Why would you ask that?'

'Because it seems to be the way of the world these days. People hurting each other.'

'Do you know something about the Armenian church that would lead you to believe that?'

His eyebrows raised. 'No, no, it's nothing like that.' He brushed it off. 'Just a feeling, I suppose.'

'A feeling? What feeling?' Jamie enquired, stepping a little closer.

He watched her, then let out a long breath. 'It's you.'

'Me?'

'You're carrying a ... weight. The weight of the lives of others. The weight of the suffering of others. I can feel it. Sense it, I suppose. I come across many troubled souls here. They're drawn here, seemingly. Whether they know it or not.'

Jamie smirked a little, amused. 'I wasn't drawn here. I came here to ask a question.'

'And you got your answer,' he replied. 'But I think that's not all you're seeking, is it?'

She narrowed her eyes then. 'Thanks for your time, vicar. I've got to go now.'

'Of course, of course, my apologies for keeping you.'

Jamie gave him another quick nod, then turned and headed for the door.

'I'll pray for them,' he called afterwards.

Jamie didn't answer.

'And for you. Good luck!'

Her hands hit the door and then she was back in the sunshine, the day warming, set to be humid and claustrophobic, the kind of heat that presses in on you from all sides, squeezing the air from your lungs with every breath.

She made it halfway to her car before her phone starting ringing.

Jamie pulled it free and answered it: Richard Rees. 'Hey,' she said, 'I found out—'

But she didn't get a chance to finish. 'Jamie,' Rees said with the sort of urgency that stopped Jamie dead in her tracks. 'You need to get to the hospital right now.'

'What? What's wrong?'

'The NCA have got that woman on me again, following me. I can't get rid of her. Can't get there. The hospital, they just called – the girl ... she ... she tried to escape. Assaulted a doctor. They're going to call Children's Services, the police. I begged them to give me an hour. You've got to get there.'

'I ... I can't? What am I supposed to do?' Jamie asked, turning in place, staring around the cemetery she was standing in the middle of.

'I don't know!' Rees hissed. 'Please, just ... if they do that, and the NCA get wind of it, who knows what will happen. She could be dead before the day's out. Jamie, please, you have to just ... do something!'

Jamie gritted her teeth. 'I ...' Her eyes came to rest on the church. She filled her lungs, knowing that letting the NCA take this was the correct thing to do. But was it the *right* thing to do?

She swallowed. 'Okay,' she said slowly. 'I'll go there. I'll do what I can.'

'Thank you,' he said, relieved, and then he hung up.

The line clicked in Jamie's ear and then she lowered the phone. 'Jesus Christ,' she muttered, then looked up at the church guiltily. 'Sorry,' she said, holding her hand up. 'I didn't mean to ...' She shook her head. 'What the fuck am I doing?' she asked herself, turning and making a run for her car. 'I'm going insane, talking to a fucking building.' She scoffed then. 'Yeah, like talking to myself is any better ... God, why can't life just be simple for once?'

But strangely, he didn't answer her.

CHAPTER
SEVENTEEN

Jamie didn't know what to expect when she exited the lift onto the paediatric ward. She knew that she was late though. Rees said be there in an hour, and it was now exactly seven minutes after that.

She tapped her foot impatiently as the lift climbed the floors, stopping to let someone on, then someone off.

When the doors opened on the right floor, however, the screams that filled the air were enough to make her explode from the doors.

There were the voices of two men, one woman, all loud, commanding, ordering someone to calm down, to stay down, to put her arms down. Down. Down!

The girl's screams pierced through everything, shrill and wild, deranged and terrified.

When Jamie reached her doorway, open and splattered with blood, smeared with a bloody handprint, her heart seized in her chest.

Inside, there were four people as well as the girl. Two burly men in security uniforms pinned her to the bed by the arms while a nurse tried to control her thrashing legs.

A doctor was frantically trying to draw a liquid into a syringe, his scrubs bloodied.

Jamie looked left, out of the door, and could see another doctor down the corridor having a wound on his arm attended to.

The forceps and gauze on the ground next to the bed told the story. How the girl had got them, Jamie didn't know, but she did know what she'd done with them afterwards.

'Hold her!' the doctor with the syringe ordered, climbing onto the foot of the bed, straddling one of the girl's legs.

She shrieked, convulsing, spitting saliva into the air like a fountain as her voice echoed down the corridor and made the windows vibrate in their frames.

Jamie had never seen a girl fight so hard, injured and weak as she was.

And then the doctor plunged the needle into her leg.

The tone of her screams changed, moved up an octave, reached fever pitch, and then softened, warbling and dying in her throat as the drug took her.

She calmed and stilled, her cries turning to pained moans.

The nurse let go, sank to her knees and sobbed a little, looking at her hands. The doctor thanked the two security guards and they released the girl, keeping their hands hovering above her arms until they were sure she wasn't about to leap up and start fighting again. Once they were confident, they backed out of the room, giving Jamie a quick, questioning glance as they did.

The doctor seemed to notice her then. He was perhaps in his thirties, with curly hair, and he looked as though he hadn't slept in two days.

'Who are you?' he asked.

Jamie's mouth opened to reply, but no words came out as she reeled through the possibilities and their ramifications. 'I'm … a friend,' was what she came out with.

'We're calling Children's Services, and the police. She'll be taken into custody, immediately,' he said, gesturing with his hands to the definiteness of the statement.

'No,' Jamie said, coming forward a step or two, heart beating harder, eyes fixed on the broken girl in the bed. Her voice caught in her throat as she watched tears roll down the girl's olive cheeks, her eyes barely able to flutter under the weight of the drugs.

'No?' the doctor asked.

'No,' Jamie said with more conviction.

'She can't stay here. She's a danger to herself, and to the staff. She needs to be in custody. She needs help.'

'I know,' Jamie answered, nodding. And then she

fished in her pocket and produced the lanyard that Richard Rees had given her, showing it to the doctor.

He just shrugged and shook his head. 'I don't know what that means.'

'It means that I'm taking custody of her.'

The doctor's eyes narrowed a little.

'I'm assuming responsibility for her, and I'm taking her out of here. Right now. You don't need to call Children's Services, or the police. I'm here, okay?'

He considered that for a moment, then looked back at her. 'She needs *help*. Serious help,' he urged Jamie.

'I know she does. And she'll get it, I promise.'

He just shook his head. 'I can't ... I can't just release her to you, I'm sorry. We have protocols to follow, and she assaulted hospital staff, stabbed a doctor. I have to report this to the police and Children's Services. My hands are tied, I'm sorry. Now, please, excuse me,' he said, walking past Jamie. 'I'll be back shortly. You can stay with her, if you'd like.'

Jamie just swallowed and nodded a brief thanks as the doctor left the room, striding quickly down the corridor.

But when he did return, he didn't find Jamie waiting, or the girl. All he walked into was an empty room, the bedsheets rumpled and hanging from the rubber mattress.

CHAPTER
EIGHTEEN

J amie left the wheelchair in the multi-storey and drove away from the hospital at speed.

Whatever they'd given the girl, it was strong. As Jamie loaded her into the wheelchair a small groan escaped her, but by the time they reached the car and Jamie hauled her into the passenger seat, wrapped in her hospital gown, she was totally unconscious. Utterly limp.

Where they were going, Jamie didn't know. But it had to be away from here. Stealing a patient from the hospital was basically kidnapping. No, actually, it was exactly kidnapping, and as Jamie wheeled the Z4 in a J-turn and squealed from the car park she racked her brain, trying to remember if she'd given anyone her name.

She didn't think so, and her lanyard just had the words 'Special Consultant' on it, along with Dyfed-

Powys Police's insignia. She hoped that might give her a little bit of a head start, at least.

She aimed for the motorway, her first thought being to take the kid back to Rees' house. But that was going to be even worse for him. Fuck! She didn't think this through. Not at all. Though she hadn't expected to be absconding with a material witness in a case.

Okay, think, Jamie. Somewhere safe. Somewhere quiet. Somewhere she can come around clothed and secure, and not immediately lose her shit. Somewhere they could communicate, and that Jamie could find out why she had the finger of a man in her mouth with an Armenian Apostolic Church ring on it.

She reached the M4 and headed west before cutting north towards Merthyr, knowing that the centre of the country was vast and intricate. Easy to get lost.

When she saw the signs for the shopping centre, she slowed and pulled in, finding a shady spot away from the other cars.

Jamie checked the girl was still out of it, shaking her pretty hard and waiting to see if there was a response. There wasn't, and she figured she had a decent amount of time before she came around. Still, she had to be quick, and sprinted from the car to the shops, returning fifteen minutes later with a few bags full of clothing. She dumped them into the boot and checked the girl was still out, then doubled back for food from the supermarket there.

And by the time she got back again, she had a plan.

. . .

THE COTTAGE WAS NORTH OF A LITTLE VILLAGE called Beulah, deep in the most rural part of the country.

She managed to book it for three nights, paid in full, and headed right there for self-check-in, pulling off the main road onto a country lane, and then off that onto what was more like a forestry than anything.

She rattled across a cattle grid, the low-profile tyres complaining at the rough ground, and trundled up the exposed track towards the stone cottage on the hill. It had a small copse of trees behind it but, other than that, the landscape was open all around for at least a hundred metres in every direction. The boggy grassland made the only way of access the road they were on, and the fact that it was so remote meant that if anyone approached, Jamie would be able to see them coming.

Was she being paranoid? She didn't know. Rees had thought she was being hunted, and Jamie guaranteed that after she'd taken the girl, the police would most certainly have been contacted.

The big question was whether they'd be able to find her here, and if so, how long did she have?

She had no answers, but she knew that she'd need to come up with some. Namely how to ensure the girl's safety. Could she call Julia Hallberg, her friend at Interpol? Explain the situation, get her out of the country maybe? Could she call Dahlvig and take the girl back to

Sweden? Hell, how would she sell that? I can't trust the police or the NCA, do me a favour?

No. That wasn't going to go down well.

Jamie was in trouble.

And as she pulled to a halt behind the cottage and exited the car, looking across the brutal and barren landscape surrounding them, glancing in through the window at the girl still passed out in the passenger seat, still clad in her hospital gown, she'd never felt more alone.

She just hoped, for once, as she turned her attention to the open ground before the cottage once more, that she could stay that way.

CHAPTER
NINETEEN

When the girl came to, it was already deep into the afternoon and the smell of food cooking permeated the cottage.

She awoke in a strange bed with strange clothes on. A red hooded sweatshirt and cargo trousers that were a size too large.

Her eyelids fluttered a little and then opened, a ceiling swimming into view. But not a hospital ceiling. There was white paint and wooden beams, cobwebs in the corners.

As her faculties returned, she tried to gain some idea of where she was.

The sound of pans and running water reached her ears and she groaned a little, realising at once her arms and legs weren't bound any longer. She was disorientated, that much she knew. But nothing else made sense to her. Her first coherent thought, in fact, was that she was at home again, her mother making food, and it was quickly replaced by the thought that she was dead. To be home, she would have to be. They killed her. The people in the hospital killed her.

But she didn't think that was the case. She could move her fingers, and her toes. And after a moment, she sat up, trying to blink herself clear.

A sheet of paper that had been laid on her stomach flopped onto her lap and she picked it up, trying to read what was written on there. The fourth line down she understood, written in her language. It said the words: You are safe.

The legibility was terrible, obviously written by someone who'd never written anything in Georgian before.

The other lines were in languages she recognised, but the legibility was even worse. Arabic, Persian, Turkish, Armenian, Hebrew, Kurdish ... But they all said the same thing. You are safe.

The girl looked up from the paper, trying to make sense of all of this, and saw her, the woman from the hospital room, standing at the sink with her back to the kitchen.

She lowered the paper carefully, heart beating hard, realising she needed to be quiet, or this woman would hear her.

Where was she? Had she been taken again? Was this the person that she was being taken to in the van? The possibilities reeled through her head. All she knew was that she had to escape. And now.

She looked around the room. Windows. Tiny. What the hell was this place? The walls were two feet thick and she didn't even know if she could squeeze through the little opening.

She let out a long breath, trying to temper her emotions, trying to stabilise the fear and the anger coursing through her.

Okay. Okay. Think.

She swung her legs from the side of the bed, looking around.

Socks. And shoes.

Not hers. But they were right there in front of her. New, white socks. And white trainers.

She put her feet on the cold stone floor, the feeling cooling against her bare feet.

She managed to reach down and grab the socks, pulling them on slowly and without sound.

The shoes came next. They were too big, her feet sliding in easily. But they'd be a lot better for running outside than going without them.

Her fingers curled into the bedsheet under her as she mustered her strength. God, she felt weak, her stomach aching with hunger, her mouth dry, lips chapped. But it didn't matter. She could find a stream and drink, find mushrooms or berries to eat. Steal if she had to. She didn't care. She just needed to escape.

But as she pushed to her feet and found her balance,

the drugs they'd put in her still riding in her system, she became distinctly aware that the sound of running water and the banging pots had stopped.

She turned her head, slowly, breathing shallow and fast, and saw her there, filling the doorway. This woman. This blonde woman with the long braid, and the black jeans and big boots and the stern look and the piercing blue eyes like ... like she didn't know what. Some sort of wraith. Ice-blue and cutting into her.

There was a moment of stillness between the two, the woman just hovering silently in the doorway as though she didn't know what to say.

Her mouth opened a little and she stepped inside.

The girl twisted to face her, half crouching, lifting her hands as though to fend her off.

The blonde woman raised her arms and backed away a step, said something in English. The girl didn't really catch it. She spoke a little, but not a lot. No one at the hospital had bothered to really try to speak to her, so she'd been quiet. That was best, always. Listen, don't speak. The smartest people listen. They learn.

'It's okay,' the blonde woman said again. 'You're safe.'

The girl's brow furrowed a little, her eyes scanning the room for any other means of escape. There was none. None but right through this woman.

So that's where she was going.

She leapt, hurdling the corner of the bed, head

down, shoulders back, driving with as much strength as she could.

When she hit the woman, she expected violence, to be struck, to be thrown, kicked, beaten down.

But all she felt was the woman's arms envelop her. The woman was forced back, heels digging into the stone floor until they were in the middle of the kitchen, where, even in the heat of the moment, the smell of food still made her mouth salivate and tears form in the corners of her eyes.

The girl tried to fight her off, trying to get loose, but the woman had her arms around her, holding fast. Her head was against the woman's chest, arms pinned at her sides, so she did the only thing she could, and bit down hard.

The woman yelled out, her grip releasing just momentarily, enough that the girl could stamp down onto her foot and get loose, shoving her off.

But she was fast, and strong, and before the girl even got two steps, the woman was on her, arms locking around her from behind this time.

She looked down, seeing the woman's right fist close over her left wrist and grip tightly.

'Ara!' the girl screamed. *'Ara!'* No! No!

But the woman wouldn't let her go, and the girl felt her weight then, pulling her backwards.

She screamed and cried, tears rolling down her cheeks as the woman took her to her knees and then keeled backwards, her legs wide around the girl so that they were both sitting, one nestled in front of the other.

She heard the woman then, whispering to her. But not in a threatening way, not harsh or violent. She was hushing her, softly.

'It's okay, it's okay,' the woman said. 'I know. I'm sorry. It's okay. You're safe.'

The girl continued to fight, with everything she had. But it wasn't enough and, suddenly, her remaining strength left her. And with a shuddering sob, she just gave up, head flopping forward, choking, mewling cries escaping her dry lips.

'Shh, shh,' the woman said, holding her. Just holding her.

The girl cried.

And before she knew what was happening, she was being turned around, her cheek resting against the woman's collar bones.

'You're okay, you're okay,' the woman whispered into her hair, one arm around her shoulders, the other cradling her head. 'I promise you're safe.'

The woman's voice quivered, catching in her throat.

And they stayed like that, the girl melting into this stranger, exhaustion taking her, dragging her down into the darkness.

Before she realised, her hands were clutching at the woman's clothes, taking fistfuls and gripping hard, pulling her closer as she sobbed fitfully, painfully. Powerfully.

Her eyes closed.

The tears flooded.

And for the first time in what seemed like a very long time – she felt safe.

CHAPTER
TWENTY

Food was soup and bread. But it looked like it was the best soup and bread the girl had ever eaten.

Jamie supposed that no one could dislike Heinz Cream of Tomato.

The girl ate two whole cans, and about half a loaf of the ciabatta she'd bought. She had no idea what the girl would be able to tolerate after so long without eating, but she didn't seem to have any trouble shovelling it down.

Jamie watched her carefully across the table. She had a heart-shaped face, with a finely pointed chin. She was olive-skinned, her complexion was smooth, her eyes bright, a deep and rich green, shaded by thick eyebrows. Her lips were full, but cracked and pale from a lack of nourishment. Her hair looked unclean and greasy, but it was thick and naturally curled. She was slight, underweight and weak, but on the cusp of becoming a woman all the same. And a beautiful young woman at that. Jamie shivered thinking of the fate that would have awaited her.

She knew nothing of the girl yet. Just that she liked soup, and she was a fighter.

She kept glancing up at the back door, but had made no further attempt to run. She kept looking at Jamie too, who was doing her best not to stare back, difficult as it was. The girl's face was still bruised and cut from the accident, her arm still in a cast.

Jamie hoped they were safe for now, so her main goal was learning more about the girl. Finding out who she was, where she was from, and how she got from wherever she was from to here. And then … what happened afterwards.

'How is it?' Jamie asked, smiling.

The girl stopped eating, spoon halfway to her mouth. She looked at Jamie, confused.

Jamie nodded to her bowl. 'Soup,' she said, smiling and nodding. 'Good?'

The girl narrowed her eyes a little. 'Soup?' she replied.

'Yes,' Jamie said, pointing to the soup with her hand, and then mimicking an eating motion. 'Soup.'

The girl looked left and right awkwardly, then nodded. 'Soup.' Then she continued eating.

Jamie sighed. 'Fucking soup,' she said. 'Great progress, Jamie.'

She looked around then, wondering how to approach this. Did the girl know any English? She could ask her. 'Do you speak,' she began, very slowly, 'any English?'

The girl swallowed a mouthful, staring at Jamie.

'English?' Jamie repeated.

'Yes,' the girl said, fishing for the word for a moment.

'Great.' Jamie grinned. 'What is your name?' She made sure to separate the words so it was clear.

'Yes,' the girl replied.

'No, no,' Jamie said, pointing to her. 'Your name.'

'Ah,' the girl said, looking down past her chin. 'Soup.'

This could take a while.

Jamie pushed back from the table and cast around a little more, looking for anything she could use.

There was a small bookshelf against the wall, filled with books and games.

She went over.

There was a notepad on top, a mug full of pens and pencils. She grabbed that.

Anything else?

Maybe Monopoly would be a stretch right now.

Books ... birds and flowers common to Wales. Walking guide of the Brecon Beacons. Cookbooks. And an ... atlas.

Oh.

Jamie grabbed it and headed back over to the table, putting the book down and the pad next to it.

The girl watched cautiously.

Jamie scooched her chair around so they were a little closer, waiting for the girl to finish her soup and push the bowl away.

Jamie cleared her throat then, writing her name on the pad in big letters. She turned it to show the girl who looked down at it curiously.

'Jamie,' Jamie said, running the tip of the pencil under the word. 'Jamie.' She repeated it, then pointed to herself. 'Jamie.' She put her hand on her chest, to reiterate.

Then she gestured to the girl, raising her eyebrows with a questioning look.

The girl seemed to understand, and took the pencil from Jamie. She flipped the page and started writing. Jamie didn't recognise a single letter.

She thought that she might have written with those characters when she put that sign together for the girl's room, but she couldn't remember which they were. It'd taken an hour to write half a dozen lines, copying the translations painstakingly from her phone screen, not knowing if they were even correct.

The girl finished writing, then pointed to herself. 'Alina.'

'Alina?' Jamie asked, confirming it.

'Alina.'

Jamie took the pencil back, then wrote under the word Alina had written: Alina.

Alina stared at it.

'Alina,' Jamie said, underlining it.

Though the girl seemed to understand that it was the English spelling, it meant nothing to her.

But Jamie had a plan. She drew a little stick figure next to it with curly hair, and an arrow from the name to the figure. 'Alina.'

This was her.

Jamie reached for the atlas then, opening it to the centre page, a large world map. She circled the Middle East, from Italy across to Kyrgyzstan. 'Alina?' Jamie asked, lifting her hands questioningly, and then started pointing to different countries.

Alina watched, trying to understand, and then she seemed to, taking the pencil and deftly planting it in the middle of Georgia. She nodded firmly at Jamie.

'You're Georgian? Great,' Jamie said, grinning. Okay, that's the first thing, she thought. She took the pencil back, then drew a circle around the UK and gestured to the room they were in. 'Wales,' she said, pointing more specifically to Wales on the map.

The girl watched.

Then, Jamie connected Georgia to Wales by a line, and put a question mark next to it. She pointed to the drawing of Alina on the notepad, and then pointed to Georgia, and dragged her finger to Wales. 'How?' she asked, shrugging her shoulders animatedly. 'How did you get from here, to here?' she asked, gesturing as clearly as she could.

Alina thought for a few seconds, then reached for the pad and pencil.

Jamie let her have it, and watched intently.

Next to the drawing of herself, she made a drawing of a larger man, then looked at Jamie. *'Babua.'*

'Father?' Jamie asked.

'Babua,' she repeated.

'Babua.'

The girl nodded.

Jamie pulled out her phone for this one, typed it in phonetically, putting 'Georgian translation' after it.

The answer popped up.

'Grandfather,' Jamie said. 'Ah.'

'Babua.' Alina put her fingers on the table then, mimed walking with her index and middle. Then pointed from Georgia to Armenia.

'You and your grandfather walked from Georgia to Armenia?' Jamie confirmed, wishing she could ask why. But she had an idea. Georgia was predominantly Christian, but not entirely. It was predominantly progressive, but not entirely. Some of the country was wealthy, some was greatly impoverished. If it was her grandfather with her, then Jamie guessed her parents weren't in the picture. Dead? She didn't know, couldn't ask. But either way, if they walked, it meant they didn't have a car. And it meant that they were desperate to better their lives. Did her grandfather have a plan? What had happened?

'Where is your *babua* now?' Jamie asked, pointing to the man in the picture.

Alina looked at her questioningly.

Jamie pointed from her *babua* to the UK. *'Babua?'* she asked, tapping on the country.

Alina shook her head, then took the pencil and drew a fast, hard line through her *babua,* the anger in the movement clear. Jamie didn't need to know Georgian to understand that.

'Dead,' she said.

'Mk'vdari.' Alina said.

Jamie let out a long, slow breath. 'I'm sorry,' she said, then typed it into the translation app on her phone. *'Vts'ukhvar,'* she said, trying to pronounce the translation.

The blank look on Alina's face told Jamie she wasn't even close.

So, she just showed Alina the screen instead.

The girl understood, swallowed, then nodded.

She'd lost her grandfather – killed, Jamie guessed, by the men who brought her here. What she'd gone through, Jamie couldn't fathom. But she'd fought so hard to stay alive. 'You're a fighter,' Jamie said then.

The girl did not understand.

But when Jamie smiled and nodded to her, the girl smiled back.

And that was something.

Then, in the quiet of the cottage, Jamie suddenly became hyperaware.

Something distant – the call of an animal, of a bird maybe. No, not that. A squeak. A metal gate hinge, the brakes of a car.

She leapt up quicker than she meant to. Alina jolted at the movement, cowered a little.

'It's okay,' Jamie urged her, turning and striding quickly towards the front door at the far end of the kitchen.

She pulled it wide and stepped into the gathering darkness.

The sky still had streaks of light in it, the clouds a deep and restless violet. But in the shadowy folds of the valleys, night had already spread across the ground like a miasma, choking Jamie's sight from her.

She squinted into the gloom, looking for something, for anything. For proof there was nothing.

And there wasn't anything. It was deathly quiet. Utterly still.

And yet Jamie's skin was alight with gooseflesh.

Her eyes twitched as she searched the shadows, unsure if she'd heard anything at all.

Could she trust herself?

She swallowed, holding on as long as she dared, and then ducked back inside, locking the door tight.

The girl was on her feet now, looking at Jamie with those wide, green eyes, stricken with fear, her narrow shoulders rising and falling quickly.

'It's okay,' Jamie said. 'We'll be okay. Everything's fine.'

She was glad the girl couldn't understand her. Because if she could, she knew she wouldn't have believed a word.

CHAPTER
TWENTY-ONE

Jamie extinguished the lights and came forward quickly, lit by the glow from the lamp that was on in Alina's room.

She tried to keep her expression calm, but she and the girl both knew that something was wrong.

Jamie kept telling herself that in a few minutes nothing would have happened, and they could go right back to eating soup. But as she approached the girl, wide-eyed in the darkness, she knew deep down that it wasn't the case.

She reached for Alina's arm and she pulled it away instinctively.

Jamie held her finger to her lips to hush the girl, then extended her hand. Don't speak. Just come with me.

The girl stared at her, fear in her face, but after a

second she took Jamie's hand and was led from the table to the bedroom.

Jamie pointed to the bed, then motioned for her to get under it.

The girl's brow crumpled and she bit her lip, but then she did it. Quietly. Quickly. Without protest. Without hesitation.

Jamie watched her, then went in and turned off the lamp, pulled the door closed and went back into the kitchen. She looked around, the place drenched in darkness, with just the dim light from the reading on the microwave illuminating it. Enough to make out shapes and little else. But Jamie knew where she was going and what she was going for.

There was a fireplace with a stone hearth next to the back door and Jamie crossed to it quickly, lifting a metal poker from the stand next to it, weighing it in her grasp as she crossed towards the sink.

She laid her hands either side of it and breathed, trying to steady herself. Her heart was hammering, a cold sheen of sweat around her collar. God, she wished she had her gun.

No, no, Jamie. Don't think like that. No *if onlys*. You're here, you've got to protect her. There's no one else.

She swallowed the rising bile in her throat and reached out for the knife rack below the windowsill ahead of her.

Outside, the trees rustled softly, the moon just

peeking between the branches. Its dim brilliance caught the blade of the knife as she dragged it from the block, fastening her grip around the handle, staring down at it.

With another steeling breath, she turned back to the room, to wait for whatever was coming next, and noticed two eyes staring at her from a crack in the bedroom door.

Alina was there, standing in the gap, clutching at the door.

Her eyes went from Jamie's to the knife, and lingered there. She looked back at Jamie then, and nodded to her.

Jamie tried to smile at her, tried to find the strength to lie, to tell her it was going to be okay. But she couldn't. She motioned her back inside instead, and the girl obliged, slowly closing the door, leaving Jamie to face whatever was coming alone.

You've battled worse odds, Jamie told herself as she took up position next to the back door, crouched against the wall, poker in her left hand, kitchen knife in her right.

What she really expected to happen, or expected to do, she couldn't say. But the image of Alina's face filled her mind. Her eyes, gleaming in the darkness. The thought that the only thing standing between her and whatever was outside was Jamie. Who these people were and what they wanted, Jamie didn't know. But they would kill the girl. And if they didn't, then her fate would be worse than death.

Jamie closed her eyes, conserving her strength and her breath. Her heart beat fast and steady, she could feel it in her temples.

She listened.

Waited.

And sure enough, a minute or two later, there was the soft crunch of stones under shoes coming from outside.

Slow, cautious steps. One or two sets. She didn't know.

She watched the front door. Listened as the steps approached it, then stopped.

A near-silent creak. The handle depressing.

Jamie held her breath.

The handle moved up and down, slowly, the door wiggling in the frame a little. Locked. Jamie had locked it.

She tried to calm herself.

There was a small, frosted glass pane at the top of the front door, and the shadow of a head crept up it, two dark hands cupping against the glass, trying to see in.

There were no voices, but she knew that if they weren't coming in the front, they were coming in the back.

Jamie waited, the poker slick in her grip from the sweat on her palm.

Another shadow swept across the window above the sink and Jamie pressed herself hard to the wall, breathing shakily.

Footsteps outside.

Right through the wall.

She looked at her hands, laid the knife on the ground, held the poker in both hands, wound it up to swing.

Go for the knees, she told herself, her eyes going to the front door now, the face still against the glass, still trying to see inside.

No, fuck. She couldn't be sure. And she had to be.

She lowered the poker, reached for the knife instead, tasting vomit in her mouth. She grimaced as she picked it up, knowing what she had to do.

And no sooner had her fingers closed around the handle that the door knob next to her head jiggled, then twisted.

The latch clicked, the door unlocked, and then the whole thing swung inwards.

Jamie watched a black-gloved hand guide it, and shrank from the door frame, fingers flexing around the blade.

She held her breath, hearing the man's. He was right there.

Breathing steadily. Listening. Looking. For the girl. For Jamie.

Then, the muzzle of a pistol nosed through the gap. Jamie could smell the gun grease.

She held the knife fast, waiting for her opening. For some open and exposed patch of flesh that she could …

And then a foot came across the threshold.

The guy took a single step inside, the polished toe of a leather shoe right next to Jamie's boot.

If he looked down, he'd see her.

If he saw her, he'd shoot her.

She couldn't wait.

With a quick, plunging strike, she sent the knife whistling towards the ground.

The leather groaned. Bone crunched. And the sound of the knife tip snapping against the stone beneath the guy's foot punctured the air.

A fine blood mist erupted upwards, filling Jamie's senses. And then her eardrums almost burst as he screamed, his curled, pained roar making her eyes shake in her head.

But she couldn't let up.

Her right hand left the knife, grabbing the poker, and then she drove the hooked and sharp tip upwards with everything she had, slamming it into the waiting wrist of the man that had come to kill them.

The gun sailed free of his grip, flying into the darkness, and as Jamie got to her feet in front of him, she saw his face, filled with fury.

He was much taller than her, filling the doorway. His eyes were wide, glowing in the darkness, his bearded face troll-like and terrible.

His arm swung then, loping and heavy, ready to take Jamie's head off.

She ducked backwards, out of his reach, his stabbed foot refusing to take his weight as he tried to rush her.

The man stumbled, still yelling.

Jamie readjusted her grip, wound up, and then swung the poker hard.

It sliced through the air, the wrought iron connecting with his temple.

There was a dull crack and his scream died in the darkness, his brutish form slumping forward onto the flagstone floor.

Jamie raked in a breath, standing over him, but before she could even process what had happened, the front door exploded inwards behind her in a shower of splinters.

Two tree-trunk arms grabbed her, one around her ribs, the other around her throat.

She kicked and fought, dropping the poker as the second man dragged her clear of the ground and shook her like a doll, his fist collapsing her windpipe with ease.

Her eyes bulged, pain exploding in her neck as he choked the life from her.

A gargled cough escaped her lips as she tried to scream, only one word coming to mind. 'Run!'

She wanted to tell the girl. Leave me. Go. Run away! Now, before it's too late.

Over the rush of blood in her ears, she heard the door to the bedroom open.

She heard footsteps.

Tears streamed from her eyes. Tears of joy. Yes! Run! Get away! Please!

But she didn't.

The girl hurled herself at the man, yelling and beating on him with closed fists, her strikes bouncing off his back.

Holding Jamie by the throat with one hand, he swiped at her with the other, knocking her off her feet.

She cried out as she hit the ground, and if Jamie had any breath in her body, she would have called out. But she didn't. He was holding her against his chest, pinning her by the neck, heels flopping six inches off the floor.

Jamie watched, vision pulsing black, as the girl scrabbled for something in the darkness.

She stood then, clutching it in both hands, the sleek black weapon wavering in the half-light of the moon.

The gun.

She had the gun.

Jamie's eyes searched for hers as she levelled it at the man. Do it! She screamed in her head. Pull the trigger!

But she couldn't. She sobbed, the pistol shaking wildly in her grip.

The man stared at her for a second, waiting for the bullet. And then he advanced, snatching the gun from her grasp, and sending a vicious back-hand across her cheek.

Jamie was on the ground then, on her hands and knees next to the dead man, coughing and hacking onto the floor, fighting for breath.

She turned her head, neck on fire, watching as the second man took hold of the girl by the hair and began dragging her towards the open door.

She screamed, the noise filling Jamie's head, making her whole body break out in a prickly heat.

He was taking her.

He was taking her!

Jamie's eyes moved to the bloodied handle of the kitchen knife, still sticking out of the first man's shoe, and she reached for it.

It scraped along the ground as she dragged it free, forcing herself to a wavering stance.

The second man was at the door now, out on the porch, pulling the girl into his arms and making for their vehicle.

Jamie flew at him, across the kitchen, through the door. She leapt from the top step, knife raised, and plunged it square into his back.

He snarled, turning. But Jamie was still on his back, still clutching the knife.

Her heels hit the ground and she twisted, hard, feeling the blade grind against cartilage and bone.

The man dropped the girl and she scrabbled away.

Jamie hooked her left hand over his shoulder, pulling the knife free with her right, and then shoving it right back in again, teeth gritted so hard she thought they might shatter.

Again!

Again!

With each attack, the man grew weaker, his noise more pained. And then he went to a knee, swayed sickeningly, and flopped onto the ground, lying still.

Jamie laid on top of him, panting hoarsely, her throat raw and bruised.

But before she could even withdraw the knife, the girl was there, on her feet, launching vicious kicks into his ribs.

She lost her footing in the loose stone and fell, but didn't stop, raining punches down onto his back with all she had, a mad and chilling shriek echoing from her mouth.

Jamie climbed off, reaching for her.

The girl swung for Jamie then.

And all Jamie could do was tackle her, taking her to the ground and holding her in her own arms, soaking her hoodie with the man's blood, staining her skin with it as she grabbed Alina's arms and stilled them.

'It's me, it's me,' Jamie whispered, feeling the girl soften against her. 'It's okay. I'm here, I'm here.'

And she felt her shudder, and then stop fighting, the last light of day now finally gone from the blackened skies around them.

CHAPTER
TWENTY-TWO

Whether he was dead before she dragged him outside, or whether he eventually died sometime during the night, Jamie didn't know.

But she was sure that Alina deserved one night of safety, of peaceful sleep before the sea of flashing lights arrived.

The first man that Jamie had struck with a poker was lying limp and lifeless on the kitchen floor, and while Alina showered, washing off the stink of the men who had tried to take her, Jamie dragged him out of the kitchen by the arms, and dumped him on the stones next to his buddy.

She found a tarpaulin that was used to cover a wood pile for the fireplace inside, and draped it over them.

Nothing moved in the darkness, but she knew their

car was parked out there somewhere. She just hoped that more backup wasn't on the way.

Two guys could handle a woman and a little girl, right? Surely no one else would be coming for them right now?

Jamie hovered at the front door, the pistol that she'd recovered from the kitchen in her grip, a bullet in the chamber, until she heard the water shut off and Alina finish her shower.

And then, with a sigh, she went back inside and closed the door. The latch had been snapped as the big guy kicked it in, so she had to drag a kitchen chair over and wedge it up under the handle.

As she turned back to the darkened kitchen, she stepped in the smeared blood trail that led from where she'd struck the first man right through to the front door.

'Fuck,' she muttered, lifting her foot, the sole covered in sticky crimson. 'There goes my cleaning deposit.' She laughed abjectly, looking up only as Alina exited the bathroom, hair soaked and hanging in loose ringlets. She was wrapped in a towel, clutching her clothes in a ball in front of her.

'You can, uh, just leave those wherever. I'll wash them for you,' Jamie said, trying not to gesture with the loaded gun. 'There are pyjamas in the bedroom, in a plastic bag next to the—'

But she cut herself off, remembering that Alina didn't speak any English.

So instead, she tucked the pistol in the back of her jeans, and went over.

Alina waited for her to approach, and let Jamie take the clothes from her grip. As she did, she stifled a little gasp. Across Alina's exposed upper arms and chest were scars and cuts, marks on the skin. Burns and nicks and grazes and gouges and who knew what else. How long had she been imprisoned? What had she gone through? Jamie hadn't noticed before. When she'd redressed her before putting her on the bed, she'd not looked at her. Tried to preserve the girl's dignity as she stripped the hospital gown from her and pulled the T-shirt and hoodie over her head. But now, in the stark light on her washed skin, Jamie could see it all.

She clenched her teeth together to stop her jaw from quivering, and then dropped the clothes in her arms to the ground and pulled the girl against her, hugging her tightly. She was stiff in her grasp, unmoving. But then she lifted her arms and gently wrapped them around the small of Jamie's back, not hugging, but holding.

Jamie resisted the urge to kiss the girl's head, so instead, pulled away, running her knuckles roughly across her own cheeks to wipe away the forming tears, and led her to the bedroom, where she pulled the plastic bag from the floor onto the bed and laid out the pyjamas that she'd bought.

The girl looked them over, then looked at Jamie, her lips trembling as though she wanted to smile, but was too frightened.

'I'll give you some privacy,' Jamie said, rubbing her back gently, feeling the ridges of the scar tissue beneath her touch. And then she left the room, pulling the door closed. And did her best to hold back the tears.

CHAPTER
TWENTY-THREE

Though they had separate bedrooms, less than twenty minutes after Jamie went to bed, Alina crept into her open doorway and hovered there, looking in.

Jamie wasn't asleep, or even lying down.

She was sitting up against the headboard with a clear view of the front door from her vantage point, pistol resting on top of her thigh, fully clothed, boots on.

She looked up at the girl, smiling a little. 'Hey,' she said, reading the look in her eyes. She beckoned her in then, and Alina came through the door and crawled over the foot of the bed, curling up on the empty side next to Jamie.

She tucked herself under the duvet, holding it in her fists, pressed to her mouth so that all that was visible were her eyes and a pool of curled brown hair.

Jamie smoothed it as the girl fell into a troubled

sleep, snatching a few minutes of rest herself here and there where she dared, ready to spring into action at the sound of a single crunch of stones, the burble of an engine, or even a single breath uttered by something outside that room.

She would have killed for the girl. She already had. And she had no remorse for it. The two bodies outside were a warning to anyone who came to their door that night. And not one that should be taken lightly.

As dawn crept its way into the cold and clear sky, Jamie climbed from the bed and went outside, pulling the chair from under the handle as carefully as she could and slipping into the cool morning air.

She'd been thinking all night. And though she would have loved nothing more than to just turn tail and run, the options weren't good. She could leave the country, but there was no way Alina had a passport. They'd never get out via any official channels. And Jamie wasn't ready to be a fugitive just yet. Whether they were traffickers, rapists, the worst scum on earth, or all three – probably all three – she had still killed two men. And that wasn't something that she could lawfully, or wilfully, run from.

So she did what she needed to.

And she called Hassan.

She woke him up, told him she needed him, that it was serious, there was a break in the case, and that he had to come right now, and alone, and all he said was, 'Okay. Send me an address.'

And within the hour, he was there.

Jamie was sitting on the front step with a cup of coffee in her hand when the nose of his Audi came around the corner and rumbled across the cattle grid, hauling itself slowly up the rocky track.

Jamie slurped the brown liquid, hot and bitter on her tongue, thumb tapping on the side of the pistol in her hands. It was a Beretta 92, Italian-made. Sturdy and reliable. They packed a punch. A common enough gun, and not surprising to find it strapped to someone involved in trafficking from the Middle East. If they were bringing things through the Med, Italy was an easy stop off for supplies.

Hassan pulled to a halt, alone as promised, about twenty yards from the cottage, and got out, eyes locked on Jamie.

He came forward cautiously, wearing a black bomber jacket, blue jeans, sturdy boots. His hair was slicked back, as normal, though his beard was a little thicker. He usually groomed it meticulously, but perhaps the urgency in Jamie's voice had taken precedent.

He stopped in front of his car and pushed his hands into his pockets. 'There's a blacked-out Range Rover parked down by the gate, just out of sight. No sign of the driver. That something to do with why I'm here?'

Jamie let out a long breath and put the coffee down, getting to her feet painfully. Apart from her throat, her hip was hurting from where she'd been thrown to the ground, and her back was aching terribly.

Hassan's eyes went to the deep bruising on her neck, then to the pistol he now noticed was in her grip.

The gears churned in his head, eyes flitting to the broken door frame, the blood smeared across the stone, and finally to the two suspiciously person-shaped lumps under the tarpaulin to his left.

He said nothing, just sort of braced himself, filling his lungs and pulling his shoulders back, and then he walked over to the tarp and crouched, lifting the corner and peaking under.

He dropped it back down and then hung his head, letting out a long and frustrated breath. He looked up at Jamie, stone-faced. 'Who are they?'

'Armenians, I'd bet,' Jamie answered, standing her ground in the doorway.

'And why are there two dead Armenians in the middle of butt-fuck nowhere, lying face down in the dirt with their skulls caved in?'

'Technically only one has his skull caved in,' Jamie said tiredly. 'The other one I had to stab.'

Hassan stood and walked towards her a little. She raised the gun slightly, not to point it at him, but just to show him this wasn't a surrender.

He stopped, lifted his hands. 'You should talk. Quickly. And don't leave anything out.'

'They came for us.'

'For … *us?* Who is 'us'?' Hassan asked, eyebrows bunching.

Jamie stepped aside then, not needing to look behind her to know that Alina was hiding in the doorway, listening.

Hassan's eyes widened at the sight of the girl.

'Who is that?' he asked, voice quiet and strained as he tried to keep a lid on his anger.

'Alina,' Jamie said, turning to the girl and motioning for her to come outside.

She hesitated, watching Hassan carefully.

Jamie gave her a smile, and beckoned her. 'It's okay, he's a friend.'

Alina took a step outside.

'And who is Alina?'

Jamie drew in a slow breath. 'She's one of the trafficking victims, we believe.'

'We?'

'Richard Rees,' Jamie said.

'Of course,' Hassan scoffed. 'This would be Rees. And he got you into this, too? Hiding a witness from the NCA? You don't see how this is interfering with an investigation? Fucking hell, Jamie!'

Alina shrank from him.

'You're scaring her,' Jamie said coldly. 'She leapt from a moving van, got hit by a car. She … she bit a guy's finger off to get away from these people. She's covered in scars! Had the shit beaten out of her before she narrowly escaped death and who knows what else.

She was unconscious in the hospital for days, tried to escape the moment she woke up, and the second she gets out of there, two hitmen show up to try to fucking murder her,' Jamie spat. 'She has been through *enough*. So, keep your voice down, and let's talk about this like adults, okay?'

'There's nothing to talk about, Jamie. You killed two people and fucked with an NCA investigation by kidnapping a witness. This is out of my hands. Well and truly.' He stared at her for a moment. 'Why did you even call me? You must have known this is what would happen?'

'I did,' Jamie replied. 'I knew that there was no way it couldn't go this way. I just wanted you to know that I tried to do the right thing. I don't believe Rees is dirty. So that didn't leave me with many other options of people to trust, alright?'

'So you decided to take responsibility for her yourself? And look how that turned out.' He tsked. 'If you think Rees is clean, then you're even more naïve than the last time we worked together.'

'He asked me to protect the girl. Why would he do that if he was on their side?' Jamie snapped, pointing at the bodies under the tarp.

Hassan came forward a step. 'Maybe because if she was in the hospital, he couldn't exactly finish her off himself. But once she was *out* of the hospital, in his care, or yours ... if they came for her, well, he could protect her … and *fail.* You see where I'm going with this?'

Jamie's mind whirled. 'You're saying that Rees planned to take her into his care just so he could kill her? No, I don't believe that.'

'Because you're not being objective,' Hassan said coolly. 'You're not seeing this clearly. But think about it, Jamie. That's all you have to do. He kept her existence from the NCA. Why? Because the moment they found out, they'd have taken custody of her, and she would have been out of Rees' grasp. And she could talk. Maybe even identify him in some way. At least identify the people that took her to begin with. If she left the hospital and then died, well, he'd want to keep that quiet, too, wouldn't he? To save his skin.'

Jamie tried to breathe, keep her cool. 'So why bring me in at all, then?'

Hassan thought on that. 'Because he knew he needed a patsy.'

'A patsy?'

'Someone to do his dirty work for him. Someone who could take the girl, and get killed.'

Jamie shook her head now. 'No. No way. My *mother* called me. You think he'd have my own mother call me, beg me to come here, just to walk me to my death?' Jamie scoffed. 'You think anyone would be so evil?'

'He's taking money from human traffickers who enslave and murder young women, so yeah, I do,' Hassan said plainly. 'I don't think there's a depth he won't stoop to. Why did you take the girl when you did? Did he ask you to?'

Jamie's mouth opened, but the words seemed reluctant to come out. 'He wanted to do it himself – the hospital were going to call the police – but he was ... but he couldn't get there. Mallory put Ash on his tail again.'

'No, she didn't.'

Realisation began to dawn.

'And these two?' Hassan said, gesturing to the dead men. 'Funny they knew exactly where to find you, wasn't it? Almost as if they were waiting at the hospital and followed you out here or something.' He glanced over at Jamie's car on the driveway. 'Whose car is that? Yours?'

'My mother's.'

Hassan nodded. 'And it's usually parked on Rees' driveway? He'd know the colour, the model, the number plate. Make it easy for them to find the right car to follow.'

'No ...' Jamie said, her resolve fading. She looked over at Alina.

'He tried to kill you both,' Hassan said. 'And it looks like he came close. I guess he underestimated you. But I don't think he'll do it twice.' Hassan sighed. 'I'm going to call Mallory. I'll tell her the truth, but if it comes down to your head or mine ...'

Jamie clamped her teeth together, a sickening pit forming in her stomach. She looked at Alina and raised her arm.

The girl walked towards her and ducked under it, allowing Jamie to hold her. 'She doesn't leave my sight,' Jamie said firmly.

Hassan looked at her sadly. 'I'm sorry, Jamie,' he said, lifting the phone to his ear. 'I don't think you're going to have a say in it.'

CHAPTER
TWENTY-FOUR

The flashing lights arrived quickly.

First, it was two local police cars carrying four uniformed officers, who quickly worked to secure the scene. Which, honestly, seemed utterly pointless considering they were in the middle of nowhere.

Then the coroner's van, trundling up the track with another van in tow, out of which three SOCOs climbed and began pulling on their white overalls. The coroner himself stood next to the van and begin filling in his reports.

Then another Audi, the same one that had followed Rees the first day Jamie arrived. Ash, the other investigator working under Mallory, stepped from it - glowering at Jamie with her arms folded. She kept her distance, thankfully. Jamie doubted she'd be able to hold her tongue if anyone spoke to her wrong that morning. She wasn't happy about how this was playing out.

Hassan stayed with Jamie the whole time, quiet but reliable. They didn't say a word to each other as the scene began to fill, but Jamie knew that they'd have to speak soon.

And she was right.

Catherine Mallory's Mercedes rounded the corner and came through the gate, leaving a trail of dust behind it.

By the time she pulled to a halt, exited the car, and walked between the other vehicles up the driveway towards Jamie and Hassan, the SOCOs had already peeled back the tarps and were examining the bodies.

Mallory didn't pay them – or the dead men – any mind. Just walked right towards Jamie and Hassan, who Jamie thought was standing a step or two further away than he had been moments ago.

'Mallory,' Jamie said, forcing a smile as Alina hid behind her.

'Shut up, Jamie,' Mallory sighed, turning to Hassan. 'You knew about this?'

He held his shoulders back, head high. 'For about thirty seconds before I called you.'

Mallory fired a cold glance at Jamie, then looked back at Hassan. 'Talk, now.'

Jamie interjected. 'If I could—'

'You can't,' Mallory snapped without looking at her.

Hassan cleared his throat. 'Detective Johansson

called me this morning at approximately 6am, and requested my assistance. She did not divulge the nature of the issue, but I gleaned from the directness of her request that it was urgent. And with consideration to her proximity to the case, and her unaccounted-for absence the day prior, I thought it prudent to come here as quickly as possible.'

'And?'

'And when I arrived, I observed that there was a suspicious vehicle parked on the entry road, signs of forced entry to the property at which Detective Johansson was staying, along with ...' he looked over at the two dead Armenians, 'the bodies of two unidentified males. Detective Johansson bared bruising and injuries congruent with a physical altercation, leading me to believe that the resulting deaths of the two unidentified males were self-defence—'

'Yeah, yeah, leave out the bullshit and get to the point,' Mallory urged him.

He risked a quick look at Jamie. She appreciated the effort.

'Detective Johansson also appeared to be in custody of an unidentified minor with ties to the investigation – specifically that she was a third, yet-unknown-to-us victim who escaped captivity and was being treated in hospital. Her testimony was such that Richard Rees asked her to take responsibility for the girl, and specifically requested that she keep her existence from the NCA for fear of her safety. However, it has now become apparent to Detective Johansson,' Hassan said, looking at Jamie, 'that this was all part of Rees' plan to get both Jamie and the girl killed without us ever knowing about her. Don't we, Jamie?'

Jamie kept quiet. Mallory didn't even look at her.

'That all?' Mallory asked.

Hassan nodded.

'Fine, good.' She nodded towards his car and he took the directive, walking quickly away.

Mallory turned to Jamie then, pushing back the hem of her blazer with her hands and planting them on her hips. 'Jesus fucking Christ,' she said, once Hassan was out of earshot. 'I mean, seriously, Jamie. Jesus fucking Christ.'

Jamie didn't speak.

'I'm sorry, you know, that this happened. That you almost died, I assume?' She turned her head to face the two dead men, both of whom were much larger than Jamie. 'But ... but ... I don't even know what to say.' She pinched the bridge of her nose and let out a long breath, and then she motioned Jamie aside so she could see the girl.

Jamie obliged reluctantly, putting her arm around Alina as she stepped forward, wide-eyed, shaking a little, but staying strong all the same.

Mallory extended her right hand, and with her left, reached inside her blazer pocket.

Alina just stared at the outstretched hand.

Mallory then produced her warrant card to show the girl – pointless as the exercise was, Jamie thought.

But Jamie knew that she had to play nice now, or it would make it worse.

She nudged Alina a little and the girl looked up at her. Jamie nodded and, slowly, Alina took Mallory's hand and shook.

'Catherine Mallory,' Mallory said. 'My friends call me Cat.' She smiled widely, repeating it. 'Cat.'

'Cat.' Alina said back.

'Do they really?' Jamie asked.

Mallory shot her a cold look. 'It's one fucking syllable, Jamie. Easier to remember.'

'Right,' Jamie said.

Mallory released the girl's hand and stood back. 'Here's what's going to happen,' she said to Jamie. 'You aren't going to move from this spot.' She pointed to the ground. 'Children's Services are going to come here.'

'No—'

'You don't get to speak.' The words were so sharp they cut Jamie off at the knees. 'You killed two people. You withheld crucial evidence. You intentionally deceived me, and the NCA. You do not get to speak.' When she was satisfied Jamie wouldn't, she carried on. 'When they arrive, their sole purpose will be to ensure the safety of this girl.'

'Alina.'

Her eyes flashed and Jamie quietened. 'They will remain with her while Nasir Hassan accompanies her to a safe location. She shall be in the presence of Hassan, or another member of my team, at all times. This location will not be known to anyone outside of my team. As such, you can rely on her safety. That much, I promise you. Do you understand?'

Jamie seethed, but nodded.

'Once the girl has been removed from your care, Ash is going to take a statement from you. You will leave nothing out. You will provide details on every moment pertaining to your involvement in this case, especially in regards to your interactions with Richard Rees and Dyfed-Powys Police, as – unfortunate as the fact is – it may well be your testimony that allows us to officially arrest Rees.' She let that sink in a moment. 'And let me put this to you in the plainest terms possible. If your testimony is sufficient in this regard, I will *consider* not putting you in handcuffs too. I don't think I need to explain the charges I can level, do I?'

'No,' Jamie said through gritted teeth.

Mallory stood there, eyes locked with Jamie's for a few seconds.

'Good. And finally,' she said, taking a deep breath. 'You are to have no further involvement in this case. You are not to have any contact with Nasir Hassan or any other members of my team. You are not to have any contact with Richard Rees or any members of the Dyfed-Powys Police. You are not to leave the country until I am done with you. And you are to remain reachable, and in a known location to me until such time. And then ... are you still with me?'

'Just about,' Jamie growled, fists clenched at her sides.

'And then, you're to go back to your own job, and take your nose out of mine. Are we clear?'

'Crystal.'

'Good.'

And then Catherine Mallory walked away, and Alina held on to Jamie a little tighter.

The rest happened very quickly. A black Vauxhall Astra arrived and a woman got out. She was short, with a bobbed haircut and a grey skirt so tight it prevented her from taking proper steps on the uneven ground. She spoke to Mallory and Hassan, and kept looking over at Jamie and Alina.

A few minutes passed as they spoke, and then all three came over. Mallory stopped next to her Mercedes and watched while Hassan and the woman from Children's Services came over.

The woman didn't even acknowledge Jamie, just reached straight for the girl's hand.

She quickly pulled it away.

'You have to come with me, sweetheart,' the woman said. 'It's alright.'

'She doesn't speak English,' Jamie said, not keeping the bite from her voice.

The woman tried hard not to speak to Jamie. Likely under orders.

'Come on, come with me,' the woman said again.

Alina shrank behind Jamie, who didn't move. She was almost sorry she'd put her gun down now.

Hassan was there then. He leaned in. 'Jamie, I know this isn't what you want, but you have to let her go.'

'With this woman? I don't know who the fuck she is,' Jamie hissed.

The woman pulled back a little, straightening her blouse, and then she glanced at Mallory.

'She's with Children's Services, and I'm going with them. I promise she'll be safe. But you have to step aside, and you have to do it *now*.'

Jamie could see that two of the uniformed officers had now come to stand by Mallory, and were watching Jamie closely.

'Don't do it, Jamie,' Hassan urged. 'She's not fucking around. She'll arrest you, and charge you. Think of your career. The next ten seconds will decide it.'

Jamie set her jaw, staring at Mallory.

She stared back, unwavering.

Jamie swallowed, looking over her shoulder at Alina, her eyes big and green and full of fear.

An ache developed in the back of Jamie's throat and she began to choke up. 'I'm sorry,' she said, barely able to get the words out, and then turned back to Hassan. 'You'll be with her?'

'Every step of the way. She'll be safe. You have my word.'

Slowly, she forced herself to nod. And then she stepped forward.

Alina tried to hold on, but the woman with Children's Services took her arm and pulled.

The sound was so sudden and so violent, Jamie physically jolted.

Alina let out a piercing scream as the stranger's hands pulled at her, swinging her arm right into the woman's face.

She yelled then, reeling backwards and almost falling.

Hassan leapt in, taking the girl in his grasp, peeling her from Jamie's back.

Jamie just screwed her eyes closed, kept her head down, hands at her sides, as much as she wanted to fight.

The two uniformed officers rushed in, boots crunching, and Jamie swayed on her feet as Alina clutched at her clothes.

It took two of them to pull her free, the third pushing Jamie the other way.

When they finally separated, Jamie was shoved to a knee, opening her eyes to see the backs of her hands in the dirt, still bloodied from the men she'd killed to protect Alina. They were blurry through the tears.

Alina howled and thrashed as Hassan carried her towards the waiting car. One of the uniformed officers helped up the woman from Children's Services. The other tried to help Jamie, but she pushed him off.

So he left her there on the ground and went after the others.

Jamie couldn't look up. Couldn't watch her get taken.

She just kept staring at the ground, tears running from the tip of her nose as Alina's voice grew more distant, and was then silenced as the car door slammed shut.

The engine started quickly, and then the churn of stones under the tyres echoed through the morning air.

When they'd died away and silence had returned, Jamie found the strength to look up.

When she did, Mallory was still staring at her, arms folded.

And just before she turned away, Jamie saw the slightest hint of a smile spread across her lips.

CHAPTER
TWENTY-FIVE

Jamie was in the dark.

Not literally – it was morning and the sun was streaming in through the window. But metaphorically it was the bottom of a mineshaft at 3am, she was blindfolded, with her eyes closed, and it was a lunar eclipse.

All she could think about was the girl. All that she had been thinking about was the girl.

It had been nearly twenty-four hours since she'd given her statement to Ash who, Jamie had decided, she didn't like very much. She was about an inch taller than Jamie, and had short dark hair, dark eyes, and thin lips. There had been an air of smugness about her as she'd taken Jamie's statement, as though she'd been pissed to see Jamie take her spot at Hassan's side, and was glad to watch her crash and burn so spectacularly. Jamie couldn't say anything about her policing skills, but she'd been merciless with her statement taking, which was all the more painful for Jamie, having to relive and recount every one of her missteps. Of which there seemed to be a lot.

At least the bed was comfortable. Though options had been limited as Ash had passed along the instruction that Jamie stay within five miles of Brecon. So she was at a small collection of tiny lodges just to the north of town. It would have been a beautiful little escape if she wasn't awaiting the possibility of getting arrested.

So when there was a knock on the door of her little cabin she jumped up so quickly her head began to spin and she nearly fell over.

Jamie crossed the floor cautiously, pausing for a second to listen before she opened it, expecting uniformed officers, Ash maybe, there with handcuffs.

It wasn't, though.

'Hassan,' Jamie said, a little surprised.

He didn't ask for an invitation before he stepped inside, the look on his face enough to get Jamie's back up a little.

She glanced outside quickly, seeing the other little cabins dotted around the wooded field, and Hassan's car parked next to her mother's. Which she really should be taking back … She figured her mother was likely on the verge of reporting it stolen. If she hadn't already.

And now, considering Richard Rees was likely in custody … that'd be a good way to thank Jamie for coming to help. Slap her with a theft complaint.

She sort of hoped that was why Hassan was there. The alternative wasn't good ...

She waited for him to speak.

He looked around the tiny cabin, paced a little, then pressed his hands together like he was in prayer, and touched the tips of his fingers to his lips.

'What's wrong?' Jamie couldn't wait.

He looked at her. 'I don't know.'

'But something's wrong?' Jamie's voice quivered a little. 'Is it Alina? Is she okay?'

He stayed quiet for a few seconds. 'I ... don't know.'

'What do you mean you don't know? What are you doing here? What's going on?' Jamie went to the window instinctively, looked through the blinds to see if anyone else was arriving.

When she turned back, Hassan was pacing again. 'It's probably nothing, okay?'

'Talk to me,' Jamie urged him. 'What happened?'

'Yesterday, we left the cottage, yeah? With the unis, and we took Alina to a designated halfway house. The government owns them all over – emergency safe spaces to place families or children in crisis.'

'Yeah, I know what a halfway house is,' Jamie said quickly. 'What happened?'

'When we arrived, Alina was silent. Catatonic. We led her into the house, showed her to her room, and she just went in and closed the door. Stayed in there all afternoon. But then ...'

'Then what?'

'The unis got called away, not surprising. I was readying to spend the night, the welfare officer too. Then Ash shows up.'

'Your partner?'

He nodded. 'Says Mallory instructed her to take the night shift. I said that it was fine, I was happy to – promised you and everything. But Ash was sort of insistent, said she was just following orders, Mallory's orders.'

Jamie's blood ran a little colder.

'I called Mallory, and she just confirmed it, said Ash could take care of it, to go home. When I started to insist ...'

'She was a fucking bitch about it?' Jamie said bitterly.

'She was direct.'

Jamie's heart was beating hard now. 'So why are you here?' she asked cautiously.

'Because this morning, I wanted to check on Alina myself. Extend an olive branch. Kid's been through enough. So, I swung by McDonalds, got some breakfast stuff, coffees for Ash and me. And when I arrived—'

Jamie's mind got there first. 'They were gone.'

'House locked up, no sign of them. Ash not picking up. I called Mallory, she said don't worry about it. It's being handled.'

'What the fuck does that mean?'

'Not a clue. But Mallory told me to drop it, it wasn't my concern.'

Jamie's head was reeling. 'Fuck.' She tried to calm herself, think pragmatically. Only one question came to her mind. 'Would she hurt Alina?'

Hassan hedged a little. 'Mallory's not cruel. That's one thing I can say about her. She wouldn't hurt a child.'

Jamie didn't know if she believed that. So, what was her reasoning? 'Maybe she's punishing you because you brought me into the investigation?'

'That's not Mallory's style.'

'So, what are the options?'

Hassan bit his lip. 'We had unis pick up Richard Rees yesterday afternoon. I expect Ash and Mallory interviewed him before she sent Ash to the halfway house, but the transcript's not on file, and I don't know where he is either. Just that he's in custody ... somewhere.'

'And where's Mallory now?'

'Don't know.'

'So why are you here?'

Hassan hesitated.

'You think Mallory's dirty.'

'We'll know for sure if Richard Rees turns up hanged in his cell.'

'That's not funny.'

'I know it's not.' Hassan sighed. 'I just don't know. Until yesterday, I would have bet my life that Mallory was straight down the line. But now? Suddenly, they're keeping things from me, icing me out of the investigation. I've been Mallory's number two for months. Ash has been the apprentice – and one that Mallory's never thought highly of. And now she's brought her into the fold, and made sure I'm in the dark. And, hell, as if that wasn't enough to make me suspect, she's ignoring good intel.'

'Good intel? What good intel? What are you talking about?'

'The police impounded the Range Rover found at the cottage, but I asked Jerry to look into it. Obvious lead, right? You mentioned the Armenians, and lo and behold, the Range Rover is a company car registered to a laundromat in Merthyr Tydfil.'

'And the police raided it this morning with armed response and a fleet of NCA officers?'

'You would think,' Hassan said. 'No, once Jerry found that out, we passed it to Mallory who said she'd look into it. This morning, she said it wasn't actionable, and we needed more information. She'd submit a surveillance requisition for it.'

'That's a brush-off.'

'Especially when I'm sitting around on my ass and could easily be doing that outside the laundromat.'

Jamie was sensing something irresponsible was going to be asked of her. 'And you want me to help with what exactly? I'm guessing you're not here for moral support?'

'No.' He let out a long sigh. 'Look, I don't know where Alina is, and my hands are tied here. Why Mallory's moved her, I don't know. Why she arrested Rees and is keeping his location under wraps, I don't know. Why she's icing me out of the investigation, I don't know. Why she's ignoring good intelligence and leads, I don't know. But what I do know is that ignoring all of that shit – that the men who came to kill you and Alina came from this laundromat, or at least are tied to it. And it only took about ten seconds of googling to find out that upstairs from that laundromat is a health centre.'

'Health centre,' Jamie repeated back. 'A massage parlour?'

'A brothel. And the question on my mind is ...'

'Whether the women working there are doing so by choice.'

He clicked his tongue. 'Bingo.'

Jamie let out a long breath. 'Shit.'

'I can't help Alina if I don't know where she is. But there could be other women, other girls there, right now. In chains, being forced to do God knows what. And those places, Jamie – fuck, I've seen my share the last year. They chew up girls, they spit them out. These guys, they're fucking animals. And knowing about this place now ... If no one else is going to go in there ...'

'You want us to?'

'No. This is just a courtesy, me being here. Because I'm going in there. And I thought you might want to have my back on this.'

Jamie nodded in agreement. 'I do owe you one.'

'You owe me about twenty.'

'Fuck,' Jamie sighed, thinking of Alina. The women

that'd been buried in those shallow graves. The others in that place, being used like meat. She found herself nodding before she even spoke.

'Good,' Hassan said. 'Let's get to it.'

JAMIE WAITED IN THE CAR WHILE HASSAN slipped into the police lot, his warrant card doing the talking, and retrieved the Range Rover.

A few minutes later, he came driving it through the barrier.

He pulled up next to Jamie and she switched cars, climbing into the elevated cabin of the Range Rover, her jeans squeaking on the leather seats.

'Human trafficking obviously pays well,' Jamie remarked, settling into the extremely comfortable seat.

Hassan was already propped up with one hand on top of the steering wheel, the other elbow resting on the leather centre console arm rest. He was massaging his mouth with that hand, looking at the road ahead.

'We going?' Jamie asked.

'Is this a stupid thing to do?' he said. 'Are we jumping the gun here?'

Jamie thought on that. She couldn't lie. 'Yes.'

'Should I trust Mallory? She's been good to me.'

Jamie just stayed quiet.

He looked over. 'I need you to answer me.'

Jamie thought back. To how Mallory had stripped Alina from her. How she'd watched Jamie fall to the ground. How she'd tried to hide that smirk as she turned away.

A fire burned in Jamie's belly.

'We are jumping the gun. But Mallory's jerking the lead to make sure you know who's in charge. Thing is, when the two guys who own this vehicle don't come back with the girl, the people who sent them are going to get nervous. They'll know that if they haven't come back, it's because they've been killed or captured. And in either case, they'll be scrambling. If we wait another day, the laundromat could be cleared out. Hell, it might be already. It won't take them long to shutter their companies, cover their tracks, and ghost. If Mallory's waiting for more information or she's just trying to remind you who's in charge, she's risking the lives of those women to do so. We already know these fucks beat them and bury the ones that don't survive. What do you think they'll be liable to do if they feel cornered? That the net is closing? You know these operations. How they work. What's their move?'

'They'll clean house. Execute them all, bleach the whole place, maybe torch it if it comes to it.'

'And if they do, we'll never catch them.'

That seemed to be good enough for him.

Hassan pushed the car into drive then and pulled away from the curb.

Accelerating hard.

CHAPTER
TWENTY-SIX

They didn't speak much on the drive. Though Jamie came to understand what had Hassan so riled up this morning.

He'd hinted at the fact that he was now estranged from his family. He'd lived in London with his wife and two kids, and it seemed like they were still there. He'd mentioned that his wife had fallen in love with someone else, and it seemed like whoever that was now was raising his kids, too.

Jamie managed to get out of him that he'd called them the night before, after leaving Alina. Nothing like dragging a screaming girl away from the person trying to protect her to make you miss your own kids.

But by the sounds of it, the conversation either hadn't happened at all, or hadn't gone well.

So either Hassan's guilt for taking Alina from Jamie,

involving Mallory and the NCA, or maybe just him missing his own kids, was driving this.

She didn't know if Hassan was seeing or even thinking clearly but, either way, she didn't like to stand idly by while people were being hurt. Not when it was well within your power to do something about it.

Hassan had always coloured inside the lines, but timid was something Jamie would never brand him. One of the bravest people she'd ever met. And one of the best-hearted. A kind man.

And there weren't many of them left.

He drove smoothly, deep in thought, as they approached Merthyr.

The laundromat wasn't on the high street, but off a long, narrow one-way road that wound through the heart of the city. The kind of road you'd have no need to drive down unless you were going to the laundromat.

Hassan slowed as they approached, looked around, and then wheeled them carefully into a narrow alleyway that circled around the back.

He eased them around a tight left-hander, and they came to a steel gate with an electronic lock.

'Fuck,' he muttered, narrowing his eyes. 'This is the place.'

Jamie checked their surroundings. Penned in on three sides, no easy way to reverse out.

The gate was locked tight in front, secured with a magnetic lock, it looked like. Spiked on top, slick metal on this side, keypad on the right, and on the left ...

'Camera,' Jamie said, careful not to lean too far forward, making sure it didn't get a good look at her. She pointed subtly to the thing, set on the wall above the gate.

'Didn't find any gate codes on those guys you handled at the cottage, did you?' Hassan asked, almost dejected.

'Nope,' Jamie sighed.

'Looks like we'll be going in the front door—'

But before he could finish what he was saying, the gate in front began to move, splitting in the middle to welcome them into a small car park. Despite the run down look of the buildings around, there was another gleaming black Range Rover, and a 7-Series BMW parked there.

'Must have recognised the car,' Hassan said, looking at Jamie. He let out a short breath, steeling himself. 'Last chance to back out. We can reverse out of here right now,' he offered.

'No,' Jamie replied. 'Let's do what we came here to do.'

'Alright,' Hassan said, letting off the brake.

The Range Rover went forward.

'Pull in with the nose to the wall,' Jamie said.

Hassan nodded and did so, parking up so the tail of the Range Rover was sticking out.

'What now?' he asked.

Jamie looked over her shoulder. 'Wait,' she said. 'Someone opened the gate, so we see if anyone comes out. I don't see any other cameras out here,' she added, leaning into the back to look around.

Sure enough, after a second or two, the door leading into the laundromat opened and a guy stepped out. He was pretty big, had dark skin, a white shirt on, with black jeans. He came to the bottom of the concrete steps leading to the door and looked at the car.

The back and side windows were tinted, so he couldn't see in.

The guy raised his hands, like, 'What the fuck are you doing?' And then came towards the car, slowly, one hand out, speaking his native tongue.

Jamie watched him come. 'You speak Armenian?' she asked Hassan.

'Nope,' he said, with a sigh. 'But I think it's clear what he's saying. Fuck. Okay, let me handle this,' he said, nodding to himself.

And then he got out, just as the guy reached the bumper, the two of them penned between the Range Rover and the BMW.

Hassan's door closed. Jamie peered over the side of the seat, watching as they engaged in conversation.

The guy looked immediately on the defensive, speaking loud and fast.

Hassan held his hands up to calm him, reached into his jacket pocket for his warrant card.

But before he even got it out, the guy had a gun in his face. He was holding it like he didn't know how to shoot, cocked half to the side, but from two feet, he wasn't going to miss.

'Fuck,' Jamie muttered, looking around the cabin. She opened the glove box, spotted a small glass bottle of aftershave. Terrible idea, she thought, then grabbed it. She clenched her fists a few times, then cracked her door quietly and slipped out, circling behind.

She could hear the guy jabbering in Armenian, and nothing from Hassan. This was going one of two ways – the guy was going to shoot, or he was going to call for backup. And either way, they'd be fucked.

Jamie swept up from behind and pressed the cold glass of the aftershave bottle against the nape of the guy's neck.

He stiffened at the touch and Jamie just hoped he wouldn't be able to tell the difference between the feeling of glass and metal.

'Don't fucking move,' Jamie said, 'or I'll pull the trigger.'

The guy didn't. He just kept his pistol trained on Hassan who, despite the actual gun in his face, looked pretty cool. And then the guy started laughing. His shoulders rose and fell a little as he chuckled.

And then he turned his head, quick enough that the bottle was now hovering an inch from his eye.

'Stupid bitch,' he laughed. 'You think I don't know the smell of Versace?'

'What about the taste?' Her thumb was already on

the spritzer. A quick rotation and squeeze sent a fine mist right into the guy's eyeball.

He turned quickly, hand flying to his eye, a pained yell escaping his lips.

But before he even managed to get the gun around, Hassan was on him, one hand under the guy's arm, the other around his throat, forcing the pistol into the air.

He drove his heel through the back of the Armenian's knee and forced him down. 'The gun, Jamie!'

She was already there, twisting his wrist backwards and peeling his finger from the trigger.

He fought, but she managed it, just in time for him to throw his free elbow into Hassan's flank with enough force that he wrestled himself free and turned to try to get up.

Though Hassan was quicker, and just as strong, and with a strike so fast and fierce it made Jamie wince to watch, he slung a right cross into the guy's cheek hard enough that he span into the ground and immediately laid limp.

Hassan sank forward, hands on knees, and swore to himself. 'Jesus, that was stupid,' he said.

'You or me?' Jamie asked, checking the chamber of the pistol in her hands.

'Both of us. Coming here.' Hassan stood straight, hands on hips. 'Come on, let's get him in the boot. In case any of his friends show up.'

'Good idea.'

'Well, I was bound to have at least *one* today, wasn't I?'

CHAPTER
TWENTY-SEVEN

Once the Armenian was in the boot, with the doors locked and the parcel shelf pulled across to hide his unconscious body, Jamie and Hassan went towards the door.

On the first step, Hassan paused.

'What is it?' Jamie asked.

'Give me the gun,' he said.

'Why?'

'Because I'm going first. And if anyone's in there and ready to shoot me, I want to have the ability to shoot back.'

'So let me go first,' Jamie replied.

He shook his head. 'No. My gig, my rules. Gun.' He held his hand out.

'You know every time you've gone through a door first when we're together you end up getting shot,' she replied.

'I learned my lesson,' he insisted. 'Gun.'

Jamie sighed. 'Fine. But if this is some bravado thing—'

'It's not,' he said. 'I just don't know what's waiting for us. And I know I'll pull the trigger if it comes to it.'

'A lot has changed,' Jamie replied. 'It's been a long few years.'

'I know,' he said sadly, as though he knew what she'd been through. 'Which is why you want to give me the gun. You don't need to add any more bodies to your conscience. Not for me.'

Jamie handed it over. 'I don't think these ones would weigh on me,' she said, stepping up after him. 'And I'm not here for you.'

Hassan offered her a final glance, then pulled the door open and stepped inside.

What Jamie expected, she wasn't sure. But what they found was that they were standing in an empty laundromat.

It was still early in the day, and a quick look around showed most of the machines were either partially disassembled, had 'Out of Order' signs on them, or just looked so run down and dirty, you wouldn't want to put your clothes in them. Which made sense considering the real money was being made upstairs.

A small counter at the back sat in front of a curtained doorway.

Hassan stepped towards it, looking around the room, seeing no people and no cameras.

So far, so good, Jamie thought as they circled the counter, an empty stool sitting behind it.

Hassan pushed the curtain aside gently, peeking through before he went in.

Jamie followed cautiously, the feeling of emptiness in her hands distinct. She didn't like it.

They came to a small room. On the left was another counter, this one with a laptop behind it. Jamie took a quick look, saw there was also a cash drawer there with a key slot, and a card machine too. Guess even brothels had to enter the twenty-first century at some point.

There was a split of four camera feeds displaying on the computer screen. One showing a view of outside the front door, one covering the alleyway outside the gate, another covering a narrow corridor lined with doors, a set of stairs at the far end, and the fourth ... which was just black - though the feed was live, the time ticking upwards in the corner. It was just dark wherever the camera was.

She reserved judgement until she knew, but it still gave her a bad feeling.

'Come on,' Hassan said quietly, motioning Jamie forward.

'Hang on a second,' she said, spotting something under the desk. She reached down, pulling out a solid steel pry bar.

Hassan's eyebrows raised. 'For unruly customers?'

'Or unruly employees,' Jamie said darkly, weighing

it in her hands. 'Either way,' she sighed, 'it'd be effective.'

He pressed onwards through the next curtain in front of them. A flight of stairs stretched upwards and wrapped around, but on the left there was another door, this one padlocked.

Jamie took the little square of steel in her hand and lifted it. 'What do you think they'd want to keep locked up?'

'Maybe not what, but who,' Hassan said.

Jamie squeezed the lock in her fist.

'We'll come back,' Hassan said. 'But right now we don't know who's upstairs or how many.'

Jamie reluctantly let it go and nodded. And Hassan went up the stairs, treading carefully.

As he neared the top, he paused, looking over the step.

'What do you see?' Jamie whispered.

He remained quiet, looking, listening.

All Jamie could see was his back, but what they could both hear was clear enough. The fierce grunts and thuds of men rutting, headboards hitting walls.

Jamie's blood pumped harder, boiling in her veins. 'You see anyone?'

Hassan pulled back. 'One guy at the end of the corridor, sitting on a chair. He's on his phone.'

'How far away?'

'Too far to rush him,' Hassan sighed. 'He's security, gotta be armed.'

'Fuck,' Jamie muttered, the sounds of male pleasure echoing in her head. Enough to drive her mad. 'Okay, I've got a plan.'

'What? What plan?'

'You'll know,' was all she said before she handed the pry bar to Hassan, shrugged off her jacket so she was just in her white T-shirt, clearly unarmed, and stepped upwards into the corridor.

'Jamie!' Hassan hissed, as loud as he dared.

But she was already on the landing and walking between the doors, brow furrowed in feigned confusion, looking from one door to the next.

When the guy at the end of the corridor noticed her, he jumped up, his bald head shining in the light above him. He was wearing a black shirt and leather jacket and immediately came at Jamie.

She froze and looked up at him, fear in her eyes.

'Who are you? What are you doing here?' he barked at her, his words heavily accented.

'I'm sorry!' Jamie exclaimed, holding her hands up.

As he reached her, she backed into the wall.

'I'm looking for my husband,' she said quickly, shaking her head.

'What? No husband here. You must go, now,' the guy ordered.

'I can't! He's here, I know it,' Jamie blathered. 'Please! I just want him to come home.' She slipped from the wall, facing the guy, but backing towards his chair. 'I'll be fast. Just look in each room. They won't even notice.'

'No, you cannot. You must leave, now,' he snapped, reaching out for her arm.

Jamie pulled it away from him, backing towards his chair.

He bared down on her, eyes narrowing. 'Who are you? How did you get up here—' He cut himself off, eyes widening as he heard the footsteps behind him a second too late.

He didn't even get to turn around before Hassan cracked him across the back of the head with the pry bar.

Jamie flinched at the sound, the guy's eyes lolling as he collapsed forward into a heap. 'Jesus, you didn't have to hit him that hard,' she said, looking down at the shining patch of blood on the crown of his skull.

'Big guy,' Hassan said. 'Don't want him getting up any time soon. What, you want to shed a tear for the pimp with an asp in his pocket?' Hassan asked, patting the guy down and pulling out a telescopic metal baton. He pushed it into his own pocket, then lifted the back of the guy's jacket. 'Merry fucking Christmas,' he said, pulling the pistol tucked in the guy's belt free. Here.' He handed it to Jamie. 'Try not to shoot anyone.'

She pulled back the slide and chambered a round. 'No one who doesn't deserve it.'

'Jamie,' he said sternly.

'Only if they shoot first.'

'Good.' He stood, grabbing the guy by the back of the jacket, and dragging him to the end of the corridor, where he just sort of left him slumped next to his chair. 'You take the right, I'll take the left,' he said, pointing to the doors.

Jamie nodded.

She went to the first door, waiting for Hassan to get in position, and then pushed down on the handle.

It swung inwards, revealing a small room. It was empty, save for a few pieces of furniture. The room was painted black, a red lightbulb burning overhead.

There was a chair at the back of the room, and next to it, a single bed with a stripped and stained mattress. Jamie grimaced, looking left.

A small table with a basin was set up against the wall, a cheap mirror above it. Next to it was a bowl full of condoms, a bottle of hand sanitiser, and a box of tissues.

Jamie looked over her shoulder, seeing Hassan standing at the threshold of an identical room, also empty.

There were three more on her side, same on his.

The next one had noises coming from beyond the door, so Jamie had no illusion it would be empty.

She pushed the handle down and opened it, revealing the fat, triangular ass of a middle-aged man. Hair grew from his back in thick bands, stretching onto his pasty bottom and down his legs.

He didn't seem to notice her enter, but the woman beneath him screamed and tried to shove him off.

When he didn't let her, pinning her arms, Jamie quickly shoved the pistol against his neck. 'Get up,' she snarled.

He froze, looking up at her, face slick with sweat. He opened his mouth to speak, but Jamie just twisted the muzzle into his skin until he winced, and then nodded instead.

He climbed off her, ugly and pale, his tiny cock flapping as he reached for his clothes, all with Jamie's gun hovering six inches from his head.

The man hurried from the room, and only when he was gone did Jamie turn back to the woman. She didn't look Middle Eastern, perhaps Russian or Eastern European judging by the high cheek bones. But she did look tired, confused. But not scared. She'd no doubt had worse people than Jamie do things far more frightening than this.

'You're free,' Jamie said, lowering the gun as the woman sat up on the bed, watching her. 'Run. Now. No one will stop you.'

'You are ... police?' the woman asked slowly, pulling the rumpled and damp bed sheet covering the mattress across her naked body.

Jamie just nodded back. 'Go,' she said then, nodding towards the door.

The woman seemed reluctant, as though it were a trap. Some cruel test designed to break her spirit.

'No one will stop you,' Jamie said, stepping towards the door.

The woman said nothing, just clutched the sheet to herself and watched Jamie leave.

She swallowed the lump in her throat, looked away, and then moved onto the next room.

Jamie had two to go, and they were both full. Similar scenes, just blurring together in her mind as she burst in, threatened to shoot the men, ordered them to leave, tried to be kind to the women …

The second woman, perhaps in her early twenties, with curly hair, took the chance. She threw on her clothes, a simple and tired dress, and ran. She was down the stairs, shoes in her hand, before Jamie could even get back to the corridor.

The last woman, older, stayed where she was on the bed. She hunched forward, naked and round shouldered, staring at the floor.

'You're free to go,' Jamie said, staring at her.

She laughed a little, abjectly. 'Go? Go where?'

Jamie paused at the threshold. 'Go to the police station,' she said. 'Tell them what happened. They'll help.'

'No one can help. They'll come for us. They always do.'

'I'll make sure they don't.'

'How?' she asked, looking at Jamie.

'I'll stop them.'

The woman's eyes drifted to the gun in Jamie's hand. 'You don't have enough bullets.'

But before Jamie could say anything else, the Russian woman from the first room shouldered past her, approaching the woman on the bed, and threw a robe around her shoulders. She muttered something to her, and then dragged her to her feet and guided her to the door.

Neither of them looked at Jamie as they went past, down the stairs, and towards who knew what future.

CHAPTER
TWENTY-EIGHT

J amie pressed herself against the frame, eyes closed, breathing slow, listening as their footsteps faded on the wooden steps and then disappeared.

There was a hand on her shoulder then and Jamie opened her eyes, seeing Hassan standing there. 'You good?'

She nodded.

'All clear up here, though we should keep moving. I don't think semen stains and used condoms are going to hold up in court as evidence.'

Jamie scoffed a little, gesturing to the unconscious body at the end of the hallway. 'Don't think we're really sticking to the code book today.'

He offered a half smile and nodded towards the stairs, heading down.

Jamie followed, catching up with him as he reached

the padlocked door. 'Last one,' he said, offering the pry bar to Jamie. 'You want to do the honours?'

She took it, and without hesitation jammed it behind the lock, pulling hard.

It burst from the wood, sending splinters across the corridor.

Jamie and Hassan paused and listened, but there was no sound at all.

She pulled it wide then, seeing a set of stairs leading down into a darkened cellar.

Jamie lifted her pistol and eased onto the first step. They were solid concrete, narrow and steep, and what little light was coming in from the corridor was all but extinguished when Hassan came down behind her.

Jamie proceeded cautiously, holding her breath, willing her eyes to adjust to the darkness.

Her mind filled in the blanks. The final camera. Likely covering this room. Locked from the outside. The smell of sweat, urine, faeces ... all thick in the air.

As she reached the bottom she stopped. A single wire had been running down the wall next to her as she'd descended, and she groped for the light switch she hoped was there.

She found it, pushed it up, and watched as a dim halogen strip hummed and then sputtered to life overhead.

Jamie had to shield her eyes from the sudden brightness, squinting until her pupils constricted enough that she could see.

But before she even opened them fully, she knew what she was looking at. Iron rings screwed into the walls, chains and manacles hanging from them in pairs. Buckets on the ground to shit in. Straw and sawdust strewn around to absorb what missed the bucket.

Piles of it were pushed into the corner, makeshift bedding for those unfortunate enough to find themselves down here.

Jamie had to clench her teeth to stop her jaw from quivering. Her throat constricted, her heart hammering as she looked around the empty room.

There was no one here.

But there had been.

She counted more than ten sets of cuffs at a glance.

Had this been where they'd held Alina?

The women upstairs ... they didn't have cuff marks on their wrists. Weren't kept down here and taken upstairs for use. No, they were living somewhere else, imprisoned ... but not like this.

This was barbaric. And the word didn't even seem to come close.

To treat humans like this ...

Hassan took the words out of her mouth. 'Jesus fucking Christ,' he whispered.

Jamie swallowed the bile rising in her throat. 'How do you feel about shooting them now?'

'My stance on that is shifting.'

'Good,' Jamie replied, pulling her phone out.

Hassan did the same, and they both opened their

cameras, started taking photos, videos. This could not be ignored, and if Mallory wouldn't act on it, there were a hundred others who would.

This wouldn't stand.

They wouldn't let it.

But the more she looked, the harder it was.

'Jamie,' Hassan said, 'that's enough. We have enough.'

She lowered her phone, tasting vomit in her mouth. She just nodded, couldn't really speak. Didn't really know what to say if she could.

Hassan started upwards and Jamie, after a moment, followed.

By the time she reached the top, Hassan was stopped, looking at the closed door, the dim light from below showing what was on it.

Marks from fingernails. Dug into the wood. Someone had got free down there, climbed the stairs, scratched and clawed, trying to get out.

Jamie shuddered, envisioning it.

She could see Hassan's fingers running slowly over the indentations, tracing the path the girl's fingers must have taken when she made those marks. When she fought for her life.

The staircase flooded with light then, suddenly, startling Jamie.

'Oh, fuck!'

The words had barely left Hassan's mouth when a gunshot rang out, all but bursting Jamie's eardrums.

She saw stars, the muzzle flash blinding her, and then felt Hassan's bulk clatter into her face and chest as he fell backwards.

Her hands dragged the walls, the wind knocked from her, but her heels were off the ground, her and Hassan tumbling backwards into the basement.

She landed on her side, Hassan half on top of her and pain lanced through her ribs and spine.

They tumbled and then hit the bottom, blowing apart from each other and rolling through the hay and God knows what else.

Jamie, dazed and in pain, rolled sideways, kicking her legs to get behind the corner as voices erupted from above.

She raked in shallow breaths, trying to fill her lungs, and searched for focus, trying to pick out Hassan across from her. 'Hass ...' she tried to say. 'Hass ...' But she didn't have the air.

He was propped up against the wall, clutching his chest, face twisted in agony.

'Hassan!' Jamie managed to wheeze. 'You ... shot ...' She coughed into the back of her hand, the pistol still miraculously in her grip.

He winced, pushing himself more upright, and then reached down, pulling his shirt up, revealing a black vest, a shining bullet plugged in the fabric. He looked over at Jamie, and grinned. 'Bulletproof vest,' he groaned.

'You fucker,' Jamie laughed.

'I told you I learned my lesson from last time.' He screwed his eyes closed, trying to breathe, but it was clear the act was painful. 'Shit,' he said then, looking across the floor at his pistol. He'd dropped it and it was about six feet in front of him, in clear line of sight to the door above. 'Jamie,' he said then. 'You have my permission.'

Jamie adjusted herself, getting to one knee at the corner. 'Finally.'

She steadied her breathing, moved towards the edge, listening for the voices above, and then popped out, levelling her gun and firing.

She put two shots, close grouping, into the idiot standing at the top of the stairs with a pistol in his hand, looking down.

He collapsed forward, the red roses on his chest enough to let Jamie know he wasn't as smart as Hassan.

He landed face down on the steps and slid all the way to the bottom, a second voice above clamouring.

Jamie couldn't see him, but by the way the door was being held half open, she had a good idea where he was.

She broke cover, climbing over the first shooter, and put four more rounds through the wood.

A pained grunt. A thud of a body hitting the wall.

Her aim was true.

She listened as he mewled, keeping her gun raised and trained on the doorway as she reached out behind her.

Hassan retrieved his gun, took her hand, and then

they moved upwards, his strength returning with each step.

At the top, Jamie found the second gunman prostrate, clutching his belly, his blood spilling onto the carpet.

She ignored him, kicking his weapon away from his hand, and stepped over him towards the curtain ahead.

She could hear no more voices, but she knew better than to rush this.

Pinning herself to one wall, she looked through the gap next to the wall, seeing the little room with the laptop clear.

She glanced back, motioned to Hassan to move up, and pulled the curtain across. 'Get the laptop,' she said, 'I'll make sure we're clear.'

He nodded and Jamie went through the next curtain, returning a second later.

'We're not clear,' she said.

'What?' Hassan asked, hands around the laptop.

Two bullets punched their way through the curtain suddenly, a few inches over Jamie's head, and she dived forward, scuttling into cover against the wall.

Shafts of light shone across the little room as footsteps thundered through the laundromat. The shafts blinked as bodies moved across them, converging on the doorway.

Jamie looked at Hassan. 'You feeling up to this?'

He rubbed his chest. 'I got a choice?'

'Depends if you want to live.'

He cracked a half smile. 'You know ballistic vests become way less effective after taking a bullet.'

'Then try not to get shot … again.'

'I don't mean to.'

'Could have fooled me,' Jamie said.

Hassan's smile faded a little. 'On you.'

'Protect that laptop,' Jamie said, and without waiting for his reply, ducked through the curtain, sliding across the tiled floor and into cover behind the counter in front of the doorway.

She counted four more guys, the Range Rover they'd arrived in parked half on the curb outside. They were spread out, hiding behind the various washing machines.

Jamie would have to shoot true. She was down six bullets, and the gun held eleven. Which meant five to deal with four guys.

She just really hoped Hassan could still shoot as well as she remembered.

Breathing hard, she did her best to still her shaking hands. 'Hassan,' she called back through the curtain. 'Any time today!'

'On three!' he called back. 'One!'

Jamie flinched as more bullets hit the wall above her. 'Fuck it! Three!' she yelled, rising over the counter and dropping her elbows onto it, firing off a well-placed shot that just ricocheted off the top of a tumble dryer, missing one of the shooters by an inch or two.

He ducked back, yelling in Armenian.

More shots rang out from her shoulder then as Hassan came through the curtain, laying down fire.

He swung left and right, putting shots right at each target.

Jamie looked up at him and he took his off-hand from the grip and motioned for Jamie to circle around.

She nodded, vaulting over the counter, and strafed right, staying low as Hassan pinned the shooters in place with his suppressive fire.

Jamie wasted no time, counting off his shots, and got down the right-hand alleyway between the machines, closing in on the tumble dryer she'd hit a moment ago.

When she rounded the corner, the guy, young and inexperienced, clutching his pistol to his chest, wide-eyed and drenched in sweat, nearly shit his pants.

His mouth opened to yell, and while Jamie would have wanted nothing more than to tell him to drop the gun and get on the ground, he didn't give her chance.

He tried to aim at her.

But she was already aiming at him.

And she knew what would happen if she didn't pull the trigger.

So she did, looking away as quickly as she could after the bullet struck him mid-chest and sent him spinning to the ground.

There were two other shooters hiding behind the machines at the end of the row here too, and seeing

Jamie, both turned their attention to her, getting into firing positions.

But before they could even loose a shot, Hassan was on top of the machines above them, and plugged two rounds into each. Double-taps, right into centre mass.

They barely made a sound before they slumped to the floor.

One left.

Jamie's eyes swept the room. Where was he?

And then, in a flurry of black fabric, he was bolting for the door.

He reached it, even managed to grab the handle before Hassan put a round into the back of his right leg.

The man shrieked, collapsing against the glass, blood pouring from the wound as he clawed his way towards the handle once more, trying to escape.

Jamie and Hassan advanced quickly but cautiously. Jamie ditched her pistol for a fresh one with more bullets, trying to ignore the fact it was slick with someone's blood.

Hassan got to the guy first, kicking away his pistol, and then grabbed his shoulder and rolled him over.

He looked up at them, pain in his face, hands raised, blathering in Armenian. Jamie didn't speak it, but 'Don't kill me' was easy to spot in any language.

'English,' Hassan demanded.

'Yes! Yes!' the guy whimpered.

'Who owns this place?'

'I can't! I can't!'

'The girls!' he yelled then, pressing the gun into the guy's throat. 'Where are the girls?'

'I don't know!' the man squawked.

Hassan pressed the muzzle deeper into his flesh. 'Don't lie to me! Where are the girls?'

'Upstairs! Upstairs!'

Hassan drew the pistol back, cracking the man across the forehead with it. The skin split and blood rushed down his face. 'The girls in the fucking cellar!' he roared.

Jamie's skin lit up with goosepimples. She'd never seen Hassan like this, losing his cool. He frightened her, for the first time ever. He was lethal, capable, and his incessant calmness and upbeat attitude were the only things that made him seem harmless. Now, he seemed as deadly as he actually was.

'I don't know about any girls!' The man actually began crying.

'I'll fucking kill you here. Like your friends,' Hassan threatened. 'Tell me where they are. Right now!'

'I ... I don't know ... They don't tell me anything ...' he sobbed. 'Please ... please! I have a family! A wife, children!'

Hassan looked up at Jamie.

She felt like telling him to shoot the fucker.

But before she could, a screeching of tyres cut through the windows, streaked and cloudy. It was clear what the source was though.

Another black SUV came to a shuddering halt on the road outside next to the other one.

Before the doors even opened, Jamie had her hand on Hassan's arm, pulling him away. 'Come on!'

He resisted, staring at the guy on the ground, tears on his cheeks.

Hassan pointed the gun at him and the man screwed his eyes closed, whimpering.

'Come on!' Jamie insisted.

Hassan let out a guttural noise of frustration, and then began to move.

There was only one way out of here now.

Jamie and Hassan raced towards the side door, bursting from the laundromat and hurdling down the stairs, noting the open gate, the missing BMW. Must have belonged to one of the men upstairs.

She circled the Range Rover and climbed into the passenger seat.

By the time the door was closed, Hassan had already turned the key and thrown it into reverse, jamming his foot against the floor.

The car launched backwards, swinging violently through the gate, the front wing crunching into the brick wall next to it.

He had one arm around the back of Jamie's head-rest, his head pointed towards the back window as he wrestled the Range Rover around the tight corner and into the street.

The gearbox whined as they accelerated backwards,

but before they reached the curb, a Mercedes slid to a halt, blocking their path, the window rolling down, a man rising from it, gun in hand.

Jamie didn't know if they expected Hassan to stop, or the guy to be faster on the draw, but either way, Hassan kept the pedal on the floor and smashed right into the side of the car.

A sharp wail of agony rose through the air as metal crunched into metal, tyres ground across asphalt, and the saloon was forced backwards into the line of houses opposite.

Jamie tried to make out what was going on through the back window, seeing nothing but sparks and shattered glass, but before she could make sense of the mauled Mercedes, Hassan was already driving forward, swinging them violently into the road and hurtling away from the laundromat and the carnage held within.

She was pinned to the seat, watching in silence as Hassan weaved around cars and down side streets, putting distance between them and the crime scene as sirens began to echo through the town.

He drove fast and deft, not speaking, just thinking.

And though Jamie was no mind reader, she knew exactly what was going through his head.

The Armenians had moved the girls.

And if they had done that, it meant that they knew someone was coming for them.

And by Jamie's reckoning, it sounded like there was

only one person in the world that Hassan had told about the laundromat.

The person who told him not to pursue it.

The person who had moved Alina without telling Hassan.

The person who had accused Richard Rees of being corrupt.

The person who they'd trusted.

Catherine Mallory.

CHAPTER
TWENTY-NINE

'Rise and shine, fuckwit.'

Hassan slapped the Armenian in the face a few times, and when that didn't work, he threw a cup of water on him.

It seemed to do the trick.

The big guy from the laundromat who'd come out to check on their car was sitting on the ground in front of the tailgate, his hands tied behind his back with duct tape that they'd found in the back seat ... along with a folded up sheet of polythene, and two spades. Considering this was the same car that had rolled up to the cottage with the intention of taking Jamie and Alina ... it spoke volumes.

At least the items were coming in handy. And if they did decide to kill and bury this fucker out here, they'd have the right equipment.

They were about five kilometres up a forestry road

on the outskirts of the Beacons, parked off the track in the trees. A long way from anything. From anyone who might hear him scream.

Not that torture was the main objective. But if he was reluctant to talk ... It wasn't out of the question.

While they both knew that looping someone in was the right call, the question of who that person was seemed pretty tricky to decide on.

The guy roused, his eyes out of focus. It took him a few seconds to come around properly – not surprising considering he'd been unconscious for over an hour. He could probably have benefited from an MRI scan. But there was no time for that. Or sympathy.

Hassan and Jamie stood back, framed by the trees, backlit by the sun.

The man squinted at them, their arms folded, expressions stern.

'Name,' Hassan said.

The guy just stared up at him, then sneered and began speaking in Armenian.

Hassan walked over without hesitation, drawing a flick knife from his belt, and opened it.

He crouched and swiftly plunged the blade into the big man's thigh. Not deep enough to hit anything important. But deep enough to really, *really* fucking hurt.

The guy howled.

'Scream all you want,' Hassan said, fingers still on the handle. 'No one's gonna hear you.' He twisted it a little to get the guy's attention and he stifled his scream through gritted teeth. 'I know you speak English. I know you understand the words I'm saying. So I'm going to ask you again, what's your name? Uh-bup-bup,' Hassan said, lifting his finger, the knife still sticking out of the guy's leg. 'Before you answer, let me just tell you that we're going to ask you a series of questions. Every time you answer truthfully, we ask another one, politely, without raised voices, and without violence. Every time you don't, or I don't like your answer, I'm going to hurt you. Hopefully this knife in your leg is proof enough that I mean what I say.' His hand flew to the blade and gripped.

The guy's eyes widened but he didn't cry out.

'You understand? Or do you want more proof?' Hassan pulled the knife into the air with a little spurt of blood, and moved it above his other thigh.

'No, no,' the guy said, panting. 'I understand.' His English was heavily accented, but clear enough.

'Good,' Hassan said, wiping the knife on the guy's trousers before stepping back and standing next to Jamie. 'So how about that name?' His knife waved gently through the air, slicing back and forth ominously.

'Vahe,' he said, hanging his head. 'My name is Vahe.'

'Good. Thank you, Vahe,' Hassan replied. 'How long have you worked at the laundromat?'

Vahe seemed reluctant to answer, but when Hassan's knife stopped moving, hanging in front of him like a viper poised to strike, Vahe's tongue loosened.

'A year. Maybe a little more.'

The knife began flowing again. 'And what do you do there, exactly?'

'I ...' He swallowed, afraid of his own words.

'I understand that you're afraid of the people you work for. But when you leave here, you're going into custody, and probably to prison. How that goes for you is going to be decided here, today. Right now.'

'This is not proper law,' Vahe said, seemingly offended. 'Not legal how you hold me here. Anything I say will be no good in court.'

Jamie couldn't help but smile. 'Does it really seem like we give a shit about what's going to hold up in court? You don't care about the law. Why should we?'

Hassan sighed. 'You want to do the honours, or should I?' he asked, holding the knife up for Jamie.

'I wouldn't mind a turn,' she said, taking it and advancing on Vahe.

She knelt, lifted it, ready to plunge.

'No! Wait!' he called, struggling against his bonds. 'Okay, okay! I understand now, okay?'

'So, talk to us, Vahe,' Jamie said.

He nodded, staring at Jamie until she moved back.

His thick, curly black hair hung over his face, moist with sweat and blood. 'I work security, okay?'

'And what does someone who works security there do?'

He deliberated over his words. 'I make sure that the

girls do their work. That they are happy, and that customers are happy.'

'How do you make sure the girls are *happy*?' Hassan asked, tone biting.

'I remind them what happens if they are *not* happy.' The guy didn't seem perturbed by what he was saying.

'You beat them?' Jamie asked now.

'No,' he said. 'Bad for business.'

'There are other ways to keep people in line,' Hassan said. 'I'm sure the other girls that are chained up in the cellar are enough of a reminder of what happens if they don't put on a brave face.'

Vahe's eye twitched a little as he tried to keep his composure.

'Oh, yeah,' Hassan said with a sadistic little laugh. 'We know all about the fucking cellar. And believe me, the *only* reason you're not digging your own grave at gunpoint right now is because I think you might have some useful information. So start being useful, because I'm losing my patience.' Hassan clenched his fists a few times. 'Where are the girls?'

'I don't know.'

'When were they taken?'

'This morning.'

'By who?'

'I don't know.'

'You're lying.'

'I'm not.'

'Jamie? Knife.'

She obliged.

'No! I promise, I do not know. People showed up, they took the girls, put them in a van. And left. I don't get told anything. Just make sure the girls upstairs do their job. Alright?'

Jamie stayed the knife.

Hassan folded his arms. 'When did they arrive?'

'Two weeks ago,' Vahe said. 'You have to believe me.'

'Is there a reason I shouldn't?'

Vahe didn't respond.

'Who brought them?'

'I don't know.'

'Where did they come from?'

'I don't know.'

'Where were they taken?'

'I don't know!'

Hassan sighed. 'Jamie, get the fucking shovel. I'm going to break his knees.'

'No! No! Please! I have a family!'

'You think I give a fuck?!' Hassan roared. 'You have a family. I have a family. She has a family,' he shouted, gesturing to Jamie. 'Every girl upstairs in your laundromat has a family. Every girl downstairs has a family! The two women you fucks buried in the woods had a family. The girl that you tried to kill two nights ago had a family. It doesn't fucking matter!' He walked past Vahe, ripping a spade from the back seat and then lifted it over his head, bringing it down with such force that the bed of pine needles danced around it.

The steel head bounced off the ground an inch from his kneecap.

Vahe recoiled and whimpered.

'Where are the girls!?' Hassan screamed.

'I don't know!'

He smashed the ground again.

'The girls!'

'I don't know!'

He moved in front of Vahe now, lifted the spade high, and brought it down, leading with the edge like an axe, the blade burying itself between his knees this time, close enough to snag his trousers.

Jamie felt like she should intercede. But she didn't want to. She was waiting for Hassan to make good on his promise. Alina's cries as she was dragged away rang in her head. Hit him, she thought. Break him.

'Where are they?'

'They'll kill me!' he cried.

Hassan lifted the spade again this time. 'I warned you.'

'No, wait, wait!'

But he didn't wait.

He led with the flat side.

The spade whistled.

Vahe's knee crunched.

Metal on bone.

A clear snap as something broke.

He screamed so loud the trees seemed to sway.

'Two hundred and six bones in the human body, shithead. I've got nowhere to be!'

'Wait, wait!'

'For what?' Hassan raised the spade again.

'There's a boat! There's a boat!'

'Not good enough!' He wound up above the other knee now.

'They were talking about a boat, okay!'

'Who were?'

'The men ... the men in the van,' he sobbed. 'When they brought the girls in ... they said something about a boat.'

'You're going to have to do better than that! What's it called? Where does it come into?'

He was shaking his head so hard that tears were flinging themselves into the undergrowth. 'I don't know! I don't know! They said that it stank! Like rotten eggs!'

Hassan's eyes twitched. Jamie's mind churned. Rotten eggs?

'The boat smelled like rotten eggs?' Hassan asked.

'No, the town!'

'What town?'

'I don't know ...'

'When was this?'

'Two weeks ago! Like I said!'

'What day?'

'I don't know .... Mid-week. Wednesday. Thursday. I don't know.'

'You don't know anything, do you?'

He just cried then.

Hassan knelt, turning the spade in his hands. 'Do not make me get up and hit you again.'

Vahe raised his head, looked at Hassan. Nodded.

It seemed he also wanted to not get hit again.

'Tell me what happens to the girls when they arrive at the laundromat.'

'We keep them. We keep them alive, okay?'

'For what? To sell?'

'I ...'

The look in Hassan's eye told him that if he uttered those words again the hitting would recommence. So he stopped himself.

'They come for them. One at a time, and take them. Sometimes two. And when they are all gone, more girls are brought in. All I do ... I feed them. I empty buckets. That's all I know. I just do my job. I just do my job ...'

Vahe wept, but it was impossible to feel sorry for him.

Hassan stood, and turned to Jamie.

They walked away from Vahe until they were out of the woods and in the sun, staring down over the valley.

'You believe him?' Jamie asked.

'I broke his fucking kneecap,' Hassan said darkly. 'I don't know many who'd lie after that. And rotten eggs? Be a pretty stupid fucking lie if it was one.'

'Lie or not, I don't know if it helps us.'

Hassan shrugged, staring into the distance, the gravity of what he'd just done weighing on him.

Jamie reached out and rested a hand on his shoulder. 'You did good.'

'Nghh.'

That was all the response she got.

'They pick girls up from a boat, bring them to the laundromat. Then they take them away one by one ...' Jamie shook her head. 'The girls that were buried? What happened to them?'

'You saw their bodies. They were beaten to death.'

Jamie swallowed. 'You think that's their business? Selling the girls off to be beaten and killed?'

'Maybe they just rent them for it, maximise their profits,' Hassan growled. It was horrific to hear, but Jamie knew he was just being pragmatic. These people didn't see those women as anything other than products to be traded and used.

And Vahe, family man or not, was a cog in that machine. As clueless as he seemed to be.

'It's not surprising,' Hassan said then, reading Jamie's mind, 'that he doesn't know shit. These operations are layered. They keep everyone in the dark about everything. Different circles of knowledge, so no one can be a liability. Vahe spilled everything he knew.'

'So, what do we do with him now? Turn him over to Mallory?' Jamie asked.

'And get arrested? Pretty sure we broke about fifty laws this morning, and killed a couple of people.'

'I'm not losing sleep over them.'

'Me neither.'

'So what do we do with Vahe?'

Hassan looked at her. 'You with me on this?'

'That seems redundant, don't you think?'

'You could get out now, run back to Sweden before all this blows up.'

She shook her head. 'I'm not abandoning Alina. I'm in this until the end. Until she's safe.'

Hassan let out a long breath. 'Okay, then you're just going to have to go with this, okay?'

'Your lead.'

He smiled a little, then nodded to her. 'I was wrong about you, you know?'

'Oh yeah, how so?' Jamie asked, smiling back.

'I didn't think you'd changed at all.'

'You're just now realising that?'

He laughed, then shrugged, walking back towards Vahe, spade still in his hands. 'I'm a slow learner.'

'You have other strengths.'

'Yeah,' Hassan said, stopping in front of Vahe and raising the spade over his head. 'I do.'

CHAPTER
THIRTY

'It's sulphur,' Jamie said, looking up from her laptop.

Hassan was sitting opposite at the dining table in Jamie's rental cabin, staring at his phone, which was vibrating in his hand.

Finally, it stopped, but Hassan's worried expression didn't fade.

'Mallory again?'

He looked at Jamie. 'Fifth call.'

'It's gonna be worse the longer you leave it.'

He sighed. 'I think I'm already probably fired. Don't know if it's gonna be worse than that.'

Jamie clasped her hands together. 'Not necessarily. There'd only be one way for Mallory to know for sure that we were at the laundromat … We took the laptop with the camera footage of us arriving. So all they know is that there was some sort of incident there – and I doubt that the Armenians are going to finger us in that. And considering you broke Vahe's *other* knee and left him in the woods to crawl back to civilisation ...' She checked her watch. 'Two hours ago ... I doubt that he's anything to do with it.'

'What's your point?' Hassan asked cautiously.

'My point is that you should answer, tell her you have flaming diarrhoea and that's why you haven't answered the phone. Play dumb about the rest.'

'Why does it have to be flaming?' He lifted an eyebrow.

'Because flaming is debilitating. You think Mallory believes you're so undedicated to your work that a regular bout of the runs would keep you from doing your job?'

He just scowled. 'And what about the Range Rover that we checked out from the police station?'

'You hope she doesn't know about it. We already took it back, there's a good chance she won't have even known it was gone.'

'Mallory doesn't miss things. She knows about it.'

Jamie sighed. 'Well, then I guess you'd better pray you're a good liar.'

'Or I could just not answer.'

'Forever?'

'Until we have something worth the mess we made.' His brow furrowed then. 'Wait, did you say something about ...'

'Sulphur, yeah,' Jamie said. 'Sulphur smells like rotten eggs.'

'Yes, it does,' Hassan replied. 'And that helps us … how?'

'Vahe said that the guys who delivered the girls complained that the place stank like rotten eggs.'

'And you think it's because of sulphur?'

'I do. And you know what kind of place stinks like sulphur?'

'Where?'

'A steelworks. When they hose out and clean the smelters.'

His eyebrows raised slightly. 'And there's one nearby.'

'In Port Talbot. Biggest in the country. And on Thursdays, they clean their smelters. Which makes the whole town smell like—'

'Rotten eggs.' Hassan grinned a little.

'Exactly.'

'And there's a port there, of course.'

'There is.'

'And there are ships and boats coming and going all hours of the day and night, so it wouldn't be difficult to slip in without anyone noticing.'

'Correct again.'

'Fuck, Jamie,' Hassan sighed.

'What?'

'If this wasn't such a shitstorm of a case, I'd really be enjoying working with you.'

Jamie looked away bashfully. 'Yeah, yeah, well, it is

a shitstorm of a case. And it's only a one-off. So don't get too excited.'

He held his hands up.

'We should go, though,' Jamie added. 'Before Mallory sends armed response to blow the windows in here and flashbang us to death.'

'Flashbangs aren't lethal,' Hassan said, getting up.

'I know,' Jamie laughed. 'But who says we don't catch a stray bullet in the confusion? Especially if Mallory's there …'

'That's not funny, Jamie.'

She pulled on her jacket, heading for the door. 'None of it's funny,' she said. 'But you have to laugh anyway.'

THEY DROVE SOUTH WEST TOWARDS LLANDEILO in separate cars – on top of everything else, Jamie didn't really want the police chasing them for the stolen Z4. So she pulled up outside the gate to Richard Rees' house so the tyres didn't crunch on the gravel, and then tiptoed across it and dropped the keys on the front mat, before tiptoeing back to Hassan's waiting car.

He was smirking as she got in.

'Shut up.'

'Didn't say a word,' he replied, laughing. 'She really that bad?'

'My knee jerk is to say yes. The fact that she's my mother makes me want to say no. But my experience of her being my *actual* mother ... yes. Yes, she is that bad. Now let's go before she comes outside.'

Hassan pulled away quickly. 'She call you or anything?'

'No,' Jamie sighed. 'Rees was in deep shit before I got here. And she begged me to come to try and help him. But I'm sure the fact that he's now in custody is somehow my fault.'

'That's parents for you,' Hassan said. 'I could never do anything right for mine, either. You think they wanted me to go into the police? Let alone armed response? The wife, too. Hell, I was already *in* the police when we met and that was still wrong.' He shrugged, guiding them out of Llandeilo and south towards the coast. 'At the end of the day, we're the ones who have to live with what we do. And people who have to make themselves feel better by deriding or judging others. Well, there's a word for people like that.'

'Pricks?'

He laughed. 'I was going to say *bullies*. But 'pricks' works too, I guess.'

Jamie allowed herself to laugh a little too. 'What do we do when we find the boat?' she asked.

'I don't know. I guess at some point we'll have to go back to Mallory, tell her what we found out. Hopefully, it'll give us some protection and, if nothing else, confirmation of whether or not she's really playing both sides.'

Jamie fidgeted a little. 'And what about the girl? What about Alina?'

'I don't know.'

'We have to find her. Have to make sure she's safe.'

'We will,' he said. 'With Mallory's help or not.'

She left it at that. Questions on how or when would only prove what a shitty position they'd got themselves into. Jamie's brain worked through all the scenarios, all the possibilities. Of Mallory being dirty, of her being clean. Of Alina being safe. Of her already being in the hands of the Armenians. Of her already being dead.

Jamie shifted nervously, looking at the sign ahead that said it was still thirty miles to go. She let out a long breath. 'Drive faster, will you?'

And mercifully, he did.

CHAPTER
THIRTY-ONE

The sky greyed as they approached Port Talbot, swinging through the narrow mountain pass on the M4 and across the bridge, high above the water.

The town stretched out ahead, spread across the coastline, shaded by the steelworks behind, the towers and stacks stretching skyward, belching steam and flame into the air.

Jamie and Hassan watched it loom off the horizon and grow in size as they neared, heading for the dock. Seagulls wheeled overhead, the roads busy as people headed for the beach.

She tapped her thumb on the sill of the window, willing the traffic to move. Thankfully, the interior of the car was cool, the air conditioning doing its work.

Hassan followed the satnav across the river, towards the steelworks, and swung them off a roundabout down towards the docks. He slowed on the road, looking around.

'Quiet,' he said. 'No residential housing, just a few industrial units.'

'Easy place to unload some sensitive cargo,' Jamie agreed.

'Port office.' Hassan nodded ahead to a small, tired building, and pulled into the little car park there.

They got out and headed for the door, pushing through.

There was a small waiting area, a faint smell of old food, and a single desk ahead.

They approached it and waited. There was no one around.

'Hello?' Jamie called out after a moment.

A man appeared, in his fifties and portly, with a moustache and glasses. He was wiping his mouth with a serviette, which he promptly stowed in his pocket. 'Yes?' he asked, pausing short of the desk, as though getting back to his bacon buttie was more important.

Hassan produced his warrant card. 'Nasir Hassan, NCA,' he said, almost tiredly, as though the title had lost its zing for him.

The guy put his hands on his hips. 'No, no, no,' he started.

'No, no, no?' Hassan replied. 'You mean, *how can I help you?*'

'Listen, I just work here, alright? Twenty-two hours a week. Got a bad back, okay. I don't know anything about anything. You're gonna have to come back when the manager's here, or—'

'Let me stop you right there,' Hassan said, cuttingly, at the counter now. 'Why don't you stop stuffing your fucking face for a second, and listen. We're looking for a boat. It arrived in the early hours of the morning two Thursdays ago. It unloaded some cargo into a waiting van, and then left. We need to see the shipping logs for that date, as well as CCTV footage of the dock. I assume you *have* some, correct? This place can't be *that* fucking useless, can it?'

The guy puffed, but looking at Hassan and Jamie, he knew he was both outnumbered as well as outgunned.

He sighed and held out his hand. 'Let me see that ID again? Don't want to lose my job here.'

Hassan fished it out and gave it to him. 'If you haven't lost it already, I don't think you're in any immediate danger.'

THEY STEPPED BACK INTO THE SUNSHINE, THE smell of steel and seawater strong in the air.

'Well, that took fucking ages,' Hassan sighed, cracking his back. 'Was he breathing on the back of your neck too, or just me?'

'Guess he must have liked you,' Jamie replied, pulling her phone out.

'Who you calling?'

'Backup.'

'Woah,' Hassan said, laying his hand over the screen. 'We're not bringing Mallory in on this, not yet. All we have is the name of the boat and the company it's registered to. That's not enough.'

'Jesus, I'm not suicidal,' Jamie replied, pulling her phone free. 'I'm not calling Mallory. I'm calling a friend.'

'What friend?'

'Julia Hallberg.'

'And who is Julia Hallberg?'

'We worked together in Stockholm. Now, she works for Interpol. Runs a team there – last I saw her, chasing down Russian smugglers and traffickers. So, if this company, Aegean Trade Enterprises, is already tied to the Armenians, owns ships, trucks, whatever, she likely already knows about it, or knows someone who does. That okay with you?'

Hassan lowered his hand. 'Fine. I just ... I want to call Mallory. When the time's right.'

'You should have already called her.'

He grumbled as Jamie dialled, listening to the international sound hum and then ring.

Hallberg, as usual, picked up. 'Jamie Johansson,' she said, not sounding particularly enthused.

'Julia Hallberg,' Jamie replied. 'How are you?'

'I'm good, but I feel like my day's about to get worse. What do you need?'

Jamie laughed a little. 'Guess I only call you when I need something, huh?'

'You and everyone else,' she said with a little sigh. 'So, what is it? Let's just skip the preamble and get to the point, shall we?'

Jamie detected the coldness in her tone. She didn't think bringing up the last case they worked would be the right move, even just to apologise. Jamie did leave a string of bodies and unanswered questions in her wake when she fled that particular crime scene. Ones that she felt like Hallberg would have been left to answer. And considering that Interpol didn't come to kick her door down, she figured that Hallberg probably worked some magic to cover Jamie's ass.

Maybe a 'thank you' would be more appropriate than a 'sorry'.

Instead, she just cleared her throat. 'I'm back in the UK, working with the NCA on a trafficking case.'

Hallberg scoffed a little. 'Just two weeks ago I heard through the grapevine you were heading up a team for the NOD?'

'I was — I mean, I *am*. This is a temporary thing. Personal favour.'

'You're knee deep in a trafficking case in a different country, already crossing the NCA, on a *personal favour?*'

'Why do you say I'm *crossing* the NCA?' Jamie repeated, a little nervous. Hassan came swooping back to listen in. 'What have you heard?'

'Nothing,' Hallberg said. 'But I assume that's why you're calling me and not asking your SO about this –

because you've gone and pissed off the people you're supposed to be helping. Am I right?'

'Uh ...' Jamie said. 'About half right. But I've got good reason.'

'You always do. So spit it out, what is it?'

'Does the name Aegean Trade Enterprises mean anything to you?'

'Should it?'

'It's a shell company that owns a boat, the *Mavi Yildiz,* being used to traffic women into the UK. They're being transferred to a van, but we don't have a make, model, or plate.'

'Blue star,' Hallberg said.

'What's that?'

'*Mavi Yildiz.* It's Turkish for 'blue star'.'

'You speak Turkish?'

'I'm learning. So what do you need?'

'It's tied to an Armenian trafficking operation, and we wanted to know if you've had any run-ins with them.'

'A Turkish shell corp running a smuggling vessel? Shit, there's about a thousand of them. We shut one down, another three spring up in its place. I can run the name, but I wouldn't get your hopes up. These guys are getting cleverer every day.'

'Can you try?'

'Always. And Jamie?'

'Yeah?'

'How are you?' The words caught her off guard,

sincere and kind, the two things that Hallberg has always been.

'I'm good,' Jamie said.

'Liar.'

'I'm getting by.'

'Just … keep a cool head. I know how you get.'

'And how's that?'

She just laughed a little through closed lips, as though the deflection was amusing. 'I'll drop you a line if I dig something up. Stay safe out there. If it is the Armenians, they don't fuck around.'

Jamie rubbed her still-bruised throat. 'I know.'

'Ha, of course you do.'

And then the line went dead.

'What'd she say?' Hassan asked.

'She's going to try,' Jamie sighed, turning and looking out over the sea, the sky darkening beyond the horizon.

'Then I guess we wait.'

'Yeah,' Jamie sighed, watching the clouds build above the ocean. 'I guess we wait.'

CHAPTER
THIRTY-TWO

have friends too – that's all I'm saying,' Hassan repeated as they queued through traffic.

'I know you do.'

'It's not just you that knows people, alright? I've made contacts as well.'

'Of course you have.'

'Not Interpol but, you know, in the NCA – and I still have lots of friends at the Met, and in AR.'

Jamie sighed, looking out of the window. She was willing Hallberg to call back.

'And like you said, Hallberg was working for Stockholm Police when you met, right? Not for Interpol.'

Jamie closed her eyes. 'Why does it even matter?'

'It doesn't.' Hassan let out a long breath. 'It's fine. It's good we have people to call on. Like you have Hallberg, and I called Jerry.'

'You called Jerry?' Jamie opened her eyes and looked at him. 'Why?'

'To see whether Mallory's about to sack me.'

'And?'

'He didn't pick up,' Hassan replied. 'But we're on good terms. So if he doesn't call back, then it means Mallory is gunning for my head.'

'Even if she's not, you keep dodging her calls and she will be.'

'Well, once Hallberg gets back to us with something, I'll shoot Mallory an email. Outline everything. Tell her we're in the hunt, it's why we haven't got back. Keep her sated. If she is dirty, then it's nothing she won't already know. And if she's not, hopefully that buys us some favour.'

'And if that's not enough?' Jamie asked.

He glanced at her. 'I hear Sweden's nice this time of year.'

She laughed. 'It is. I'll put in a word for you, shall I?'

'Might be worth doing.'

Jamie watched him for a moment, wondering how the tables had turned. She was usually the one acting on impulse, and Hassan had always been cool headed. But now, it seemed to be the opposite. Or maybe she was overselling herself and they were both just out on a limb here.

That seemed more likely. But if it was the case, then they were definitely skating on thin ice. And it'd likely already cracked beneath them, and they just didn't know it yet.

Jamie was still trying to figure Mallory out. Her actions weren't encouraging, but then again, Jamie had displayed more than poor judgement with Alina. Keeping her existence from the NCA was a bad call. A tough call. But a bad one. She put faith in Rees, and if what Hassan said about Ash not tailing him when he called Jamie held water, then that painted him in a bad light. The Armenians knowing where to find Jamie, too? Even if they didn't follow her, they could have tracked her mother's car ... And the only one who'd know it was gone was Rees ... All signs pointed to him.

But Mallory? The way she'd acted after removing Alina.

And that smirk.

That hint of a smirk.

Enough to make Jamie's blood boil.

But was it because she took joy in seeing Jamie pay for a bad decision? Or because she'd made good with the Armenians by getting Alina away from her?

Either way, spiriting the girl away and locking Hassan out of the operation was a difficult move to comprehend. Unless she was just testing Hassan's loyalty ...

Fuck.

Jamie stared at her partner, her fellow fugitive. Had she cost him his career?

He'd come to her, raving about Mallory's decisions, how guilty it made her look …

But Jamie couldn't help but wonder whether Mallory was playing some larger game. If she was withholding information from Hassan because she didn't trust him any longer. And if that was the case, then he'd definitely just got himself sacked.

The laundromat was a shit show. Dead bodies. Gunfire in the middle of Merthyr … The only bright side would be that the police would have descended on the place en masse, and would have discovered the brothel, the prison in the cellar … The armed men … Handling it with more care would have been preferable. But Mallory had denied Hassan that.

Going over her head was another bad move in a string of them, but what was done was done. And Jamie couldn't help but feel like it was time to face the music.

Dirty or not, Mallory was still in charge of this game, and if they wanted to keep playing they needed to do it by her rules.

'We need to see Mallory,' Jamie said then.

'What?' Hassan laughed.

'I'm serious. If we don't, we'll have warrants out for our arrest, and getting sacked will be the least of our worries. Think of it as two birds, one stone. We get back to the office, hat in hand, see Mallory, relay what we learned, and hope for the best. That way, we can get a better gauge of where her allegiances lie, and you can speak to your best pal Jerry at the same time. See if we can't get a lead on Alina.'

He was thoughtful for a moment, lips puckered as he drove. 'Fine,' he said then, sighing heavily. 'But you've gotta do me a favour, just in case.'

'What's that?'

'Help me translate my CV into Swedish?'

Jamie laughed.

Hassan didn't. 'I'm serious.'

'Oh, I know,' she said. 'I just can't wait to see you face down a proper Swedish winter.'

CHAPTER
THIRTY-THREE

Jamie had never seen Hassan nervous before. But as they walked into the office in Brecon he was fidgety, shiny, and kept wiping off his hands on his thighs.

'Relax,' Jamie urged him. 'Just breathe.'

'I've never been sacked before,' he muttered as they walked across the office, empty save for Jerry sitting at his desk. He looked up, stopping his work, clearly surprised to see them.

Jamie had to laugh a little at Hassan's statement. 'First one's the worst, you get used to it after that. They all sort of blend together after a while.'

'You're used to getting chewed out,' Hassan whispered as they approached Mallory's door. 'But you keep coming back. What's the play?'

Jamie sighed, stopping as they reached the threshold. 'Solve the case. It's hard to be pissed at the methods when the results speak for themselves.'

'And if they tell you to stop investigating before you crack it?'

She shrugged. 'Ignore them and do it anyway. Works for me.'

He tried to force a smile, but seemed to struggle. Then he knocked, and they went in.

Mallory was sitting behind her desk, and though she didn't seem shocked to see them, she didn't look happy either.

'You, sit,' she said to Hassan. Then she turned to Jamie. 'And you, get out. I told you I'd send for you if I wanted you.'

Jamie lingered.

'Wait,' Hassan said, taking the seat. 'Jamie's been assisting me.'

'Oh, I'm well aware of what Miss Johansson's been doing. And I'm pretty certain it includes shooting four Armenians at a fucking drycleaners in Merthyr Tydfil. The same one I told you explicitly *not* to go near.' The bite in her voice was clear and sharp, her eyes boring into Hassan.

Jamie felt like she needed to dive on the grenade.

'Technically it was a laundromat,' Jamie said, bringing Mallory's gaze upon her instead. 'Not a drycleaners. And I didn't shoot all of them.'

Mallory scoffed, indignant at Jamie's brazenness.

'But we acted purely in self-defence. We discovered

where they've been imprisoning the women they smuggle into the country, as well as disrupting a prostitution ring.'

Mallory seemed unmoved. She looked slowly at Hassan. 'What reason do you think I would have for not wanting to move on the laundromat?'

He stammered a little, searching for the words.

'Is it because you think I have some sort of deal with the Armenians? That I'm taking bribes or money under the table to allow young women to get abused and sold?'

The colour drained from his face a little.

'Or do you think it's because the laundromat was already under surveillance, and we were waiting to see what happened next?'

Jamie felt her heart beat a little harder.

'We've been running a joint surveillance operation with DP for two weeks now. And you and your assistant' — she cast a quick look at Jamie — 'just shit all over it. And now, we have nothing. Except some dead Armenians, and an empty fucking cellar.'

Mallory was clearly furious, but she was keeping her cool.

'We're set back months on this operation. The Armenians know we're looking at them. They know we're on to them now. And if their pattern is anything to go by, then they're about to close up shop and move their operation elsewhere. So, thanks for that, Hassan. You've been a wonderful asset to the team for months now. Less than two days with your former partner here, and your decision making has gone utterly to shit. I chose you because I thought you were reliable. But this is a *string* of bad decisions now. And one I can no longer ignore.' She took a deep breath, and Jamie knew what was coming next.

'Wait,' she interjected, pulling her phone from her pocket. 'There's more.'

'More?' Mallory's eyebrows raised. 'It's going to have to be a golden fucking goose egg if you intend to stop me from saying what I'm about to.'

Hassan had his jaw set tight, fists clenched on his lap. He knew his rashness had got the better of him, and likely cost him his job. Maybe he'd be going to Sweden after all.

Though Jamie didn't want to let this go just yet. 'We managed to question one of the men from the laundromat,' Jamie said, strategically leaving out the fact that they'd abducted him, broken his legs with a shovel, and left him in the woods. 'And the information he gave us led us to the Port Talbot Dock, where we were able to identify the boat that was bringing the women in. It's called the *Mavi Yildiz,* and is registered to a shell corporation out of Turkey called Aegean Trade Enterprises. I have a contact at Interpol who's digging up some more information on them. Which we should have soon.'

Mallory seemed nonplussed. 'That it?'

Jamie swallowed.

'It's not enough.' She turned to Hassan. 'Suspension, alright?'

He nodded.

'You think that's fair?'

He nodded again.

'You know I could do more. That you'd never work again, for me or anyone else?'

He nodded, hung his head.

'Think about why that is, the decisions you made. You needed to trust me. And you didn't. And you cost me, and a lot of other people, hundreds of hours' work. As well as endangering the lives of all the women that we now will likely not find and rescue as a result of your impetuousness.' She cleared her throat and sat back. 'That's all.'

Hassan pushed back from the desk and left the room, leaving Jamie there. She felt like Mallory had more for her, too.

'I know you don't *try* to fuck up investigations. Your intentions are good, undoubtedly. As are your instincts. And your skills speak for themselves. But everything you touch turns to shit.'

Jamie straightened a little. 'I think that's probably confirmation bias.'

'It's not. It's a matter of ratios. All the cases you've worked on. The number solved. The number solved without issue. And the ones which have caused harm – either to victims, to witnesses, to persons of interest, to property, to the agency or service you're working for, to co-workers themselves and, of course, to *partners*. Your success rate is almost perfect, and the speed at which you solve them is also unparalleled. But most talented investigators don't tend to *not* solve their cases, they just do so by following protocol. It takes longer, but it's safer for everyone involved. So, tell me; is it purely a lack of impulse control that leads to this pattern of reckless-ness, or is it that you're so arrogant that you truly believe the rules that bind us and everything we do as arbiters of the law just don't apply to you?'

Jamie said nothing.

'I can't suspend you because you don't work for me. And regardless of what you achieved, the fallout of your actions outweighs that. As well as being just a total fucking shit show – I mean, four bodies on a Friday fucking morning? – the political, diplomatic, and legal repercussions are going to be colossal.'

Jamie couldn't help but feel her anger bubbling over. 'So you just wanted to allow it all to go on? Those women, imprisoned, forced into sex slavery above that laundromat. You're just happy to sit idly by while they're abused like that? And the women below? If you've been watching them for weeks, then where are they? Hmm? The information we gathered today told us that they were removed in a van from that location. Within the last twenty-four hours. So where are they? Tell me that. You know, don't you? And you have proof of them being brought in too? Two weeks ago. We know the date and the time that the boat arrived. So, surely, you know the make, model, and number plate of the van that brought them in?'

Mallory was stone faced. 'I can see you're frustrated.'

'Did you rescue those women? Do you have the van drivers in custody?'

'You'd do well to remember who you're speaking to.'

'You'd do well to remember who *you're* speaking to,' Jamie snapped. 'I don't work for you. And right now, all I know is that you've done a lot of talking, but achieved exactly nothing. You're moving pieces around the board, but you're not doing your job.'

'And what exactly is my job, tell me?'

'It's to help people. It's to protect them. That's it. That's all you have to do,' Jamie almost laughed.

'My God, you are naïve, aren't you?'

'Sometimes, I think I'm the only person in the world with my eyes open.'

'As much as I'd love to sit here and continue this discussion, I don't really think it's very useful. For either of us. I'm sitting in this chair because I'm entrusted to know what the right call is. Objectivity is the nature of my job. It should also be the nature of yours. I'm not the villain because you can't control your emotions, Jamie. It's a shame really, because I thought you may have been an asset to my team. My judgement was flawed. But I'd appreciate it if you didn't poison Hassan while you're at it. He was doing well until you arrived. And now, I think it's time for you to leave. This building, and the country. I'll extend you the professional courtesy of taking your word for the fact that your actions this morning were self-defence, and I'll also do you one more personal courtesy – the girl, the one you're so fond of. She's safe. You have my word on that. Now please, leave my office, and don't come back.'

Jamie ran her tongue around her teeth, trying to keep herself even. There were many things she wanted to say, wanted to ask, to yell even, but she knew that it would solve nothing and likely only do Hassan more harm.

All she could do was leave, go back to her old life. Back to the NOD and her team. Trust Hassan – trust Mallory, she supposed – to handle this in the way they saw fit. To do it right.

And as Jamie turned around and left the room, that was truly, honestly her intention.

CHAPTER
THIRTY-FOUR

Hassan might have been angry with her, but he wasn't an asshole.

He was standing outside the office, and when Jamie exited he simply said, 'I'll take you home.'

They walked out in silence, got in his car, and he drove back to Richard Rees' house, stopping at the cabin on the way to grab Jamie's bag.

It had never even been unpacked.

When they arrived back in Llandeilo, Jamie just said, 'I'm sorry.'

He nodded. 'It was good seeing you. If you're ever back in the UK socially ...'

'Yeah ...' Jamie replied. 'And if you want to see one of those Swedish winters ...'

He just offered her a brief smile and then drove away, leaving Jamie standing on the driveway.

She watched him go, the sun setting over her left

shoulder. She felt a certain sadness, a sudden emptiness. It was always the same when a case ended. Especially when the ending was sudden, and even more so when it wasn't on her terms.

'She returns.'

The words echoed from behind Jamie and her chin sank forward immediately. 'Shit,' she said, head hung.

'Back to steal my car for a second time?'

Jamie turned, putting on a smile. 'Hi, Mum,' she said, walking up the drive.

'Hi, yourself. You've got some gall coming back here.'

Jamie dropped her bag next to her, staring up at her mum on the front step. 'Do I?' she asked tiredly.

'We ask for your help, and you go and get Richard arrested?' she scoffed.

'That wasn't my fault. He was keeping secrets from the NCA that he should have—' She cut herself off. 'And anyway, you know how many times I've almost been shot in the last two days? I'm fine, thanks for asking!'

Her mother folded her arms and rolled her eyes. 'So dramatic. Just like your father.'

Jamie didn't know if she had the energy for a fight.

'Well, are you coming inside? The neighbours will be wondering what the hell's going on, you standing out here like this, ranting and raving.'

'Ranting and raving?' Jamie repeated.

'What are you, a parrot? Come inside. Dinner's on.'

Jamie realised then how hungry she was. She hadn't eaten all day. So she picked up her bag.

'Didn't expect you, mind,' her mum said, turning away. 'Doubt there's enough for two.' She paused, halfway through the door. 'A phone call would have sufficed.' She shook her head, beckoning Jamie into the kitchen. 'Manners cost nothing, you know?'

HER MOTHER HAD BEEN SERIOUS.

There was not enough for two. So, Jamie ended up eating some leftover pasta bake that was in the fridge. Despite her nauseating presence, her mother's food was actually pretty good. Likely one of the things Jamie's father had fallen in love with her for ... Which made it all the more painful for him when he'd come home late from work and found she'd scraped his portion into the bin instead of a Tupperware box.

They didn't actually eat together, though. Something about, 'If I wait for you, mine will go cold.'

As such, as Jamie fed herself, hunched over the kitchen island, her mother blared Britain's Got Talent in the living room.

She finished, dumped her plate in the sink, gave it a quick wash – feeling her mother's eyes on her – and knew that after she put it in the rack her mum would come in and rewash the thing anyway.

So, as soon as she was done, she went to bed. And didn't even bother to check the time. She just showered, and then climbed under the sheets, pulling them over her head to drown out the sound of Simon Cowell's ruthless appraisals of the would-be stars baring their souls in front of him.

She thought of Alina as she drifted off to sleep, her mind fractured in two. She had one foot in Sweden, in her job, her real life, and one foot here, in this strange place. The country she'd once called home, with an old partner. It felt natural and alien at the same time. Like reliving a memory. And yet the thing that felt new, that felt different this time, was the girl.

She had got under Jamie's skin, sunk her hooks in. The way she'd been at the cottage, the way she'd hurled herself at the man trying to kill Jamie ... the way she'd screamed when they'd taken her away.

That noise felt like it was still ringing in Jamie's head.

And then her phone was buzzing, and she was sitting upright in bed in the darkness, the girl's name still on her lips.

She looked at her phone, vibrating on the nightstand, and rubbed her eyes, heart beating hard. You didn't get phone calls at one in the morning unless something was wrong.

Jamie didn't recognise the number, but she snatched up the phone anyway and answered.

'Hello?' she asked into the darkness.

'Do you know where Hassan is? He's not picking up.'

It took Jamie a moment to recognise the voice. 'Ash?' she replied. 'What is … what's going on? What's wrong?' Jamie swung her legs from the bed and sat on the edge.

She seemed to pause before answering, as though weighing up whether to tell Jamie. She was likely under orders not to. Hell, calling Jamie was probably the *last* thing she was supposed to do.

'Is it Alina?' Jamie asked quickly. 'Is she alright? What's happening?'

'She's fine,' Ash replied then. 'I just need Hassan, alright? Is he with you?'

'No, he's not. Tell me what's going on.'

Ash swore under her breath, away from the phone. 'Fuck! okay,' she said, coming back. 'I'm at the house with Alina. She's asleep, but … but there's a car parked outside. Black SUV. It's a little up the street. But it arrived about four hours ago. Then, a van parked in front of it. And when I checked just now, it's moved. In front of the van.'

'To maintain a clear line of sight to the house,' Jamie said.

Ash just let out a long breath. 'I'm here on my own. No one's supposed to know about this place, let alone that it's being used. Not the police, not Children's Services, no one. Mallory was emphatic about it, in case there were any leaks. Just Alina and I. That's it.'

Jamie's mind worked furiously. Mallory was freeing up her more experienced investigator, Hassan, to continue working the case, leaving Ash with babysitting duty. Shit.

'Do you know where he is?' Ash asked then. 'Hassan? It's not like him not to pick up.'

Jamie bit her lip. Ash didn't know he was suspended, obviously. 'Have you tried Mallory?'

Ash scoffed. 'No, I definitely haven't called her twenty times already. What do you think?'

'Okay, okay,' Jamie said calmly, getting up and switching on the bedside light, hunting for her jeans. 'I was with Hassan earlier. It was a long day. He's probably just asleep. I'll get over to the house now and wake up him. Can you text me the address?'

'Sure,' Ash sighed.

'Good. All the doors locked?'

She scoffed. 'Yeah.'

'Windows, too. Curtains all drawn?'

'Yes.'

'Okay, and Alina?'

'Asleep.'

'Good,' Jamie said, shimmying into her jeans. 'Could be nothing, after all.'

'Right.'

It seemed neither Ash nor Jamie believed that.

'You armed?'

'Yes.'

Thank God for that 'Alright, good. Is there a safe place you can fortify? Bathroom, or closet maybe?'

'Yeah, sure,' Ash said, her voice shaking a little.

She was strong and competent – Jamie had surmised that from the interview Ash had conducted – but facing down a crew of trained killers, on your own, even armed ... no fun at all. Terrifying, in fact. Jamie could attest to that.

'You'll be fine,' Jamie said, brightly as she could. 'Text me Hassan's address, the address of where you are, I'll swing by and grab him, and we'll be there before you know it. Okay?'

'Uh-huh, yeah,' Ash said.

'Good. I'm heading out of the door now. See you shortly.'

She just heard Ash swallow on the other end of the line, and then it went dead.

Jamie descended the stairs quickly, the calmness she'd displayed on the phone immediately gone, her palms slick, and her heart pounding.

She ran to the key rack next to the front door, putting her hand on it and just feeling the bare wall.

She patted all along it with both hands. No car keys. Gone. 'You've gotta be fucking kidding me,' she muttered, looking around in the dark, just a few dim shafts of moonlight streaming in through the windows. 'You hid the fucking car keys?' Jamie hissed, cursing her mother.

It came back to her then. Visions of her childhood.

Of her mother hiding her father's keys, mostly just to fuck with him. To mess with his head, convince him that his drinking was addling his mind. She'd take them off the side table when he came in, sneak them off to a different location, passive aggression in its purest form, and then sit at the breakfast table the next morning with a cup of tea, listening with a smirk as he stormed around the house, hungover and angry, as he always was, shouting about it.

Threatening that if she moved them again, he'd lose his fucking shit.

And he often did. But violent as he was, in his job, in his life, he never raised a hand against her mother. Not even when she raised hers first.

So it would always end the same way, with him coming to the doorway, pleading with her to tell him where they were. Her saying, 'If you didn't drink so much, you'd remember.'

And then he'd look at Jamie, exhausted by it all, a shell of himself in those moments.

And Jamie would mouth ... 'Vegetable drawer,' she said aloud, now in Richard Rees' kitchen, and raced to his fridge.

She ran to the hulking American thing and pulled both doors open, dragging the drawer at the bottom open, and fishing around behind the avocados.

Her fingers found cold metal and she pulled them free, holding them up in the pale light to check they were the right ones. 'Time to get some new tricks,' she muttered, closing the fridge and turning towards the door.

Up until that moment, she'd felt a little bad at the idea of stealing her mother's car twice.

Now ... not so much.

And a few seconds later, she was ripping out of the driveway in a shower of gravel, and hurtling through the deserted streets, orange streetlights strobing overhead, and a dark and starless night ahead.

CHAPTER
THIRTY-FIVE

Jamie raced out of town and along the A40. She knew it was more than forty minutes to Brecon, but she did it in thirty.

Ash had sent her the address and she pulled up in front of the house, a modest detached cottage with a white exterior, leaving the engine running, and jumped out.

The car smelled hot behind her, like metal and oil, as she pushed the buzzer. Jabbing it repeatedly. She'd been calling Hassan on the way but, like Ash, there was no answer.

She thought she probably knew why, but she hoped that banging on the door would be enough to wake him.

When the buzzer didn't work, she started hammering. Both fists, heels of her hands.

She was about to resort to hopping the side gate and smashing a window when the light in the hallway came on and a big shadow loomed behind the frosted glass.

Hassan opened the door, one eye closed, swaying despite the fact he was holding on to the frame. She could smell the booze coming off him in great waves.

'What?' he asked, not trying to hide the disappointment and anger in his voice.

'Ash is at a safe house with Alina, and the Armenians have found them.'

Hassan processed the words and then hung his head. 'For fuck's sake, seriously?' he asked. 'So why are you here?'

'Ash can't reach Mallory, Mallory explicitly wanted to keep the police out of it, and she couldn't reach you, either.'

'So she called you?' Hassan asked, half drunk, leaning on the frame now.

'To come and get you.'

'I'm suspended.'

She stepped forward and socked him in the gut.

He let out a puff of air, doubling a little and clutching his guts. Rage flooded his face.

'Grow the fuck up,' Jamie snapped, shoving him by the shoulder back into the house. 'Get your damn shoes on. Right now. We're going.'

'Fucking hell,' he groaned, stumbling inside. 'Okay, okay. You didn't have to hit me.'

'I think I did,' Jamie replied. 'Now hurry, I don't know if we have much time.'

Hassan looked up at her, one foot in his boot, hands on the laces. 'Is Ash okay?'

Jamie fidgeted in the doorway. 'I don't know. I called her a minute ago,' she said, urging him faster. 'She didn't pick up.'

IT WAS ANOTHER TWENTY MILES AND THIRTY minutes to the safe house, which meant that over an hour had passed since Ash's phone call, and the time they pulled into Abergavenny.

Hassan had sobered some, hanging his head out of the window and slapping himself in the face every few minutes. In the time between, he'd been calling Ash. But she wasn't picking up.

Jamie couldn't drive fast enough.

They pulled into town and Jamie wrestled the car around a bend and down a narrow residential street lined with trees and houses.

Hassan was holding his phone up between them, scanning the front doors. 'A little further down,' he said. 'On the right.'

Jamie spied the black SUV parked in front of a van, just as Ash had described.

Her heart missed a beat.

Maybe they weren't too late.

But as she drove by it, slowing to glance into the cabin, she saw it was empty.

'Shit,' she breathed, standing on the brake.

Hassan lurched forward, almost fumbling his phone. But before he could say anything, Jamie was out of the car and running across the road.

She didn't need to be told what number the house was – it was the only one with the door open, the jamb splintered and broken.

Jamie tried to breathe steadily as she leapt up the front steps and pushed into the darkened hallway, grabbing the edge of the door so it didn't slam.

She stopped in her tracks, trying to listen over her ragged breathing.

Nothing.

Nothing moved.

There was a creak behind her and she jolted a little, relaxing when Hassan put his hand on her shoulder.

They'd done this dance before and fell into step. Hassan, still a little unsteady on his feet, motioned Jamie forward down the hallway while he gestured that he'd go in the front room.

Jamie crept along, noting that the house was sparsely decorated, dated, but clean. Non-threatening pictures of flower pots and pastoral scenes dotted the walls.

She reached the entrance to the kitchen and leaned through the open doorway, glancing around.

No movement.

Back door, locked and undamaged.

Pizza box on the counter.

No signs of a struggle, or of Ash or Alina.

By the time she turned back, Hassan was already at the foot of the stairs, looking up it. He caught Jamie's eye, gave her a nod, and then beckoned her towards him.

She moved steadily, keeping her steps light, and then froze.

A thud rang out somewhere above and they both lifted their eyes to the ceiling.

Something falling? A shoulder being thrown into a door?

Before Jamie could decide, a scream cut the air. Shrill and frightened.

Alina.

Jamie raced forward, swinging around the balustrade and climbing upwards, nearly on all fours.

A woman's voice rang out – something that wanted to be a word, but was cut off halfway through. Extinguished with a hard strike. It echoed through the halls.

The girl's scream continued to carry, and then was muffled. Jamie envisioned a hand over her mouth, and as she crested the top of the stairs, Hassan panting heavily behind her, she realised she was right.

There at the end of the hallway, in the doorway to the bathroom, three men were standing, their backs to Jamie and Hassan.

Three.

Fuck.

Well, they obviously learned their lesson from last time.

One turned at the sound of their arrival and Jamie saw past him, to the second man, standing over Ash, her body slumped in the bathtub with a bloodied nose, and the third, with one hand around Alina's mouth, the other gripping her wrist above her head, her body pinned against his as he meant to carry her away.

They all stopped what they were doing and turned to face Hassan and Jamie.

And then, there were guns in their hands, hanging loosely at their sides. A show of force.

Fuck.

Jamie *hated* being unarmed.

The men advanced. They didn't want to shoot; wanted to keep it quiet. Wanted to be in and out without firing. Wanted this to be quiet and clean.

But Jamie had no doubt they'd pull the trigger if Hassan and Jamie stood in their way.

She saw Hassan's hands begin to rise next to her and she did the same, her brain working furiously to try and come up with a way out of this. But she didn't see one. There were three of them, and they were armed, in close quarters. There really was no way out.

The men were just a metre or two away now. The girl was with the one in the middle. They were all in black blazers and pressed trousers, big and serious looking. Not average bruisers. These were paid security, trained and dangerous by the looks of them.

Whoever was pulling the strings really wasn't messing around this time.

Jamie's hands shook as they closed in, the man at the front motioning with the muzzle of his raised gun for them to get out of the way.

Hassan pushed Jamie to the side, into the doorway of a bedroom, and the man at the front stepped into the frame, holding them at gunpoint while the others moved past.

Alina's eyes were wide, her body frozen and still in the iron grip of the middle man, his fingers digging into the flesh on her face so hard they were leaving white welts in her cheeks.

Jamie couldn't tear her eyes from the girl.

And then there was a flash.

The bang came next.

A single shot, ringing in Jamie's ears.

She blinked hard, staring at the man in front of her in the doorway, gun in his hand.

She threw her hands to her stomach, not feeling it, but checking anyway.

Had she been shot?

There was blood splattered on the wall in front of her.

She tried to comprehend, looking at Hassan, who was doing the same.

Checking himself for a bullet that hadn't come.

They looked at each other, then realised, just in time to see the gun pointed at them drop to the guy's side and his knees give out.

He sagged forward and then hit the ground, blood

pouring over his ear from the hole in the side of his head.

Jamie and Hassan stared at the two men on the stairs in front of them, looking back at their comrade in shock.

They looked at Jamie and Hassan, whose faces were screaming, 'That wasn't us!', their hands still raised.

But it didn't seem to matter.

The first guy, the one not holding Alina, lifted his weapon.

Before he could get them in his sights, Hassan was already charging.

He leapt forward, hands raised, and shoved the guy's hand skyward just as he pulled the trigger, driving him backwards into the wall at the top of the stairs, plaster raining down around them as the bullet buried itself in the ceiling.

They tangled, grabbing at each other's clothes, and then lost their footing, tumbling with a series of heavy bangs, hitting every step on the way down.

That left one.

Holding Alina.

'Let her go!'

But it wasn't Jamie shouting.

The guy's eyes turned towards the bathroom and Jamie stepped onto the landing to see Ash, nose broken and face covered in blood, leaning against the doorway, a concealable pistol in her hands, her trouser leg rolled up to the calf, exposing the holster strapped there.

The guy holding Alina had a choice.

Drop the girl and reach for his gun.

Try to keep hold of the girl and reach for his gun.

Or, run.

He elected for the third option, and turned towards the stairs.

Alina and Jamie locked eyes for a moment before she was shielded by his back.

A muffled cry rang in the air and she started thrashing, legs kicking outwards, bracing on the top balustrade post and the banister attached to the wall.

She kicked back hard, forcing the guy backwards.

He stumbled, hitting the wall with a grunt, and shook her. A violent movement that jarred her hard enough that she went limp for a moment in his arms. Enough time for him to take her down the stairs.

But enough time for Jamie to react too.

She dashed forward, sling-shotting herself from the doorway, hands on the frame, leading with her heel.

It sliced through the air, aimed right at the guy's knee, and connected.

He yelled in pain, fumbling Alina.

She bit down hard then, her white teeth flashing against his brown skin as she sank them into the heel of his hand.

The yell turned to a yowl and she got free, landing on the top step and sliding down the stairs on her stomach, clear of the melee, leaving just Jamie, Ash, and the third Armenian.

Whose hands were now free.

And already reaching for his gun.

Jamie looked at Ash.

She was already aiming for him.

But the guy was fast.

They fired at the same time.

Ash struck him in the shoulder.

He hit her right in the centre of the chest, his gun bigger, his aim better.

It damn near threw her off her feet and she stumbled backwards landing hard in the gap between the toilet and the wall.

Her heel caught the door on the way in and it swung closed on her, leaving just Jamie and the gunman.

She knew she had to be fast, and before Ash had even hit the ground, Jamie was charging.

Jumping off the top step, she led with her knee, hoping to land it hard into his guts. The space was too tight for any kind of kick in her – her go-tos for knocking someone's head off being the crescent or axe, neither of which were going to fly.

But this wasn't just some enforcer, and the training showed.

He caught Jamie, mid-air, trying to wrestle the pistol in between them, trying to put bullets in her.

This wasn't a fair fight.

So she didn't play fair.

Her hands were free and she wasted no time

jamming her thumbs into his eyeballs, trying her best to throw the toe of her boot into his wrist.

The pistol snaked through the air, finger pulling the trigger, sending shots into the ceiling. Stars danced in her vision, the feeling of his hand on her ribs, nails dug into her skin hard enough to make her call out.

He toppled forward then, onto the landing, and slammed Jamie down onto her back.

The air was kicked from her lungs, her grip on his head coming free.

He reeled backwards, blood on his cheeks, running from his eyeballs, and rubbed at his face, cursing in a language Jamie didn't understand.

The gun came at her again and Jamie rolled sideways.

He fired blind, and missed, taking chunks out of the carpet this time.

Jamie saw her opportunity, wound up a kick, and sent it hard into his testicles.

He wheezed, doubling forward, and Jamie sent another into his chin, snapping his head backwards.

He lost his footing altogether then and hit the floor next to Jamie, face down, teetering on unconsciousness.

But Jamie knew he'd regain it quickly, and if he did, she was in trouble.

She clambered onto him, fighting his already strengthening grip, trying to wrestle the pistol from his hand as he pushed himself to his knees. Fuck, he was strong! And this gun was not coming free!

Gun. She needed the gun! She needed *a* gun!

Her eyes flitted sideways, searching the landing.

There!

Ash's gun. In front of the bathroom door.

She had to decide.

She did, scrambling forward.

As she hit the carpet, she turned, lancing a kick out behind her into the guy's chest.

He keeled sideways, still groggy, and Jamie reached for the weapon. Glock 43, subcompact, 9mm.

Would it be enough to stop him?

Jamie grabbed it, throwing herself onto her back, gripping tightly with both hands, pulling the trigger before she even found her target.

Ash had fired twice.

The gun held six.

Bang.

Bang.

Bang.

Bang.

She kept the grouping tight, hoping her shots were striking true.

Click.

Empty chamber.

She blinked, fast, trying to clear her vision of the muzzle flash.

His mass loomed out of the ether, her pupils tightening and bringing him into focus.

The guy swayed, gun in hand.

He tried to raise it, but couldn't.

His eyes, bloodshot and wide, dimmed in his head.

And then he staggered backwards into the wall, and slid down, leaving a trail of blood smeared on the magnolia paint.

'Fuck,' Jamie breathed, holding her ribs. She was hurting all over. The slam into the ground had really taken its toll.

She groaned, getting to her knees, teeth gritted.

A creak on the stairs.

She raised her empty gun, pointing it at the head between the banister posts.

'Jesus Christ,' she muttered, lowering it. 'A little warning next time.'

Hassan pressed his face against the wood, eye split and bruised, lip swollen. 'Sorry, a little preoccupied.' He looked at the two guys on the landing. 'Dead?'

Jamie nodded. 'Yours?'

'Probably. And they need a new lamp downstairs.' He grinned through bloodied teeth.

Jamie laughed a little, then winced. 'Shit.' She blinked, her faculties returning then. 'Alina! Where's Alina?'

Hassan's eyes widened. 'She's not up here?'

Jamie shook her head, getting to her feet as quickly as she could and jogging down the stairs, holding her torso. Damn. Cracked rib, she thought, but fought through it.

She reached the hallway downstairs, seeing the first

gunman lying on his back near the kitchen door, a broken lamp next to his body, his skull near split open.

The front door was open and Jamie stood on the step, bracing herself. She tried to fill her lungs, pain flooding through her body. 'Alina!' she panted, trying to shout. 'Alina!'

Her voice echoed in the darkness and then died, the street outside quiet, except for the barking of a dog and the slowly growing cry of sirens.

There was no sign of Alina though.

Jamie sank backwards, leaning against the frame.

Hassan was on the stairs, kneeling, still catching his breath. 'Where's Ash?' he asked, the worry in his voice apparent.

Jamie lifted her eyes towards the ceiling, where the bathroom was.

'She …?' Hassan asked.

Jamie looked at him, briefly shook her head, then sort of shrugged.

Hassan, with a tired grunt, turned and climbed the stairs, quick as he could, his lumbering steps above carrying along the landing.

There was a squeak of the bathroom door then.

A thud as he fell to his knees.

The clack of the toilet seat as Jamie imagined him pulling Ash's body from the gap, attending to her.

Jamie didn't think she'd been wearing a ballistic vest. But maybe she had. Hopefully, she had.

The last two times that they'd engaged with the

Armenians, they'd been armed. It would have been foolish not to have a vest on.

Jamie leaned against the wall and then slid down on tired legs until she was sitting with her knees in front of her face.

She closed her eyes and rested her head against the paint, listening as Hassan urged Ash to wake up, to 'come on'.

She became aware then that she wasn't alone.

Her eyes shot open.

In front of her, standing in the doorway, still shrouded in the darkness of the night, was Alina.

Jamie swallowed, staring up at the girl.

Her lip was quivering, her eyes wide with fear.

They moved from Jamie to the guy on the floor by the kitchen, and then back.

She could hear Hassan above, and looked upwards, taking a little step back.

'No, no,' Jamie said gently, 'It's okay … they're gone.'

The girl's mouth twisted into a strange shape as she tried to speak. 'S … safe?' she managed.

Jamie's eyes filled with tears and she forced herself to a pained stance, extending her arms. 'Safe,' she said back.

And then, without warning, Alina stepped inside and hugged Jamie tightly.

The pain was blinding, but Jamie didn't care. She pressed her face into the girl's hair and held her as hard as she could.

'You … stay?' Alina whispered into her chest.

Jamie nodded, choked. 'Yeah,' she said. 'I'm not letting you go again.'

The sirens wailed louder now and Hassan appeared on the stairs, descending quickly.

Jamie looked up at him and he shook his head, visibly shaken by what he'd seen upstairs.

Ash was dead.

Jamie steeled herself, knowing that staying and waiting for the police would only be worse. Alina would be ripped away again. They'd all be taken into custody, and there was no way Mallory would protect them.

And Hassan seemed to feel the same way.

So, without a word, they walked into the night, got in the car, and drove away.

CHAPTER
THIRTY-SIX

Alina lifted her legs onto the tiny back seat to save herself from being wedged behind Jamie and curled up.

It was late and she was exhausted. They all were.

In a few minutes the girl was asleep, curled up in a tight ball.

Hassan watched the police cars whip by, lights flashing, as Jamie drove, steady and cool, out of town.

Where they were going, she didn't know, but they needed to go somewhere. Somewhere they couldn't be easily discovered. Somewhere they could finally get answers.

Jamie didn't want to say it, but this whole thing stank. Ash had said it herself; no one was supposed to know where they were. And if she hadn't called Jamie, then Alina would be gone. Back in the hands of the Armenians.

She didn't want to jump to conclusions here, but Mallory not answering just didn't feel right.

And originally, before Ash had interrupted them, before she'd shot at them, they'd only struck her. Not killed her. Had that been part of a deal that was struck?

Jamie couldn't say. She didn't want to say. Because if she said it out loud, then it would make more sense. It would make sense that Mallory set the whole thing up. Leaked the location, walked Ash into the firing line to hand Alina back to the Armenians. But why? What purpose did it all serve? What did she get out of it? Money? Was it that simple?

Like always, Jamie felt like she was putting together a puzzle without half the pieces and no picture on the box. She was just slotting pieces together, hoping they fit, trying to guess what she was looking at.

Right now, she was at a loss.

The police would arrive, they'd see the bodies, find Ash … And then, she didn't know. She expected that a warrant would be out for their arrest before dawn. Which meant that they were likely on their own now.

Perhaps it was time to try and get out of the country.

She scoffed silently to herself. Had it really come to that? She didn't have anyone's protection this time around, she didn't think.

Options. Options. Okay. Try to flee the country with a girl with no passport in tow. She'd get stopped at any and every border and Alina would be detained. Unofficial channels? Well, that'd be one way to add another felony to her growing list.

She could stay in the country and hide? That didn't go so well last time. And with no job and no income, their exile would be short-lived.

Jamie glanced at the girl in the rear-view.

Shit. If she brought any other agency in, she'd just be handing Alina over to them, and best-case scenario she'd be granted asylum and then placed into the care system. Worst case, she'd be deported back to Georgia and then God knows what would happen to her.

Fuck. That only left one option.

Make sure that the people chasing her couldn't hurt her anymore. And then ... Try and find somewhere safe for her. Somewhere loving. Somewhere she could just ... be a kid. That's what she was. A kid. A child. Fourteen, sure, and maturing. But no fourteen-year-old should be forced to grow up.

Jamie wiped off her cheeks and kept driving, heading south. Towards the city.

She didn't know anyone who spoke Georgian, and official channels would raise suspicion. Which left one option – go underground. Find someone through unofficial channels. Find someone who could translate for them, and then get Alina talking. Get her singing. And if it was enough, Jamie could maybe take that to Interpol, to Hallberg, to barter for Alina's safety and freedom. Maybe even enough to get her an emergency passport.

And then she could fly out, at least. To ... to Sweden?

Jamie blinked, watching the road stretch out ahead. Into the unknown.

Could she take the girl with her? Did she want to?

Hell, Jamie'd never thought about kids. Never wanted them. A baby? She couldn't imagine anything worse.

But she saw something of herself in Alina.

She saw a scared and yet fearless little girl, who no one understood.

But Jamie did.

Jamie understood her. And though she didn't know what she'd been through, she knew that she could still love her, not only in spite of it, but for it.

Alina was a fighter, like Jamie.

And if that was what Alina needed, then Jamie would be there.

She watched the girl sleep behind her, her knuckles clutched to her mouth, her brow creased, almost in pain.

'It's okay,' Jamie whispered. 'You're safe. I promise.'

CHAPTER
THIRTY-SEVEN

At the height of summer, dawn seems to approach from deep in the night. Even from before four, there seems to be a flicker of light in the sky, growing and warming as the seconds tick by.

Nowhere seemed safe, and as Hassan and Alina slept off the events at the safe house, Jamie thought.

They were pulled off the main road, parked in front of a farm gate up some country lane somewhere.

Jamie drummed her phone against her palm. It was off. As was Hassan's. Though she didn't think that would prevent the NCA from catching up with them if they really wanted to.

Jamie stood against the cool steel, looking at the girl through the window. What did she know that made her so important? What had she seen and survived? Jamie struggled to believe that one lone girl with no grasp of English could really be such a liability that multiple attempts would be made to extricate her from NCA custody. Jamie didn't want to believe that Mallory was behind this, but she didn't know what other option there was?

They were in the middle of nowhere, and it wouldn't be long until the net closed in once more. They needed answers, and they needed them fast.

It would be a while before the sun was up and businesses opened, but that gave them some time to find what they were looking for ...

Someone who spoke Georgian.

As Jamie entered the car, Hassan roused a little. Jamie patted him on the arm. 'Just sleep,' she said.

He didn't need much encouragement and quickly fell back into a stupor, the bruising on his face really beginning to show after his run-in with the Armenian at the house.

Jamie sat, watching the clock tick towards five in the morning, wondering how she'd find what she needed without the Internet. How did people find information out before smartphones?

'They spoke to each other, they used their eyes, and they used their brains,' she muttered to herself. 'Get your head out of your arse, Jamie.'

And then she pulled back into the lane and drove south.

A city would be the best bet. Jamie didn't think that

there was likely to be a Georgian family living in Ebbw Vale. Though she'd been wrong before.

Cardiff was the likely culprit though, and all roads seemed to lead there.

She drove quickly but carefully, keeping her eyes peeled for flashing blue lights and roadblocks.

Though there didn't seem to be any.

Were they suppressing what had happened? Were they trying to keep it quiet? She half expected the roads to be flooded with police cars.

And yet, they were empty. And with each sign she passed, Cardiff grew closer, the trees replaced steadily with houses, then commercial buildings. And before she knew it, they'd crossed the M4 and were pulling up at traffic lights, signs for different areas pointing in different directions.

Jamie didn't know the city well, but there were a few early morning commuters walking the streets.

The first ignored her, the second just shrugged when she asked, but the third was more obliging. A young man bent at the waist to listen to her question.

'Do you know of any Georgian shops or restaurants in the city?' Jamie asked.

He looked at her quizzically, then looked at the bruised and still-sleeping Hassan in the passenger seat, the girl curled up in the back, the desperate, bagged eyes of the woman driving.

'Uh, bit early for breakfast, innit?'

Jamie smiled as best she could. 'When you've got a craving, you've got a craving, you know?'

He stood straight, massaged his chin a little. 'I dunno about Georgian,' he said. 'But I know the main road in Plasnewydd has like a million Middle Eastern places. All restaurants and supermarkets and that. Probably your best bet.'

He pointed the way and she drove on.

Jamie wasn't sure where she was going, but she recognised the street when she got there.

She chose a side street about halfway down and pulled in, tucking the car behind a box truck that was parked up, and gently shook Hassan awake.

He sat up, rubbing his eyes, the light in the sky bright enough to make him squint. 'What's up? What's wrong?' He looked around. 'Where are we?'

'Uh, Plasnewydd. Cardiff.'

'Why?'

'Because we need answers,' Jamie said tiredly. 'Stay here, keep Alina safe. I'll be back, alright?'

He nodded slowly. 'Need me to come with?'

Jamie looked at the girl in the back seat. 'No, stay with her.'

He nodded. 'Be safe.'

'Always am.'

Jamie ducked into the pre-dawn air, breathing deeply, and jogged across the road towards the main drag.

She stopped at the corner looking left and right, trying to figure out where to go first. She didn't know much about the nuances between the dialects, but from what she did understand – especially from looking up how to write that message to Alina in the cottage – there were lots of them.

'Fuck,' she muttered to herself, seeing probably two dozen Middle Eastern places to choose from.

She began walking, seeing almost all of them shut. But before long, she spotted a small supermarket with a '24/7' sign in the window, and zipped towards it.

A small bell over the door rang as she entered, the smell of spices thick in the air.

A young man sat behind the counter, hunched over it, reading a comic book. He looked up at her and lifted his chin in welcome.

'Hi,' Jamie said, lingering for a second, and then approaching.

'Good morning,' he said politely, sitting a little more upright.

'I was wondering if you could help me,' Jamie began.

He gave her a quick appraisal, guessing she wasn't here for anything he was selling. 'Sure,' he said, a little cautious.

'I'm looking for someone who speaks Georgian.'

'Georgian?' He seemed a little surprised. 'Why?'

'I have a ... friend. Who's Georgian. And I need someone to help me translate.'

'I know someone,' the guy said quickly, smiling. 'He's called Google.'

Jamie made an effort to laugh at the joke. 'It's not quite that simple. We'd prefer the *personal* approach.'

The guy looked at Jamie for a while, then sighed. 'Uh, alright.' He shook his head a little, probably wondering who the hell this woman was at 5am asking for a Georgian translator.

Jamie hoped he didn't think too hard about it.

'There's a seamstress,' he said then. 'Yeah, about ... two, three hundred yards down, I think. It's above the, um ... the takeaway place. Fuck, it's ... I don't know. The Lebanese take-out. They do a *banging* chicken shish.'

Jamie nodded. 'Right. Seamstress above the Lebanese place. Got it. Thank you.'

'Sure,' he said, sitting back down. He looked around then. 'So, you gonna buy anything, or what?'

JAMIE SLAPPED THE ROOF OF THE CAR AND Hassan jolted awake so quickly he banged his head against the window.

Groaning, he rubbed his forehead and opened the door a crack.

'You're supposed to be keeping watch,' Jamie said, a little annoyed.

'I was,' he complained, climbing out and cracking his back.

Jamie sighed. 'Alina okay?'

Hassan looked over the seats. 'Still sleeping.'

'Must be contagious.'

He grumbled a little bit. 'Find anything?'

Jamie nodded. 'Yeah, Georgian lady living above the Lebanese place down the dry here.' She hooked a thumb over her shoulder.

Hassan checked his watch. 'Still early. She'll be asleep.'

'Mhm,' Jamie said. 'But can we afford to waste time?'

Hassan thought for a second. 'It's been a long night. I could crush a McMuffin and a hash brown.'

'Seriously? You're thinking about food, now?'

He shrugged. 'I wouldn't expect you to understand. You've never been hungover.'

'I *have* drunk before. I just don't now.'

'When was the last time?'

'I don't know. When I was twenty-two?'

He laughed. 'Fuck, twenty-two? Jesus. Yeah, you don't know what a hangover's like until you hit forty. I'll tell you that much.'

'So why drink then?'

'Because ... Because it's a really efficient way to punish yourself when you're feeling shitty.'

'Sounds healthy.'

He pulled down the neck of his T-shirt, showing off a huge purple mark on his chest. 'Healthy is not getting fucking shot point blank in the chest,' he said. 'So I think a few bottles of beer and a hash brown is the least of my worries. And plus, the kid would appreciate it. What teenager doesn't appreciate a Maccy D's?

Jamie put her hands on her hips. 'One with sense?'

Hassan smiled and clapped her on the shoulder. 'Sorry, Jamie, you're outnumbered on this one. Come on, I'll buy you a bacon roll.'

She pursed her lips. 'And a coffee?'

'Biggest one they've got.' He spread his arms wide.

'Fine. But let's make it quick.' Jamie circled the car and got in, trying to look like she was doing it begrudgingly. But really, she was almost glad of a few more minutes of pseudo-normality before they found their translator.

Because Jamie knew that once they got the kid talking, things were going to change.

And not for the better.

CHAPTER
THIRTY-EIGHT

Jamie wasn't sure if Alina had ever had a McDonalds before, or if she ate meat, or what she liked, so she got her two McMuffins – one with and one without meat – an orange juice and two hash browns.

She looked into the bag cautiously, but upon seeing Hassan just tear into his food like a wild animal, she took a chance, and then promptly inhaled the entire contents.

Jamie ordered an egg wrap without the wrap and the cheese. 'So just the egg then?' the girl in the window asked.

'And a couple of bags of fruit.'

'For your daughter?' the girl asked, peaking at Alina through the gap between the seat and the door.

'Yeah, sure,' Jamie said.

The egg was rubbery and the fruit not especially

fresh, but it was fuel in her belly. Enough to keep her going.

The smell of fast food filled the car as she drove back towards the Lebanese place, parking in almost exactly the same spot.

Alina was awake now, and looking around tentatively, not understanding what was going on.

It took a while to coax her from the car. Jamie offered a hand and she took it, climbing out of the tiny back seat.

Jamie let go, but Alina didn't, holding tight as they walked to the curb, sighting their destination across the road.

It was still early, but they crossed to the door that led to the apartment above it and hovered at the threshold.

There was a small handmade sign in the window that just said 'Alterations' with a little dress drawn underneath it.

'Guess this is the place,' Hassan remarked, looking around. 'We knock?'

'Doorbell,' Jamie said, nervous suddenly. Alina was still clutching her hand, looking up at her. Jamie tried not to look at the girl. She just tried to make sure her grip was firm yet comforting, and that her hands weren't sweating too much.

She reached up with her free hand and pressed the button. A buzz rang out distantly through the door.

Jamie kept her finger on it for a few seconds, then released.

She counted to ten in her head, and then pressed again.

And again.

'Maybe she's not here,' Hassan muttered after the third press.

Jamie clenched her hand a few times. 'She has to be here.'

She pressed again, laying on the buzzer this time until there were footsteps on the stairs.

'Movdivar! Movdivar!' Came the woman's voice.

Alina's grip tightened. Jamie wasn't sure if it was the angst at a new person coming, or that she understood the words.

A lock clicked and the door swung inwards, revealing an older woman. She was short, hunched over, with long, grey hair and dark, lined skin.

She looked at Hassan, the six-foot-two English-Pakistani built like a bull ox with a black eye, Jamie, the five-foot-six, ash-blonde-haired Swede who looked like she hadn't slept in days, and Alina, the skinny Georgian girl with the wide eyes, bruised and grazed face, and cast on her arm, and did a double take.

There probably weren't three less likely travelling companions in the world.

'Not open yet,' the woman said in heavy English, waving her hands. 'Very early. Come back.'

'Wait,' Jamie said, as the woman made to close the door. 'Please, we need your help.'

'Not open, come back later,' the woman said, waving

them off, making to push the door closed with her old, boned hands.

'*Gtkhovt,*' Alina said then, and the woman paused. '*Daekhmare chems megobrebs.*'

The woman stared at her and Alina stared back, gripping Jamie's hand so tightly it almost hurt.

Jamie didn't know what Alina said but, slowly, the old woman opened the door, and beckoned them inside.

Alina looked up at Jamie and smiled, then nodded.

They went inside and climbed the stairs into the small apartment, the smell of food permeating up from below.

The sitting room was small, and the two shabby sofas were covered in clothing and fabric strips. In the middle of the room there was a rail with customers' clothes hanging on it, and against the wall a sewing machine and a table with fabric sheers and spools of coloured cottons.

The woman gestured to the sofa, and the three of them sat, squeezing in, trying to be careful not to crush the woman's clothes too badly.

She went to the kitchen and started busying herself filling the kettle and taking out teacups.

Alina watched her curiously while Jamie watched Alina.

Hassan just belched quietly to Jamie's left.

'Sorry,' he whispered. 'Acid reflux.'

'Probably because you didn't chew your breakfast.'

'I was hungry.'

'I know. I'm surprised you still have all your fingers.'

He pounded his chest with his fist. 'Fuck,' he grunted. 'Beer and fast food. Bad combo.' He hit his chest a few more times.

Jamie took the opportunity to elbow him in the gut.

He flinched in pain, then let out a loud, unintentional burp.

'Better?' Jamie asked.

'Weirdly, yeah,' he replied, rubbing his stomach. 'Don't do that again, though.'

'Yeah, one's enough,' Jamie remarked, waving her hand to clear the smell.

She caught Alina smirking at her and she smiled back.

And then the seamstress returned with her tray and set it down on the small coffee table.

She looked at Alina, said something in Georgian, then snapped her fingers.

Alina jumped to attention, pouring cups of tea while the woman settled into an armchair.

She watched Alina as she worked, and then asked something else.

Alina paused momentarily, looking up. 'Alina,' she replied.

The woman nodded, then put her hand on her chest. 'Muzhdar,' she said. Then looked at Jamie and Hassan. 'Muzhdar,' she said again.

Jamie thought that was her name, but she wasn't totally sure.

'Thank you for allowing us into your home,' Jamie said then, separating her words a little so the woman could understand.

'Mm,' the woman said. 'What is so important that you bang down my door this early, hmm?' She took a cup of tea from Alina, who then handed one to Jamie and Hassan.

It smelled like herbs Jamie didn't recognise. She just held on to it, resting it on her lap.

'My name is Jamie, and this is my partner, Nasir. We're working with the police on a delicate case, and we're looking for someone who speaks Georgian. We understand that you do?'

The woman slurped her tea, regarding them over the rim of her cup. She struck Jamie as the type of woman not to want to beat around the bush. 'The police?'

Jamie nodded.

'Aren't police supposed to introduce themselves, show their badges before coming into someone's home?'

Jamie smiled a little. 'Police in the UK don't actually have badges,' she said. 'They carry warrant cards that are …' But she trailed off, seeing the unimpressed look on the woman's face.

Jamie noticed now that she was still wearing a nightgown and robe. She'd been woken up, probably adding to her prickly demeanour.

Jamie cleared her throat instead. 'I'll be honest with you.'

'I'd appreciate it.'

'We saved this girl,' Jamie said, putting a hand on Alina's shoulder, 'from some very bad people. She was brought to this country and imprisoned.'

The woman watched Jamie carefully.

'She managed to escape. But the people that brought her here are searching for her, and they want her back. They have already made several attempts, and there's no one we can trust.'

The woman drank more tea, then lowered it. 'And you believe you can trust me?'

Jamie swallowed. 'I don't know. But she's in danger, and we need someone who can speak to her. She has no one, and we have no idea what she's been through. We just need someone to ask her some questions, find out if she has any living relatives, and if she can tell us anything about what happened to her so that we can figure out how to keep her safe.'

The seamstress just stared at Jamie, as though deciding whether or not to help.

But after what seemed like a full minute of silence, she turned to Alina and asked her something in Georgian.

The girl looked at Jamie, as if for confirmation.

Jamie could only nod.

Alina took a deep breath, clasping her hands in her lap and picking at her thumb nail.

And then she began talking.

Slowly at first, but then with more speed, never lifting her eyes from her knees.

The seamstress listened, nodding. Her eyebrows began to rise and then she spoke, interrupting the girl. She cleared her throat, and then looked back at Jamie. 'I'll translate,' she said. 'As best I can.'

'Thank you, we appreciate it.'

The woman nodded, then exhaled, brow crumpling as she thought of the right words. 'Alina says she travelled out of Georgia with her grandfather after her parents died. She said an ...uh ... a sickness, from the water in the village.'

'Jesus,' Jamie muttered.

The woman glared at her and Jamie immediately noticed the crucifix hanging on her wall above the sewing machine.

'Sorry.'

The seamstress shook it off and continued. 'Her grandfather took her across the border, where they met up with some men who promised they could get them to the UK. That they had friends here that could help.'

'Friends? Did she say who?'

The seamstress looked at Alina and asked.

Alina shook her head, then said something else.

'She says that the men took the information from her grandfather, and put her in the back of a truck with other girls. When her grandfather tried to join her, the men stopped him, told him that there would be another truck coming. That this one was full. She says as they drove away, she heard her grandfather call her name. Then ... gunshots.'

Jamie swallowed, looking at Alina. She took her hand and squeezed a little. Jamie had pieced that story together, but hearing it now didn't make it any better.

Alina kept her eyes down, and kept speaking while the seamstress translated.

'They travelled for days, with little food or water. Many girls and women from different places. All scared. But when they asked for water, or to leave, they were threatened. She said one girl tried to run, but they ...' She seemed to listen for a second, nodding along. 'They hunted her. Like a dog.'

Jamie tried to keep her composure.

'They drove through the mountains until they reached the sea, and then took a boat. Many days. She did not see the sun or stars until they arrived, and were then unloaded next to ... towers, with blue fire spitting from the top.' The seamstress shook her head, not really understanding the reference.

But Jamie did. She'd seen the same blue flames coming from the steelworks.

'They were put into a van and driven to a building, where she was kept in a ... basement. In chains.'

'The laundromat,' Hassan whispered at Jamie's shoulder.

She nodded.

'And then ... they came to collect her,' the seamstress said.

Alina had stopped speaking now and was once again picking at her fingers.

'What happened next?' Jamie asked, voice a little choked.

The seamstress asked.

Alina's hands stopped moving. She muttered something.

'She says she does not want to say.'

Jamie laid a hand on her arm again. 'It's okay,' she said, encouraging her. 'You can tell us.'

The girl's eyes seemed to shimmer in the dim early morning light. She bit her bottom lip, then let out a shaky breath. And then she spoke.

'She doesn't know how long she was there. But when they came for her, it was late,' the seamstress said. 'Everyone was asleep. The men came every week, and took a few girls. Two. Three. Four sometimes. And they would not come back. When they took her, they placed a bag over her head, and tied her hands behind her back.' Even the seamstress seemed to be struggling to speak now, her bony hands clutched tightly around her teacup. She'd lived a long life, but no matter who you were, this was harrowing to hear.

'They drove her out into the hills,' the woman carried on, voice quietened. 'They went over a bumpy road, and then she was dragged from the van and walked across sharp stones with bare feet. The other girls cried. She could hear wind in the trees, could smell the countryside, the night air. But then, a heavy door opened, and they were taken down steps, into the ground. It was cold, and smelled like grease and metal.

They were walked to another room, and pushed inside, the bags removed. There were some other girls here already. Not chained up, though. Throughout the night, there was more and more noise. People. Lots of people. Shouting and cheering.

'One by one, the girls were led out of the room by two men in black through another door. Some time would pass, the crowd growing louder, and then silence. And then, another girl. And another. Until it was her turn ...' The seamstress trailed off again.

Alina was physically shaking.

Jamie's hands were clenched tight on her lap. She nodded for the seamstress to go on.

She said something in Georgian and Alina's face screwed itself up tight. But she kept talking, the words coming out strained and sporadic.

'She says ...' The seamstress went on. 'That when they came for her, they led her down a long corridor, and then into a wide space, with a fence all around it. They were still underground, and she could see machines in the background, great machines. There were people beyond the fence, lots of people. Cheering and shouting. The floor was covered in sand and bright lights shone down from above. The sand was wet, though. With red ... with shining red.'

Jamie set her teeth, heart beating harder.

'There was another person in the space, another girl. She was a little older, a little bigger. She was bleeding ...' The seamstress held her shaking hand to her cheek.

'From her face. And her hands were covered in blood, too. Everyone was screaming so loud ... And then ... the older girl leapt at her and she ... she ...' The seamstress swallowed, then readjusted herself in her chair, setting the cup on the arm as she wiped her eyes of the tears forming there. 'She was forced to fight. To fight ... for her life.'

Alina had stopped speaking now and was curled over on the sofa, hair hanging around her face so her eyes were completely covered. But the tears spotting on her jeans told Jamie she was crying.

'She killed that girl,' the seamstress said. 'And two more. That night.'

Jamie's throat had all but closed up as she listened to the words. She thought they'd been using the girls for sex trafficking or slavery. But it was something else, something just as horrific, if not worse. They were using them for blood sport. Pitting teenagers against each other to fight to the death. That is what Alina was used for. And she'd fought. Hard. Fought for her life. Killed for her own life.

Jesus Christ. Jamie couldn't imagine.

But she'd been right – Alina was a fighter.

She just hadn't known to what extent.

But now she knew. And she was even more sure now that she'd do all she could to protect her. These people, the ones who did this to her ... they had to pay.

Alina had survived that night, but she'd been taken from there to somewhere else, had escaped en route.

Were they taking her to the next arena? Or somewhere else?

Why did they want her so badly? Could she identify where that place was? Or ... perhaps more importantly, *who* was there. A crowd. Screaming and cheering.

Jamie had been a detective long enough to know that the kinds of people who indulged in the sickest of pastimes were often the most well connected, the most influential, the richest. Those to whom the rules of the real world didn't apply. Those who could have whatever they desired. Fulfil whatever those desires were, no matter what they were.

Is that why Alina was such a liability for them?

Could she identify faces in that crowd who would do anything to remain anonymous?

Hassan touched Jamie's shoulder and she looked around at him. Even as seasoned as he was, he looked shaken, too.

'We should talk,' he said quietly. 'Figure out our next move.'

'Yeah, we should,' Jamie said, putting her arm around Alina and pulling her in close, tasting bile at the back of her throat, feeling a familiar, cold fury course through her. 'But we're going to do a lot more than talk.'

CHAPTER
THIRTY-NINE

Jamie looked at Alina through the driver's window of the car.

She was sitting in the back seat, knees curled to her chest, cheeks pressed against them, staring vacantly into space.

Jamie had to peel her eyes away from the girl. Looking at her just made Jamie want to scream, want to cry, want to hug her, hold her, wanted to make her kill every single person who had anything to do with what was done to her.

Hassan was shifting from foot to foot, watching Jamie as she called Hallberg, her contact at Interpol. It went to answering machine again. 'Fuck,' Jamie said. 'She's not picking up.' She let out a sharp exhale. Frustration. 'Any word from Mallory?'

Hassan checked his phone again, then shook his

head. 'No,' he said. 'Maybe she doesn't know we were there. I mean, Ash could have fought them off alone. But one survived, took Alina?'

'No,' Jamie said. 'That won't fly. She'll see Ash's calls to you, to me. My calls to you. Your calls to her. My calls to Ash. The Armenian's car is still there ... She knows what happened.'

'So why hasn't she reached out?'

'Probably because we're radioactive?' Jamie shrugged. 'If I was her I'd want nothing to do with us. There's going to be an investigation, for *sure.* And we're unaffiliated with any law enforcement agency right now. We killed three people, just last night, and abducted a girl from NCA custody.'

'We protected her by killing three human traffickers,' Hassan corrected her.

'That's what we know. But what is it on paper? Murder and kidnapping. Mallory isn't tied to us, and nor will she want to be now. If she's in contact with us, though, she'll need to explain why to whoever's desk this ends up on.'

Hassan licked his lips. 'But that doesn't explain why she didn't answer when Ash tried to call her.'

'No, it doesn't.' Jamie thought of that for a moment. 'But it doesn't matter now. We're going to have people looking for us. A lot of people. On both sides.'

'So, what are we going to do?'

Jamie held her phone up. 'I'm working on it.'

. . .

THEY DROVE NORTH OUT OF THE CITY, STAYING off the main roads, and wound their way back into the wilderness. Out there, among the hills, the feeling of isolation was comforting.

They kept moving, stopping every now and then to turn their phones on and try to call Hallberg again.

By the third time, they'd pulled in at the side of a road next to a small river, carving its way through the moon-like landscape of the Beacons.

The day was going to be hot, and Alina had taken the opportunity to stretch her legs after a few hours of silence, walking down to the water's edge and taking her shoes off.

She rolled up the legs of her jeans around her calves and walked out into the water, crouching there, unaware of the cold, and began turning over rocks on the riverbed. She was deep in thought, trapped by her own memories, oppressed by them, unable to escape the ghosts. Jamie knew. She'd been there. She'd seen that look. She'd had that look.

Jamie glanced down at her screen, willing it to boot up. And when it did, a flood of missed calls came through from Hallberg.

She dialled immediately and Hassan stepped closer to listen.

Hallberg answered almost immediately. 'Jamie, where the hell have you been?'

'Sorry, sorry. We've been laying low—'

'No shit! Three dead Armenians and a dead NCA investigator? You love making my life a living hell, don't you?'

Jamie's brow crumpled. 'Your ... what? What do you mean?' Jamie could hear chattering in the background. 'What's going on? Where are you?'

'I'm in London,' Hallberg said then.

'London? What the hell are you doing in London?'

She sucked air through her teeth. 'Trying to clean up your mess? The usual, you know.' She laughed then. 'But seriously, could you shit the bed any harder if you tried?'

Jamie chuckled nervously. 'I could, uh, give it a go?' She looked at Hassan, totally confused. He looked just as perplexed.

'Please don't.'

'Sorry, as glad as I am to hear from you ... can you tell me what the hell's going on? We're in some trouble here, and we need some help.'

'You're damn right you do. Do you know what you've stumbled into here? After we got off the phone, I started digging a little more into the names you gave me, of that shell company? Turns out we've got a half-dozen active investigations tied to this thing. It's just one arm of a world-wide trafficking operation. You filled in some blanks for us – we didn't know how they were moving so many people and so much product through the UK, but now we do, thanks to you.'

'That's … That's great,' Jamie said, a little hesitant. 'But we're kind of out on a limb here.'

Hallberg sighed. 'I'm not heading this up; it's above my pay grade. But I managed to shoehorn my way in here, thanks to you.'

'You sound excited?' Jamie questioned, trying to keep up.

Hallberg scoffed. 'Excited? Of course I'm excited. This is a career-maker, a case like this.'

'I'm happy for you.'

'Well, I do have you to thank. And I hope you don't mind, but I told the NCA and Interpol that you were here at my behest to look into a tip we got.'

'You told them I was … working for Interpol?'

'Yeah – I mean, I would have checked with you if it was okay, but things were moving fast and I had to think on my feet. The good news is that it seems like you were at least operating on the right side of this, and not just doing … what you normally do. You know?'

'Thank … you?'

'You should be thanking me. You'd be looking at twenty-five to life if I didn't intercede.' Hallberg scoffed. 'You have to be the luckiest person I've ever met.'

'I feel lucky,' Jamie grumbled, looking at Hassan.

'Anyway – where are you? We need to meet, debrief. Your witness, the girl? She needs to be brought in, secured, interviewed. We need everything on paper. These guys may be human scum, but we still have to nail them in court. You can't shoot them all, you know?' Hallberg seemed too excited for Jamie's liking.

'I could if I had a big enough gun.'

'Yeah, I don't doubt it. Can you hold fast for a few hours? We're just gearing up to get out there.'

'Uh, yeah, yeah, sure,' Jamie said. 'Uh, so ... the house? With the Armenians ... are we ...?'

'Are you at risk of being arrested? No, not yet. We're running a joint-op with the NCA on this now. You're under my purview.'

'And what about Catherine Mallory?'

'She's rolling out the welcome mat for us. We'll be setting up at her office in Brecon. Meet us there?'

Jamie swallowed. 'And Mallory will be there?'

'Of course,' Hallberg said. 'What, you didn't burn your bridge with her already, did you?'

Jamie laughed. 'No, no, of course not.'

There was silence. 'Jesus Christ, Jamie.'

'I didn't mean to.'

'You never do.'

Jamie could practically see Hallberg pinching the bridge of her nose.

'Alright, alright,' she said. 'Just ... don't do anything until we get there. Don't speak to anyone, don't shoot anyone, don't do *anything*. Alright?'

'Okay.'

'No, seriously, Jamie. Just sit on your hands. It's a few hours. I'll check back in when we're on the road.'

And then she hung up.

Jamie lowered the phone, blinking, dumbfounded. She'd gone into that believing she was going to have to beg for help. Beg Hallberg to protect her from the police and ... Mallory. But now it seemed like the opposite. Hallberg had used Jamie as a springboard to help herself.

It wasn't that Jamie really minded. She didn't, in fact. She wanted nothing more than for Hallberg to succeed. She was just surprised. Even more surprising was that she was now working *for* Hallberg all of a sudden.

'Well ... that went well,' Hassan risked.

Jamie just nodded. 'Yeah, no ... I, um ... I'm just ...'

'Yeah, me too ... But you know ... It's good news, right?'

'Yeah, yeah. We're not in trouble. So ...'

'Right. And we're helping. We wanted to solve this, right? Save the girl? The other girls?'

'Of course. I'm just ...'

'Mmm. Me too ...'

They looked at each other then, equally at a loss for what to say. But both thinking the same thing.

'Fuck, I really don't want to see Mallory,' Jamie said, bursting out laughing.

Hassan sank to a crouch and pressed his fingers to his lips. 'Me neither. She's going to be so pissed.'

Jamie looked over at Alina, who was still messing around in the water. She lifted a hand and waved to Jamie.

Jamie waved back, and suddenly, all her angst melted away.

So long as Alina was safe, nothing else seemed to matter.

Which, honestly, was the most surprising thing of all.

CHAPTER
FORTY

Paperwork was the last thing in the world that Jamie wanted to do, or thought she should be doing, just then.

But a very direct text from Hallberg told her that it was the difference between making this whole thing fly, or her ending up in handcuffs by the end of the day.

Hallberg needed reports to pass up the chain, specifically detailing the conversation that Hallberg had with Jamie prior to her travelling to Wales, her concerns about the chain of custody regarding some key information, as well as suspicions of corruption – hence the secrecy of the whole thing.

As Jamie was writing this fiction, she couldn't help but feel that they were wasting time. But she knew that she couldn't do anything from jail.

Hassan and Jamie made sure their stories lined up,

checking their work against each other's at Hassan's place in Brecon before they headed to the office.

Jamie wasn't sure if she wanted Alina to come with them. She didn't want to risk losing her again, but just hoped that Hallberg would be more human about it than Mallory was.

The other option was leaving her here alone. Which wasn't acceptable either.

When Hallberg said that they'd arrived, Jamie and Hassan geared up. Jamie had nothing with her and was still in last night's clothes. For a brief moment, she had considered taking something of Ash's. But that didn't seem appropriate. So instead, they called in to Tesco and Jamie picked up a few things, realising only as she was browsing the shelves how different Swedish and British supermarkets were. And how she preferred Tesco …

They arrived at the office with Alina in tow and entered the building.

As they rode the lift upwards, Alina took Jamie's hand and held fast.

On the fourth floor, they stepped out and headed inside.

Where before it had been empty except for Jerry, now, the place was bustling. Half a dozen new faces were all talking and gesturing, comparing documents, hunched over each other's screens. But as Jamie and Hassan entered, one by one, they quietened and looked up, watching as they approached Mallory's office.

Hassan knocked, looking back at Jamie, giving her a

little nod of encouragement. Probably as much for himself as for her.

'Come in,' came Hallberg's familiar voice.

It eased Jamie's nerves some, but as they entered, seeing Mallory and Hallberg, along with a man standing at the back of the office, having what looked like a stern conversation, they returned in earnest.

Hallberg was around five-foot-three, with tanned skin and a tight, dark ponytail. She looked older, thinner than Jamie remembered. She gave Jamie a brief smile. Mallory just glared.

The man turned to face them, gesturing to the two chairs in front of the desk. 'Please, sit,' he said.

It was clear it wasn't a polite request.

He was in his fifties, tall, with pronounced cheek-bones and a narrow, wrinkled mouth.

Alina had shrunk behind Jamie now, but Jamie gently guided her towards the chair in front of her. The girl sat, and Jamie stood at her side, one hand on her shoulder.

Hassan sat on the other chair, pulling a satchel he'd brought onto his lap.

The man deigned not to sit. 'My name is Walter Braun,' he said in perfect English, the slightest hint of a German accent betraying him. 'I'm supervising this operation. Thank you for coming.'

Jamie and Hassan nodded to him.

'I believe you have some paperwork for me?'

Hassan fished in the satchel and produced the reports, handing them over.

'Thank you.'

'We also have this,' Hassan said, withdrawing a laptop and offering it to him. 'We recovered this from the laundromat where they were keeping the trafficking victims captive.'

Braun just gestured for Hassan to put it on the desk, which he did.

'Anything else?'

'Yes,' Jamie interjected. 'We also uncovered information relating to what seems to be an illegal ... fighting ring.' She didn't quite know how to phrase it. 'They're pitting young women against each other, bare-knuckled. To the death.'

Braun looked up from the paperwork in his hands at Jamie. 'You have proof of this?'

'First-hand witness testimony,' Jamie replied.

Braun's eyes fell to the girl in the chair with the curly hair. 'The girl? She saw?'

Jamie swallowed. 'She fought, sir.'

Braun considered this for a moment. Then held the papers up. 'It's all in here?'

Jamie nodded. 'Yes, sir.'

'Her testimony will have to be verified, of course.'

Mallory's eyes burned into Jamie from the background, but Jamie didn't even look at her.

It was clear that Braun wasn't all too impressed with the way this had been handled. But it was hard to argue with results, and Hallberg's story seemed to be holding up so far. At least so much that they hadn't been arrested, yet. Much to Mallory's chagrin.

Braun took his time, reading through the papers.

'Uh ...' Jamie started. 'What now?'

'Now, we review, we take stock, we confirm suppositions. Investigative work,' he said plainly.

Jamie looked at Hallberg, who had perfected her 'expressionless' face.

'We'd like to continue to pursue the investigation ourselves,' Jamie said.

Braun sighed, but didn't look up.

'With the new information that has come to light, we feel that we can correctly identify the location where the fights are being held, and further disrupt their operations. Their continued attempts to find and retrieve Alina – the girl,' Jamie quickly corrected herself, knowing that if she showed too much familiarity, they'd separate them immediately, 'lead us to believe that those involved are fearful of being identified. And, with their ability to locate the girl even when in protected custody, we suspect that they may have contacts within either the NCA, or the police, or both, who are feeding them information.'

'A mole?' Braun asked, raising his eyebrows.

'I don't know, sir. But whether there is a specific person to blame, or not, we need to act quickly. If we prolong the investigation, then there's a chance that the Armenians may learn what we know, and shutter their operation, if they haven't already. We need to act, and we need to act now.'

Braun stared at Jamie for a few seconds, and then turned to Hallberg. 'You did say she was impetuous.'

Hallberg's poker face broke. 'I told you she works fast.'

'And leaves a trail of bodies in her wake.' He looked back at Jamie. 'Impetuous.'

'But successful,' Jamie reminded him. 'My methods may not be ... conventional—'

Mallory scoffed under her breath.

'— but the results speak for themselves.'

'They seem to, yes. You've certainly got a knack for shaking the right trees. And I can see why Hallberg here wanted to bring you in on this. Even if she did so without prior approval.' The way he said it made it clear he didn't really buy a word of it. 'The escalation from information gathering to full-blown engagement isn't exactly how I would have wanted things to go. But, we're nothing if not adaptable.' He didn't smile, but Jamie thought that this was positive. 'Is there anything else?'

'Uh ... No,' Jamie said.

'Then you're dismissed. Hallberg will take care of the full debrief and interviewing of the girl. Continue with your investigation and keep Hallberg looped in. She'll inform me if she thinks it's worthwhile.'

The way he immediately went back to looking at the papers in front of him told Jamie it was time to leave.

She wasted no time, feeling Mallory's daggers in her back as they headed out of the door.

Hallberg followed them out, but didn't stop, just kept walking until they were all out of the main office and back in the corridor.

She jumped on Jamie then, hugging her tightly.

Jamie stiffened, then returned it, while Alina watched.

'You're a fucking idiot, you know that?' Hallberg said, chin on her shoulder.

'That went well, didn't it?' Jamie asked, stepping back.

'As well as expected.'

'I didn't think he'd let us keep going with it …'

'No?'

'No, I thought it'd be this whole protracted process, lots of red tape and planning.'

Hallberg tsked a little. 'Well, Braun's smart. And you're still not officially on the payroll. You're not on anyone's payroll. You're rogue operatives, currently, ramming your … noses into the … business … of some very nasty people.'

'That's one way to put it,' Jamie said.

'It was for the kid's benefit.'

'She doesn't speak English.'

'Oh, then in that case – you've basically fisted the hornets' nest. To the elbow. And now they're buzzing.'

'Lovely.'

'You don't see what I'm saying?'

'I *see* what you're saying fine. It's hard not to picture, honestly. I just don't quite know what you mean by it.'

Hallberg put her hands on her hips and drew a slow breath. 'Braun wants you to keep going because he wants to see what happens. Disrupting a trafficking operation is no easy feat. They do their very best to make sure that they fly under the radar. And they don't like it when people make their lives difficult. You've prevented them from getting what they want' — her eyes went to Alina — 'and in the process, you've killed a bunch of their guys. You, a white woman.'

'Ah.'

'You see what I'm saying now?'

'That they're the type to bear a grudge.'

'Exactly. You've done more than just ruffle their feathers, and based on what we know of how these guys work, they're not above putting a price on someone's head. And they're not usually short of takers either.'

'So, I'm bait.'

'You are a worm on a hook, yes. And Braun wants to catch some big fish here.'

'Right.' Jamie suddenly felt less good about Braun's support. 'But I suppose a strike team and air support; helicopters and armed response ...'

'Out of the question.'

'Fuck.'

Hassan was keeping quiet.

Jamie looked down at Alina. 'They keep coming for her. And they won't stop.'

'They'll be coming for the three of you now. There's no way to stop that.'

'So, what can we do?'

'Braun wants to wait to see how this shakes out. I'll give this to him, he's smart, and he's ballsy. He's been on the right end of a lot of big calls. The guy knows what he's doing.'

'I'm questioning if I know what *I'm* doing, that's the thing.'

'Don't kid yourself, Jamie. You never know what the fuck you're doing. You just do it.'

Jamie saw Hassan nod in agreement out of the corner of her eye. She scowled a little.

'So, what, you're my handler in all this?' Jamie asked.

'That's the long and short of it.'

'Okay, so what're we doing here?'

Hallberg looked from Jamie to Hassan. 'Officially, Interpol's not involved in this yet. But unofficially ... I'll give you what support I can.'

'And how's that going to look?' Jamie asked tentatively.

Hallberg rolled her head side to side. 'If we get the right place for this fighting ring you described ... I'd say probably a small surveillance team would be doable. With the aim being to get inside, record enough footage to build a solid case.'

'A small surveillance team?' Jamie repeated it back, incredulous. 'You know they're fighting girls to the death, right? You heard me say that?'

Hallberg looked down at Alina. 'Yeah,' Hallberg said, 'but that's coming from a child who doesn't speak English. How did you even get that information?'

'From … a translator.'

'Who?'

Jamie kept quiet.

Hallberg sighed. 'Exactly. So, it's not exactly 'actionable intelligence' right now. And Braun's not going to expend resources and risk the lives of Interpol agents on a leap like this.'

'But he'll risk ours?' Jamie asked, gesturing to herself and Hassan.

'No more than you've been doing yourselves. And you can always walk away from this. Any time you like. Hand it over to me, go back to Sweden. To your life.'

Jamie didn't answer.

'Didn't think so.' Hallberg shook her head, as though to realign her thoughts. 'Okay, so then it's settled. We'll find out where these fights are and then we get you and …' Hallberg looked at Hassan.

'Nasir Hassan,' he said, introducing himself and shaking Hallberg's hand. 'Pleasure.'

She smiled at him. 'Julia Hallberg.' Then she looked back at Jamie. 'We get you two inside, with cameras, and you cover the whole thing. Then, slip out without making a scene, and if what you say is true, Braun will be dying to throw money and resources at this thing. Okay?'

'No.'

'That's the spirit.' She squeezed Jamie on the shoulder. 'Now, let's go over everything that's happened so far. From the top.'

Jamie sighed. 'Everything? We'll be here a while.'

'Well then, we'd best get to work. We're burning daylight.'

CHAPTER
FORTY-ONE

The last light of day warmed Jamie's skin.

And then, all at once, darkness closed in, choking the life from the sky, and dragging them into the night.

Jamie turned back from the crash barrier, looking down over a sweeping valley, steep-sided, the bottom mottled with trees and the dim lights of buildings dotted along the road.

The sun disappeared behind the western ridge and there was a sudden coolness to the air.

She checked her watch. It was getting late, the height of summer dragging daylight out as long as it could.

'Jamie,' Hallberg called, waving her back towards the box van parked in the layby. Innocuous, white. No one would know it was filled with electronics and surveillance equipment.

Jamie climbed inside, seeing Hassan and Alina sitting at the back on the bench, playing slapsies. They were sitting facing each other, hands together like they were praying, fingertips touching. Hassan was trying to teach her the game, it looked like. But Alina was cheating. Slapping his hands before he could even put them back into place. He was trying to speak, but she was laughing, and he couldn't help himself either.

Jamie smiled at that, felt warm for a moment, was reminded why she was doing this, deadly as it clearly was.

'Okay,' Hallberg said, directing Jamie to a seat next to a guy wearing a VR headset, with what looked like a video game controller in his hands. The screen in front of him was displaying a live feed from the drone he was controlling as it circled a building – an old water treatment facility, in the deepest reaches of the Beacons, about five kilometres from where they were sitting right now.

Aegean Trade Enterprises was just one of several shell companies owned by a larger corporation called Black Sea. A holding company that had its fingers in everything, including a UK-based property management subsidiary, which invested in disused commercial properties, and whose commercial function was 'green energy and carbon neutral initiatives and investments', whatever the fuck that meant. Just words that made buying old warehouses and collieries and mines and quarries and factories and refineries and water treatment plants appear above board.

Though what was happening here was nowhere close to that.

Hallberg had arranged for a Georgian interpreter to arrive at the offices and then they'd gone through the whole thing from the top with Alina once more. And once they found the property management company and what they owned, it wasn't tough to narrow the list down.

Alina had described a short drive, being walked across sharp stones, hearing trees and smelling the countryside. She'd described being walked down stairs so she was underground, the smell of grease and machines, the feeling of cold concrete on her feet. She'd described seeing large machines. There were only two properties within fifty kilometres of the laundromat that they owned, and only one of those fit the bill. The other was just an old defunct mine that had been sealed up years ago.

A drone-flyover showed that not only did the water treatment facility fit Alina's description, but that despite it being totally disused and locked up, there were several vehicles parked there. And as they watched, more arrived. One by one. And not work vehicles either. Sleek saloon cars, from which men and women were climbing, clad in suits.

They were welcomed by armed guards at the door, shown through the entrance.

They disappeared below ground.

And they did not re-emerge.

Jamie watched on screen as yet another car arrived and a man with a woman on each arm, greyed hair and tanned skin, walked across the stones and was welcomed cordially.

'We know who any of these guys are?' Jamie muttered, squinting at the image. It was high resolution, but taken from several hundred feet in the air so that the guards wouldn't be alerted by the noise of the drone.

Hallberg just shook her head. 'No,' she said. 'No way to run facial rec. But it looks like they're gearing up for an event.' She pulled her phone out and checked it. 'Care package is still about fifteen minutes out. You still up for this?'

Jamie let out a long, steadying breath, then looked at Alina again, nodding. 'Yeah,' she said. 'I am. Thanks for the support on this. You're a good friend.' Jamie reached out and put her hand on Hallberg's arm.

'Touching,' the guy with the VR headset said.

'Shut the fuck up, Tom,' Hallberg sighed.

He grinned, his mouth visible below the headset.

Hallberg motioned Jamie out of the van and down onto the gravelled layby, the sky above the mountains now a bloody red.

'You sure you're ready for this? You're going to be in there with no backup. There's still time to back out – we can submit the footage we have to Braun, see if we can't get something more official set up ...?'

Jamie swallowed. 'No, there's no time. You said it yourself, it's all red tape and hoop jumping to get anything done. And by the time that goes through, if they get wind that we're coming then they could scatter and we'll never catch up to them. And Alina will always be looking over her shoulder. Interpol won't help her, she'll just be handed back to the Georgian Embassy, deported, probably.'

Hallberg folded her arms. 'And that's not going to happen if you go through with this?'

Jamie didn't answer right away.

'Jamie ... You're not thinking about keeping her, are you?'

'What? No, I mean. No. Not adopting her or anything, Jesus. Me, a mother? Could you imagine?' Jamie laughed.

Hallberg just smiled sadly. 'I could. But she's ... she's not ...'

'She's not what?'

'She's been through a lot.'

'So have I. Maybe I'm the only one who understands.'

'Okay, okay,' Hallberg said, speaking softly. 'I just don't want to see you rush into anything.'

'I'm not. I'm just focused on making sure she's safe. And if, for the time being, that's with me, then so be it.'

Hallberg watched her carefully. 'And you think that doing this, tonight, is the best way to achieve that?'

Jamie shrugged. 'The people running this thing

want Alina back, or they want her dead. And if going in there tonight means that by the time the sun rises they'll be in cuffs, or in the ground, then it's worth it.'

'In the ground? What are you planning here, Jamie? This is intelligence gathering. Documenting. Case building.'

'Of course it is. But it's also the hornets' nest, and you're not sending us in there unarmed.'

'No ...' Hallberg's brow crumpled, then she looked down and sighed. A quick check over the shoulder to make sure they were out of earshot. She leaned in, grasping Jamie's arm. 'Just ... don't shoot first, that's all I'm asking.'

'I'm not stupid,' Jamie whispered back.

'No, you're not. I'll give you that.' She looked out at the darkened sky. 'But if you do this ... it's not going to stop. You're not going to stop them, you're just going to shift their focus. They may not come after Alina, but they'll be coming after you.'

Jamie let that hang in the air for a few seconds, and then turned her back on the mountains and walked back towards the van, towards Alina, her words ringing in the night air.

'Let them try.'

CHAPTER
FORTY-TWO

The care package was about as close to Christmas morning as Jamie could have imagined.

Glock 45 compact pistols and ballistic body armour.

Hassan was quiet and methodical, checking his weapon and pulling his body armour on in silence.

Jamie did the same, weighing the weapon in her hands. 'Gen five?' she asked Hallberg, reading the engraving on the side of the barrel.

'Yep, fresh off the production line,' Hallberg said with a sigh. 'Improved design, with—'

'A flared magwell for faster reloading, their marksman barrel with enhanced rifling, and a reversible magazine catch,' Jamie said, inspecting the weapon.

'Right,' Hallberg said. 'I forgot you were a gun nut.'

'I'm not a gun nut,' Jamie said, almost defensively.

'I'm just … I'm subscribed to their newsletter. What?' She looked at Hallberg. 'It's for work.'

'Sure.' She held her hand out between Jamie and Hassan, who were both sitting on the bench in the van adjusting their concealable holsters, which would allow them to carry the guns in the small of their backs. In Hallberg's palm were two small skin-coloured devices.

Jamie and Hassan both reached for theirs and picked them up, pushing them into their ears.

'We'll be with you the whole time,' Hallberg said. 'They know your faces by now, so you're going to have to alter your appearances, at least somewhat.' She pulled a case onto her lap and opened it, rotating it to face Hassan. 'Take your pick.'

'A wig?' he asked, raising an eyebrow.

Alina smirked a little, covering her mouth.

'You sort of stick out in a crowd,' Hallberg said. 'Here, this one'll work best, cover your earpiece, too.'

Hassan took the long black wig from her, looking at it disappointedly. 'A ponytail. Shit, seriously?' He pulled it onto his head and adjusted it, his close-cropped hair making it easy.

Despite the initial revulsion, Jamie thought it actually looked fairly natural.

'These, too,' Hallberg said, handing him a pair of glasses with thick, designer frames. '4k cameras on either side,' she said, pointing to her temples as Hassan pulled them on.

'How do I look?' he asked Jamie.

'Like you're having a midlife crisis,' she said, truthfully.

'Don't listen to her,' Hallberg interjected. 'There's a suit for you, too. It'll tie the whole thing together.'

He hummed with apprehension as Hallberg gestured for the Interpol agent who delivered the care package to hand it to her. She did so and Hallberg passed it along to Hassan. It was Alina, sitting next to him, who was first to the zipper, though, seemingly excited by the whole process. Jamie was surprised that Hallberg had allowed her to be here, but Jamie had been pretty emphatic that she'd not be letting her out of her sight. Though during the op, she would be in the van. Jamie didn't think she trusted anyone in the world more than Julia Hallberg, though. Alina would be safe with her.

'Got a wig for me, too?' Jamie asked.

'Aha, not quite,' Hallberg said, offering her a bag.

Jamie fished around in it. 'A headscarf and a sari?'

Hallberg nodded. 'You can wear it over your regular clothes, it'll hide your hair and the pistol, and you can keep your head down. Hassan's heritage is ... Indian?' she asked him.

'Pakistani.'

'My apologies.'

He shrugged. 'I don't care. Never been there. I'm from London.' He grinned. 'Far as I'm concerned, I'm more British than either of you two.' He looked at Jamie and Hallberg.

They looked at each other.

The man had a point.

'Right,' Hallberg went on. 'The guards will understand Eastern convention. They'll address Hassan, probably won't even look at you. Just keep your eyes on the floor, and your hair covered. It's a dead giveaway.'

Jamie nodded, holding the scarf up. Alina leaned across and felt it, smiling and nodding at Jamie, as though approving of the choice.

'Last thing,' Hallberg said, holding up two short metal tubes, bulbous in appearance. 'Flash-hiders.'

Jamie and Hassan took one each.

'They're not suppressors, but they'll mask the sound somewhat, hide the muzzle flash. I hope you won't need them,' she said, looking right at Jamie. 'But just in case.'

Jamie brought hers onto her lap along with the pistol and held onto them tightly.

Hallberg let out a long breath then, her hands shaking a little. 'Alright, I think that's it. Time to get ready.' She looked at Hassan and Jamie. 'Last chance to back out.'

'Very tempting ...' Hassan said, standing up, the suit draped over his arm. 'But I'm already wearing the wig. And it's starting to grow on me.'

CHAPTER
FORTY-THREE

Hallberg stood on the side of the road with Alina at her side, raising a hand to bid them goodbye, to wish them luck as they pulled away from the surveillance van and drove towards the water treatment facility.

The drone had been overhead there for the last hour, and people were arriving thick and fast. None of them seemed to be showing any kind of ID or invitation, there was no guestlist being checked. Hallberg surmised that this was invite only, and the kind of place where no names were exchanged. So they hoped that all it would take was walking towards the door with confidence.

They hoped.

Hassan drove, with Jamie sitting in the back seat. Everything had to seem right here. And while Hassan's role wouldn't be tough to sell, if they got one good look at Jamie, she'd be in trouble. Big trouble.

The roads were quiet.

It was past eleven now, and night was laying heavily on the Beacons.

The satnav took them in.

Jamie readjusted her position in the seat, the plush interior of the S-Class they were driving immaculate and space-age around them. The final part of the care package. They couldn't exactly roll up in a Vauxhall Astra.

Hassan was quiet on the drive.

Jamie remembered this from their time together at the Met. It had been short-lived, but positive. Except for Hassan getting shot. But that was a risk of the job – he was armed response, after all. It wasn't like it wasn't on the table to begin with.

But his experience put Jamie at ease. He was cool in the face of danger, and a highly skilled operator. The best person for the job by far. And sure, they were going into the lions' den here, but Jamie couldn't think of anyone else she'd want watching her back on this one.

As they closed on the facility, they came up behind a Bentley, chugging slowly through the hills. It was sleek and black, with a private number plate and darkened windows.

And before long, another car came up behind them. Jamie couldn't tell what it was, but the elevated position of the blinding headlights told her it was something big and expensive.

Hassan slowed a little, just a part of the procession now.

'Easy, easy,' he muttered to himself as they made their final approach.

The Bentley slowed to a crawl and then eased off the road onto the gravel track that led to their destination. There was a big sign that said 'Private Property – No Entry – Trespassers will be prosecuted – CCTV in operation'.

'Bollocks,' Hassan said, reading it.

'Mhm,' Jamie added. 'A little ironic.'

They followed the Bentley up the track for a few hundred metres, until they'd completely lost sight of the roadway behind them, and then came to a gate.

It was chain link and reinforced with steel poles, topped with barbed wire.

It had been pulled back, and through the gap, Jamie could see cars and cars lined up in the makeshift car park. Two dozen, at least. Maybe more. And there were two cars behind them now, too.

No one was manning the gate, and Jamie didn't see any cameras. Though she still kept her head bowed and the scarf pulled far enough forward that her hair and features were completely hidden.

Hassan guided them in after the Bentley, which seemed to know where it was going, and parked next to it, killing the engine.

He waited, wiping his hands off on his trousers, and looked left and right. A big Porsche SUV pulled in next to them and two guys got out. They had the square jaws, high cheekbones, and burley builds of a pair of Russian Bratva, and the black stars on the backs of their hands, visible below the cuffs of their shining grey suits confirmed that.

Jamie turned her head away as one of them cast a glance in her direction.

His receding footsteps on the stones told her he'd moved on.

She glanced at the guy getting out of the Bentley, too. He looked Middle Eastern, and was in a black suit with a white shirt, a silk scarf draped around his shoulders, a selection of gold rings and jewellery on his hands.

He looked around disdainfully, and then strode towards the door on thin legs.

'Alright,' Hassan said, when they were clear. 'Let's go. I don't want us to be the last ones in.'

Jamie made to open the door.

'Wait, don't,' he said. 'I get out first, you follow me. We have to make this look like it's supposed to.'

'Right,' Jamie said, steadying herself. She'd been in tough positions before, but the nerves still came. Unavoidable really.

Hassan pulled the rear-view towards himself and did a few practice smiles, locked in the right one, and then got out, holding his head high and his chest back.

Jamie just hoped the black eye wouldn't be too noticeable in the dark.

She exited after him and walked at his shoulder but one step back, so she was all but hidden on the approach.

Hassan sped up a little to get closer to the man in the scarf in front.

He crunched his way towards the door through the gravel, arriving just as it closed behind the two mafiosos.

He barely acknowledged the two Armenians at the door, just kept walking.

They opened it for him and he strode inside, disappearing.

Hassan stayed his course.

Easy, right?

He got near, glanced at the guy who'd opened the door, but then slowed.

It wasn't opening.

The other bouncer stepped in their way and lifted his hand, as though to stop Hassan.

Jamie tensed, mapping the route her hand would take to the pistol in the small of her back. She wondered if she could find it in all this material.

But before the guy could lay a hand on Hassan's suit, Hassan's hand came out of nowhere and slapped it away. Pretty hard.

The bouncers both froze, but before they could do or say anything, Hassan just let forth with a stream of what Jamie thought was Punjabi. She didn't know the language, but by the fierceness of the tone, she assumed it was both derisive and seasoned generously with swear words.

He didn't bother letting them get a word in edge-ways before he stepped between them and pulled the door open for himself, still speaking fast and mean.

He entered first and Jamie ducked in afterwards, keeping her head down and scarf tight around her face.

The door closed and she felt Hassan's hand on her back, guiding her down in front of him.

She could feel his fingers shaking, as he urged her down the stairs quicker.

The bouncers didn't follow though, thankfully, so Hassan's reaction had likely been the sort of thing they were used to.

'I didn't know you spoke Punjabi,' Jamie whispered as they reached the bottom of the stairs.

'My grandmother would kill me if I let it lapse,' he responded. 'She won't speak anything else to me.'

'Lucky for us.'

'Mm,' Hassan said, straightening his suit and brushing some of the long strands of hair that had come out of the ponytail out of his eyes. 'I hate long hair. Haven't had it since I was eighteen.'

'You used to have long hair?'

'It was the nineties,' he replied, pressing forward.

They were in a dimly lit corridor with another door in front of them. The smell of grease and metal was already strong in the air, like Alina had described.

Hassan moved quickly, keeping his eyes forward.

Again, Jamie didn't see any cameras, but she wouldn't be surprised if they were hidden. If there were people here who didn't want to be identified, having them on video would certainly be the kind of leverage people like the ones behind this would want to have. So Jamie kept her head down.

When the next door opened, the noise was all at once deafening.

They entered into a massive room, onto a catwalk that stretched the length of the back wall. At the far end, there was a set of metal steps that led down to the floor, as well as a steel door with a padlock on it. Jamie guessed this was where they were keeping the girls. Alina hadn't described going down a second set of stairs until the fight itself.

Hassan was already leaning against the rail, staring down over the scene in front of them.

Along the walls there were pipes and pipes, running into large machines – pumps and filters and who knew what else. But in the centre, a ring had been set up. The kind that you see in UFC matches. It was hexagonal, with a wooden frame and a chain link fence on the inside. Above, heavy industrial lights hung in strips suspended from the ceiling by chains.

The ground was covered with sand and sawdust and straw, and around the outside, all of the spectators milled around. Some stood, others were sat. Mostly men, dressed smartly. But women were dotted through-out, some scantily clad – arm candy – heavily made up and fawning over the men they were with. Others were dressed more conservatively. Either in more expensive gowns, or in more traditional dress. In hijabs or niqabs.

And moving between the crowd were waiters with platters filled with little finger foods and champagne flutes.

Jamie and Hassan moved slowly along, scanning the whole place for anyone of note, but there was so much to take in.

Jamie reached up and touched the bud in her ear to turn it on. 'You seeing this?' she asked under her breath.

Hallberg's voice came back to her. 'Yep, feed is coming through clearly from the glasses. Keep moving, don't draw attention to yourselves. Find a place in the crowd and don't get spotted. We'll keep radio silence unless we need something.'

The line clicked off as they reached the stairs.

From here, Jamie could see that above the ring, there was a glass-fronted control room that looked down over the spectacle.

Two men were sitting on plush chairs. One was smoking a cigar. He was older, with a bald head and dark lips. The other was younger, with a full head of hair and a finely manicured beard. Jamie thought they were both Armenian, but not all the other men in the room were. There were probably half a dozen others in there, including the two men that had pulled in just after Jamie and Hassan, the two Russians with the star tattoos. Along with a group of other men that Jamie didn't recognise. One of them was tall. He looked European, tanned, Spanish, maybe.

He seemed to feel Jamie's eyes on him, and suddenly looked over, through the glass.

She turned her head away quickly and carried on down the stairs, wondering, hoping that Hassan got a good look at them all.

'Let's find a spot,' Hassan said.

'Close to the exit, preferably,' Jamie added.

He let out a little sigh, shuffling through the building crowd. 'My thoughts exactly.'

CHAPTER
FORTY-FOUR

They walked towards the back, with Hassan skilfully moving through the crowd, getting a good look at as many faces as he could, before choosing a spot under the catwalk that allowed them to stand mostly in shadow. It was, strategically, a solid choice. They had the ability to duck behind the cover of a bank of machines that Jamie assumed had something to do with regulating flow judging by their various dials, levers, and turn wheels. But if it came to it, they'd also have a clear run to the stairs to get back up. They wouldn't have to circumvent the ring for it. And finally, from where they were, they could see the control room and the men inside.

Hassan took a glass of champagne off a tray as it went past, turning his head so it looked like he was speaking to Jamie, but actually just pointing his cameras right at the guys in the booth.

It seemed like they'd just found their spot when the old man in the booth with the bald head motioned for someone to approach. A big Armenian bodyguard in a black suit approached and leant in while the old man spoke to him. Then the bodyguard nodded and promptly disappeared.

Jamie shielded the side of her head from them, pretending as though she was coughing, and activated her earpiece. 'Hallberg – any idea who the guys behind the glass are?'

She came back. 'We're running facial rec and searching the database, but nothing so far. Will keep you posted.'

Hassan cleared his throat then and Jamie turned back, the crowd hushing around them.

A door in the far corner, under the control room, opened, and the big guy in the black suit appeared. He was holding a rope in one hand and the crowd parted for him. He walked towards the cage, pulling one side of the hexagon open and stepped inside.

It was only then that Jamie saw what the rope was attached to.

Made into a makeshift noose at one end, it was around the neck of a girl.

She was maybe seventeen or eighteen, with her hair hacked short, clumps torn out to the root. Her face was dirtied and swollen, her nose crooked, her lip formerly split but healing now. She was wearing a tattered vest and men's shorts tied tightly at the waist.

Her hands were loosely wrapped in what looked like bloodied cloth bandages and she was shaking them out, like boxers do before they fight.

Everyone watched in silence as she walked into the centre of the ring and the bodyguard turned, taking the noose from her neck. As he walked past, he pulled her by the shoulder, shoving her deeper into the ring.

And then he left the ring and the girl standing there. She looked at the crowd in turn, the corners of her lips turned down into a contemptuous embrace while the spectators sipped their champagne, pointing to her and whispering to the people next to them about this or that.

Jamie's heart was beating hard and fast as she waited, knowing what was coming next.

There was noise above them then and Jamie looked up through the grate of the catwalk, seeing another black-suit-clad figure at the door where the girls were kept.

He pulled a key from his pocket and unlocked the padlock, stepping inside.

There were faint gasps, a few hushed voices, high pitched and frightened. And then a squeal.

He reappeared, gripping a girl by the back of the head, his hand in her hair. She was in dirtied jeans and a tattered red T-shirt. She had dark skin, black, frizzy hair, and wide eyes that betrayed her terror.

She was frogmarched down the stairs, gripping the wrist of the man walking her, sobbing and begging in a language Jamie didn't know.

When they reached the bottom of the steps, they turned right, towards the open door of the cage.

Jamie knew she was looking at one of the girls from the laundromat. One of the ones they'd just missed when they'd been there.

Alina flashed in her mind. She'd lived this exact hell. Been walked down those same stairs, probably by the same man, and pushed into the same ring.

The girl in the red T-shirt was shoved through the fence and under the lights.

She stumbled, crying out, and then fell onto her knees.

The crowd fell silent as the cage was closed.

Jamie stepped backwards so she was fully in the dark, and touched her ear. 'You're seeing this, right?'

'We are,' Hallberg said.

'You have to do something.'

There was silence.

'Hallberg. You know what this is.'

She didn't respond.

'You have to get people here, now. Interpol. Armed response. The NCA. Someone. Everyone.'

There was a shaky breath in her ear. 'There isn't anyone, Jamie,' Hallberg said. 'My hands are tied. We need proof.'

'Proof? What do you think we're looking at?'

'It's going up the chain. I promise you that. Just hold on a little longer. Wait for it to start. And then ... get out of there.'

'Fucking hell,' Jamie breathed. 'You're seriously going to let this happen?'

'What did you think this was, Jamie? You knew what it was going to be going in there.' Hallberg's voice quivered. 'You knew that this was intelligence gathering. We had that conversation, outside the van. Remember?'

Jamie set her teeth, watching as the girl with the shortened hair turned around to face the girl in the red T-shirt.

She lifted her hands, waving them at her opponent, begging her for help.

But she wasn't there to help her.

She was there to kill her.

The first strike was swift and brutal. Her leg shot out, the bottom of her shin connecting with the girl's cheek, sending her spinning to the ground.

She wailed, tried to crawl away, and all at once, the crowd erupted, cheering and shouting their approval.

The girl with the short hair, the true fighter here, lifted her hands in triumph, and advanced on her victim, reaching down and grabbing her by the back of the shirt, dragging her to her knees and then throwing her onto her back.

She descended on her, the girl in red batting her away weakly, her face bloodied already, tears streaming from her eyes.

The fighter took hold of one of her hands and then

slapped her in the face with the back of her knuckles, straddling her.

She tormented the girl in red, allowing her to try and swipe back as the fighter avoided her swings, amping up the crowd, grinning at them, some of her teeth missing, the remaining ones yellowed.

And then she punched the girl in red once more. Right in the nose.

Blood splattered the ground and the girl in red sobbed and mewled like a stuck animal.

Then the punches came. Right. Then a left.

Hard enough to hurt her, to make her bleed, but not so hard as to kill her. Just yet.

This was a spectator sport. And the fighter had been kept separate, in her own room. The better she did, the more rewards she got, Jamie guessed. Alcohol, or drugs, a more comfortable bed, better food. Incentives to keep fighting, to keep winning. She was their prized bull.

And then her hands fell on the girl in red, finding her throat, choking her. Strangling her.

The bodies of the girls she saw at the coroner's office invaded her mind. The thought of Alina doing this to another girl came with it. Like waves. Crashing over Jamie. Turning her sick, stealing her strength and balance. Her knees shook and threatened to give out.

'Jamie,' Hallberg said then, steadily. 'Don't do anything. I repeat. Do not intervene. This is not an active operation. Do not intervene.'

She knew Hallberg had to say that. But she knew that Hallberg didn't want anyone to die. Didn't want this to just be intelligence gathering.

Jamie knew that, because she knew Julia Hallberg. And she knew she had a heart.

It takes more than three minutes to strangle a person to death. And Jamie would be ready in twenty seconds.

She crouched in the darkness behind the control units and shed her sari, pulling the pistol free from its holster and fishing the flash-hider from her pocket. She screwed it into the barrel as the crowd built to fever pitch, intoxicated by the blood sport in front of them.

When Jamie felt the thread bite tight, the flash-hider secured, she pulled back the slide, chambering a round, and stood. Hassan hadn't taken his eyes off the fight. He knew his job. Knew not to look at Jamie and document her going against orders.

But he already had his weapon in his hand too.

She stood next to him, squeezed his arm.

He let out a long exhale, grip re-tightening around his weapon, and then reached up, pulling off his glasses and holding them against his leg so they'd only see black.

He glanced down at her, gave her a small smile, and then nodded.

No words were exchanged. They couldn't, or it would be on record.

Jamie mapped the room quickly, chose her shots, counted the guards. Two at the side of the ring, two more in the control room, two at the front door. Any more in the crowd? Can't tell. No time.

Jamie steeled herself and chose her first target. Then, she took a final breath, lifted her gun, and fired.

CHAPTER
FORTY-FIVE

T he flash-hider did its work, the spit of the small calibre pistol swallowed up in the screams.

The bullet leapt from the muzzle, zipping through the hot and stale air, connecting with the hanging strip light above the ring.

The glass shattered and shards and sparks rained down over the competitors.

Screams of fervour turned to screams of terror as people cowered, unsure what was happening.

Everyone except Jamie and Hassan. And the bodyguards.

Their eyes fell on the pair, their hands diving into their jackets for their firearms.

Hassan tossed his glasses onto one of the control units, lenses facing into the room, capturing the whole thing as he drove Jamie sideways behind cover, just in time to avoid the hail of bullets.

They pinged off the units and pipes and people went mad, shoving and pushing their way towards the stairs in a mad scramble.

Hassan peeked, saw the bodyguards caught in the flow and knocked off balance, and stepped from cover, keeping low, moving with the crowd.

Jamie went after him, seeing the two girls in the ring now separated and going for the exit themselves.

Both alive, thankfully.

Hassan popped up ahead of Jamie, six feet in front of the two guards, and plugged two rounds into each of them, sending them reeling backwards and tumbling to the ground.

Above, the control room was in frenzy as the VIPs battled towards the door.

Except for the two men in the chairs, whose eyes were locked on Jamie, their expressions steeped in loathing.

A cold fury burned in Jamie suddenly and she raised her pistol, zeroing in on the old man first. She put him right between the sights and fired. Once. Twice. Three times.

Spiderwebs lanced across the glass as the bullets struck, but the man remained unmoved.

He got to his feet, stepping closer to the safety glass – built strong enough to withstand an exploding hydro pump, and strong enough to take a few 9mm bullets, it seemed.

He pocketed his hands, staring down at Jamie with something like amusement now.

But before Jamie could fully take him in, Hassan tackled her to the ground, just in time for automatic fire to fill the air.

They rolled to the side and Hassan dragged her into cover.

One of the guards from the control room had appeared, a sub-machine gun in his hands, and was letting off a stream of bullets.

He winged two of the spectators, blood misting in the air as they shrieked and scrambled up the stairs, fighting each other to get to safety.

By the time Jamie caught her breath and looked back at the control room, the two men in the chairs were gone. Though they hadn't appeared from the doorway behind the ring – there must be another exit. A fire escape that led out the back in case of emergencies.

She cursed as the guard with the sub-machine gun advanced, letting off burst after burst of fire as he came at them.

Above, the two other bouncers from the front door were racing along the catwalk, all but hurdling the escaping crowd.

Jamie aimed upwards and squeezed off a well-placed round, the bullet zipping through the grate and catching one of them in the leg.

He staggered sideways, into the rail, and leaned over it, face pained.

Hassan put him out of his misery with a shot right between the eyes, sending him tumbling right over.

He landed with a heavy thud in front of them.

The second managed to reach the stairs and make his way down.

Two on two, now. But they were outgunned. And they both knew it.

Hassan and Jamie were crouched behind one of the control units, but they'd be vulnerable any second.

'We need to take out the guy with the sub.'

'How? He's got a fucking MP5,' Jamie hissed, more bullets peppering the other side of the machine.

'Ever been skeet shooting?'

'What?'

Hassan turned and threw his elbow into the glass panel on the wall next to him. It broke and he pulled out the miniature fire extinguisher inside, turning and hurling it through the air, over the top of the control unit.

'Now!' he yelled.

Jamie twisted from cover, staying low, and raised her pistol, firing at the canister as it arced towards the guy with the sub-machine gun.

The first bullet missed, the second striking true, puncturing the side.

It immediately began whirling with the sudden expulsion of gases, filling the room with white smoke.

Jamie felt Hassan brush past her and then watched him charge into the cloud.

She swore, scrambling after him, just in time to see him drive his shoulder into the gunner's stomach and send him back through the chain link fence and into the arena.

They both landed heavily, locked in a death grip.

But there was one more, and before Jamie could turn, he was on her, looming from the fog, pistol raised.

The muzzle flash blinded her and she was blown off her feet, all the wind knocked from her chest as the bullet struck her centre mass.

She fired back, landing hard, finger rebounding off the trigger as her diaphragm seized up.

The guy wobbled, then sagged forward, crumpling on top of her, his hot blood pouring over her legs as she tried to kick herself free, coughing and hacking.

In her peripheral, she watched Hassan wrestle the MP5 from the gunner's grip, take a hard punch to the jaw, and then return one, even harder.

The guy's head hit the ground and his eyes lolled. But Hassan wasted no time, diving to the side for his dropped pistol, taking it, and then rolling onto his side.

He fired once, point blank, into the side of the gunner's ribcage. He convulsed once, and then fell still.

Hassan settled on his back, panting hard, and then looked for Jamie, squinting in the mist.

'Shit!' he yelled, clawing his way towards her, getting to his knees.

She felt his heavy hands on the straps of her ballistic vest through her shirt and he dragged her from under the dead Armenian, the both of them collapsing, Jamie nested between his knees.

He inspected her quickly, pulling the hem of her shirt up to find the bullet hole. When he did, he dug the round out of the Kevlar, laughing.

'Fucking hell,' he said, sitting back and sighing with relief. 'I thought you'd gone and got yourself fucking killed then.'

Jamie just tried to breathe, but it wasn't working.

'Glad you finally got a taste of your own medicine.' He got to his feet and pulled Jamie upwards. 'Though you still owe me one more before we're even.'

Jamie doubled forward hacking and coughing, trying to fill her lungs. She couldn't speak, but she had an even more appropriate response – she held up her middle finger.

Hassan slapped her on the back. 'I think that's all of them. Though it looks like the brass got away.' He gestured to the empty control room, and then reached up to the control unit and grabbed the glasses back, pulling them on. 'Guess I can lose this now,' he said, dragging the wig from his head. 'Itches like crazy.'

'The …' Jamie started, finally feeling air enter her lungs. 'The girls …'

'Right.' Hassan went to work, heading across the floor to the guy who'd brought the girl in red down. He patted him down until he found what he was looking for, and then held the key up for Jamie. 'You want to do the honours?'

He helped her up the stairs, his arm under her shoulders, and steadied her in front of the door.

Hassan laid a hand on her stomach and straightened her back with his other. 'Just breathe. You get used to it.'

'I'd rather not,' she managed.

'Hey, everyone needs to pop their cherry some time.'

'I've been shot before, you know,' she said defensively.

He clapped her on the back – which really fucking hurt. 'Not really something to be proud of, Jamie. Usually means you did something wrong.'

She grumbled, pushing the key into the padlock. 'Coming from the guy who gets shot every five minutes.'

'Only when I'm working with you.'

Jamie turned the key and the padlock clicked open.

Hassan pulled the door wide and Jamie squinted into the dimly lit interior.

She didn't make them out at first, their heads all turned away, their bodies hunched over, making themselves as small as they could. But then, one by one, they looked up. Jamie counted them as they did. One, two, three … nine girls in all.

It took her a moment to regain herself, but then she managed to finally fill her lungs, raising her hands to show she wasn't a threat.

'It's alright,' Jamie said. 'You're safe now. You're free.'

They didn't seem to understand at first.

'It's okay, we're with the police. Police,' she repeated.

'Police?' came a voice from the darkness.

It was followed by more voices. Police. Police? Police?

Jamie nodded. 'Yes, police, come, come,' she called, stepping aside and offering the door.

They rose tentatively, cautiously, and came forward.

'Go,' Hassan said. 'I'll make sure there are no stragglers.'

She put her hand on his shoulder and squeezed. 'Thank you.'

He nodded.

'And Hassan?'

'Yeah, Jamie?'

'You know ... Those glasses look really fucking stupid.'

He laughed. 'Eh, I'm making them work.'

She gave him a final grin, and then started towards the door, pistol still in her hand.

The girls followed her up the stairs, and then Jamie pushed open the final door, and led them into the night.

CHAPTER
FORTY-SIX

The air was cool and fresh. Jamie hadn't realised how stale it was below, but now she could finally breathe again. Literally. The pain had somewhat subsided in her chest, but it still hurt like hell to draw a lungful of air. She didn't think a rib had cracked, but she was definitely going to be sore in the morning.

With the girls in tow, Jamie strode forward from the water treatment plant and into the now empty car park. Clouds of dust still wafted through the still summer air, but everyone had cleared out, driving as quickly as they could in any direction they could. Desperate to escape. Sirens hadn't begun to sound in the distance yet, but they soon would.

Where the VIPs had gone, Jamie didn't know. But rats always had their own way out. A back door, a track through the mountains, waiting cars ready to whisk them away should anything go awry.

They'd scurry back into their holes to regroup, no doubt. But for now, at least Jamie felt like she'd taken them out at the knees. She had their faces on camera, their participation dead to rights. They'd have to shutter a dozen businesses, leave the country for fear of being arrested. Their operation would be set back months, if not years, the encroaching tide shoved back behind a suddenly erected seawall.

How long it would hold, Jamie didn't know. But for now, there was solid ground beneath her feet, and the shadow of the impending wave was gone.

Headlights flashed, blinding Jamie, as a vehicle skidded into view, barrelling up the track.

Jamie raised her pistol, the girls all cowering and clustering behind her.

She stood at the head of the pack, gun raised, trying to pick out a target through the glare.

The vehicle hit the brakes, skidding on the stones, and slid to a halt.

Jamie braced, narrowing her eyes, gripping her pistol more tightly.

'Jamie!' Hallberg's voice echoed through the air as a car door opened and closed. 'Jamie, it's us,' she called.

Feet crunched on gravel.

A dark shape loomed from the light.

And then, suddenly, Alina was hurling herself into Jamie.

Pain rippled through her body where she'd been hit as the girl wrapped herself around her.

Jamie grunted, staggering backwards, and then hugged her back, the pistol dropping to her side.

'Jay-mee,' Alina said, the name stunted on her tongue.

'Alina,' Jamie said back, resting her chin on the girl's head, sighing with relief.

There was some chatter behind Jamie then and Alina released her, as though recognising the voices.

She stepped around Jamie, looking at the faces of the girls in front of her. For a moment they were all silent, and then Alina walked into their ranks and hugged them. Some seemed not to recognise her, but others did, yelling with joy and grabbing hold of her.

What they'd lived through together was nothing short of hell. And they could only have thought Alina was dead or living some other type of waking nightmare.

Jamie felt a hot lump form in her throat as she watched them, and then tore herself away to face Hallberg, who was now in front of her.

'You know I nearly had to cuff her to the inside of the van to stop her from coming after you,' Hallberg said, raising a hand to gesture to Alina. 'Once it all kicked off, she nearly lost her shit.'

Jamie nodded. 'Thanks for taking care of her.'

Hallberg nodded back. 'Thanks for not taking orders.' She punched Jamie in the arm playfully. 'And for not dying. That would have been a *lot* of paperwork.'

Jamie laughed a little, hearing Hassan emerge from the door behind them. 'All clear,' he called, stepping forward to join them.

'You two both in one piece?' Hallberg asked, placing her hands on her hips.

'Just about,' Hassan said. 'We *gather enough intelligence* for you?' He put that in air quotes.

'And then some,' Hallberg said. 'We got some hits back on the facial recognition software already. A couple of foreign faces of note, and some domestic ones too. A few people are going to get their doors knocked on in the next few weeks, I'll tell you that much.'

'What about the old man in the control room?' Jamie asked. 'There were two of them, sitting in chairs.'

Hallberg nodded. 'The young one, I don't know. But the bald guy is Aram Petrosyan, an Armenian business magnate. He's not even supposed to be in the UK right now. He owns a slew of businesses across Armenia, everything from hotels and hospitals to logistics and trucking companies. He owns construction conglomerates, agriculture complexes, hell, he's even got his fingers in pharma and tourism, and is a big political supporter too.'

'Shocker,' Jamie sighed. 'And this guy's whiling away his time in some underground fighting dungeon in the Brecon Beacons? Why?'

Hallberg could only offer a shrug. 'I don't know. But

I bet it has something to do with the other people in the control room. We'll work to identify them. But having Petrosyan there can only mean this thing is bigger than we know. Guys like Petrosyan don't make themselves vulnerable for no reason, and if he's there for the spectacle, there are far easier places he could get this kind of entertainment. No, if he's here in the UK, and here tonight, then there's something building. Something big.'

'Something Braun's going to be interested in?'

Hallberg scoffed. 'You can say that again. Jamie, if we're right about this, then it could be huge. Guys like Petrosyan don't come to the table unless it's worth it for them. And what more could a guy like that need?'

'Power. It's always power.'

Hallberg nodded. 'Petrosyan's been tied to a lot of bad shit over the last few decades, but he's always got away clean. He doesn't like to lose, and he'll take this personally. He's dangerous, Jamie, and he's got infinite resources, infinite reach. He's got a line on what the NCA are doing, and probably Interpol too. He'll know we're opening this investigation sooner or later. And he won't like it. He'll want retribution.'

'You think he'll come after me?'

She licked her lips. 'If I was a betting woman … yeah. But look, tonight, whatever they were working towards – we shit all over it. We caught it all on film, and now the NCA, Interpol, they're going to pool resources, there'll be hundreds of people on this by

Monday morning. We set back their plans months, maybe years. And ... you saved all these girls. Look.'

Jamie turned to watch them, smiling and grinning, hugging each other and dancing in circles.

It filled her heart to watch. Made it all worth it.

'It's not too late, though.'

Jamie looked back at Hallberg.

'You could go, now. Disappear. We could help. New name. New identity.'

'No,' Jamie said. 'We finish what we start, right? Like old times?'

'Right,' Hallberg said, smiling at her. 'Just like old times.' She swallowed then, staring off into the desolate landscape. 'I just hope you're ready for this, Jamie. It's going to be dangerous. More dangerous than anything you've faced before.'

Jamie scoffed a little, putting her arm around Hallberg, glad to have her at her side.

'Welcome to my life.'

EPILOGUE

I t seemed to take an age for the call to dial out.

There was that light, familiar crackling as the signal made its way out of the country, and then that alien ringing tone to signify that it was going through.

It wasn't the first time she'd heard it. More like the tenth. She had called, and called, and called. But he wasn't picking up.

She didn't expect him to now, either. But, God, did she want to hear his voice. She knew now that she wasn't going back. At least not for a while. She had dreaded speaking to Dahlvig, telling him that the team would need to go on without her for just a little longer ... that she was extending her stay. Staying to finish what she'd started here. The fact that she was helping Interpol seemed not to matter at all to him. He just sighed, and told her to remember who gave her a chance. And that she could only spit in the faces of the people who helped her for so long. She promised him she would be back.

But she thought they both knew she was lying.

Still, they said goodbye amicably, Dahlvig ending the call with a simple question; 'Should I reassign your team?'

Jamie's lack of a response answered it for him.

'Got it. Keep me updated. Your holidays only stretch so far. After that, my hands are tied.'

'I know.'

'Good luck, Johansson. Hope you know what you're doing.' The words sounded embittered. And Jamie didn't blame him. She was walking away from a job that he'd gone out on a limb to give her. But beyond that, she was leaving him without his lead homicide investigator. And she knew her shoes would be hard to fill. Who knew, maybe she would go back. Maybe this would be over soon. Maybe hell would freeze over, pigs would fly, and an overweight lady would start bellowing *Carmen* from the rooftops.

There was always hope.

But as agonising as that actual call was, it was somehow much less painful than just hearing the phone ring into nothingness.

But then he answered.

'Thorsen?' Jamie asked quickly. 'Thorsen?' she repeated into the silence, hoping to God that it wasn't about to click over to the answering machine.

'No ...' came the reply after a moment. 'This is Nathalie.'

'Hi ...?' Jamie responded, a little thrown. 'Is this ...' She pulled the phone from her ear, looked at the screen to double check it was the right number. The name said 'Kjell Thorsen'. She couldn't have dialled anyone else. 'Is Kjell there?' she asked.

The woman took a moment to respond, as if considering her words. 'No, he's ... he's not available. I'm sorry.'

'What? Who are you? Put Kjell on the phone,' Jamie said, trying not to sound demanding. But, seriously, who was this person?

'I'm Kjell's nurse,' she said then. 'He ... he said that he doesn't want to speak to you.'

'What?' Jamie laughed a little. 'Come on. You're kidding. Let me speak to him.'

'We spoke at length, Jamie,' Nathalie said. 'It's not good for his recovery.'

Jamie didn't like the way this person said her name. Not at all. 'Not good for his recovery?' she practically spat. 'Listen—'

'No, I'm afraid it's you who needs to listen,' Nathalie said, a little more abrupt now. A door closed in the background, so Jamie thought she'd left the room, or at least gone further from Thorsen. 'What happened to Kjell ... It wasn't your fault. But ... but it happened. And he's doing his best to get better. He spoke a lot about you. All the time, at the start. It became clear. He loved you. He still does. But ... you aren't good for him.'

Jamie just listened, too choked to speak.

'You know that, don't you? He knows it. And the last few months, the distance between you two has been good. He's turned a corner. He's walking better, speaking better. And I think if you come back into his life, all his progress might be derailed.'

'That's ... that's not true,' Jamie whispered, her voice small.

'He can be well again. And he can be happy. Don't you want that for him?'

'I ... Of course,' Jamie said. 'But—'

'I'm sorry. Sorry to be the one to tell you. He wanted to do it himself. But ... but he's not strong enough. Not yet. He will reach out. When he's ready. But right now? You ... you just need to leave him alone. Let him heal. His wounds. His mind. His heart.'

Jamie swallowed, then wiped the tears from her cheeks with her knuckles. She nodded, unable to speak. And then, with all her strength, she managed just one word. 'Okay.'

Nathalie said nothing more. She just hung up.

The line beeped in Jamie's ear and she took a moment, then a minute, to process all that.

She stared down at the phone in her hands, standing on the side of the road somewhere in the Brecon Beacons. Alina was across the tarmac, holding some grass she'd plucked from the ground out towards a wild horse. She walked towards it slowly, the thing unsure of her, nosing forward, and then backing up, champing and huffing.

Jamie smiled, watching her as she giggled, turning and grinning at Jamie. She waved back and Alina pressed on, trying again with the horse.

Jamie looked at her phone again, and then dialled Thorsen once more, knowing that he wouldn't pick up. But, she didn't want him to.

She waited for it to click through to voicemail, languishing in the sound of his voice until he asked her to leave a message. And then she did, not thinking about when or if he'd even listen to it. But needing to tell him all the same.

'Hey, Kjell,' she said quietly, turning to face the mountains, the endless sea of green stretching out before her. 'I'm in the UK. In Wales. Some, uh, some stuff has happened. My mum called me, said she needed help with something – she married a superintendent with the police. Can you believe that? Guess she has a type.' Jamie chuckled a little. 'I know you never met her and I probably never said ten words about her – and they were all probably bad. But ... she is that bad. I thought she might not be. Might have changed. But she hasn't. Her husband was suspected of being involved with a trafficking ring. They found some bodies, then lost some evidence, the NCA had to step in. It was a whole thing. I can't say too much. But anyway, it was a mess. He was arrested, but is out on bail now. And neither he or Mum are answering my calls. Seems to be a pattern here.' She harrumphed sardonically. 'Anyway, the NCA are still investigating him, but I think they're just as bad. The intel officer in charge of the investigation, Mallory ... I don't trust her. Not a bit. I think she got one of her investigators killed. A woman named Ash. Jesus, Thorsen, I don't like doing this without you. I met up with an old partner, Nasir Hassan. Great guy, would trust him with my life. But he's not you. And I don't know which way is up. You were always so good at that. At reading people, you know? You always kept me straight, tempered me, were always my lighthouse. I miss that. I miss you. And ... I'm sorry. Sorry I wasn't there when you needed me. Sorry I'm not there now.' She let out a long, shaking breath. She laughed a little to herself then. 'Fuck, my conversation with Dahlvig was fun. Bet you can imagine how that went? He didn't blow up on me, which was surprising. But it was more like when your parents tell you they're not angry, just disappointed. Somehow worse. But, you know, I don't regret it. Don't regret coming here. Interpol got involved, and we managed to do some good. Managed to find where they were holding the girls – kids, Thorsen. Dozens of them. It was ... it was bad. But we got to them. Got them out. Not easy. But we did it. And there's this one – God, Thorsen. She's ... She's something. A fighter. Alina. She's amazing. So strong and wilful. So bright. It's been days, but she's already learning English so fast. More words every day. She's staying with me. Or, at least, I'm not letting her out of my sight. The other girls were sent home, to their families. But she has no one. And they wanted her so badly. I don't know why, I can't wrap my head around it. I could use your brain right now, I know that much. She doesn't know either. She's alone, and she's scared. And I'm looking after her. We're still in Interpol's protective custody right now. Just taking a break, getting some fresh air. For Alina. For me. Because … I wanted to call. I've been thinking about you. About how you're doing. I hope you're doing better, and that you've got good people around you. I'd love to hear from you, but I know … I know that's not going to happen. And that's okay. I understand. It's good, you know? You've got to get right. And I want you to get right.' Jamie swallowed, but the lump in her throat wouldn't shift. 'Okay, then …' she said, out of words and suddenly exhausted. 'I … bye …'

And then she lowered the phone and hung up, filling her lungs with the warm summer air that drifted across the mountains.

She watched Alina for another few seconds, the horse getting close, nose extended, Alina's hand flat, presenting the grass to it.

Jamie watched in silence, a smile spreading across her face.

In that moment, everything was okay.

She thought that maybe, just maybe, they'd be okay.

If they could stay in that moment forever. Here. In the open hills, under the blue skies.

But she knew that wasn't to be. That right now, beyond the horizon, black clouds were gathering. And that sooner or later, the skies overhead would darken. The light would fade.

Jamie knew that, deep down.

That, just like always: a storm was coming.

AUTHOR'S NOTE

Whether this is your first or eleventh Jamie novel, thank you for reading! I really hope you enjoyed what was a little bit of a different Jamie book, I think. Writing two, three, or even four novels a year is a lot of work, but it's really, really rewarding, too. The thing I find most interesting about it is how the books change and develop, how their style evolves in line with what I'm reading personally, or even just because as I write, I improve and change as an author, but also my idea of what kind of author I want to be changes.

Over the last year or so, I gained representation with my agent, and have written and agreed a deal to publish a wholly different type of book – a US-set murder mystery that's nothing like these novels. And when I was writing that, it felt great. New, exciting, even. Something different to explore and sink my literary teeth into. But, after finishing it, I realised that, actually, I really missed the Jamie formula. I missed walking in her shoes. And I missed this type of story.

I've written a lot of different types of books over the last decade or so, from romance to science fiction, from fantasy to dystopian, from crime to mystery, and a lot in between. I never really had to consider 'what type of writer' I wanted to be, because as an indie author without a huge following, I was sort of free to do whatever I wanted. But now, especially since working with a publisher, I've had that question asked of me – not directly, but because publishers want several more books like the one you just gave them. Which forces you to consider that: is this the kind of author I want to be? Are these the books I want to write?

I loved writing those more intricate, character-driven stories, but, heck, I'm just going to say it. I like the pulpy action-heavy thrillers too. And so, with this book, I just threw caution to the wind, and told myself I wasn't going to try to limit the pace or the action, I wasn't going to try to meander around inside the character development, too much. I was just going to deliver a slick, fast paced thriller that sort of left the light procedural elements at the door and instead pursued something more exciting. More page-churning and midnight-oil-burning for the reader. Something that couldn't be put down, and which couldn't wait to be picked up.

My goals changed, and my methods did, too. I spent longer planning and working out the beats of the story, ensuring that each chapter was pared down to its cleanest form, so that the story could just flood from the pages when the book was in hand.

In 2021, I left my home of Wales and moved to Canada. Since then, a lot has happened that's pushed me and really shown me a lot about myself. Moving country, leaving friends and family behind, is a pretty harrowing thing. And it really gave me so much perspective, and so much drive. I've loved every moment of what's been a crazy journey, and though it's come to an end, and we're now taking off on the next leg of our big adventure (myself, my partner, and our Welsh collie!), headed for the Spanish hills and whatever fresh experiences await us there, I'll always be grateful for what this place, and the experience, has taught me.

It probably doesn't have a lot to do with writing, but it's shown me a different part of the world, and it's changed my outlook on life. I really have a much clearer understanding of what's important and the type of person I want to be, and I feel like that has a trickle-down effect into my writing.

Lots of writers come to writing much later in life. I was probably about twelve when I decided to be an author. I'm thirty now, and I've written more novels than years I've been on this earth! Most of them were garbage (seventeen-year-olds can't write good novels!), but after all that practice, I feel like I'm finding a groove and a style I really like. And I hope you like it too. I've been meandering, or at least going in circles, trying to figure things out. But now, I feel like we're there. The last ten Jamie novels have been a hoot, and I've loved writing each one of them – and I think the readers have enjoyed them too – but now … now we're levelling up. Now we're changing gears and we're really moving.

That's why this is book one in a new series. It draws a line under everything we've accomplished so far, and it shows itself to the world as something different. I can't wait to finish the next one, and the next one, and bring new characters and stories to life. And I hope that you're ready for that, too.

The next book is out just six weeks after this one. So if you're ready to dive back into Jamie's life, there's not long to wait. And if you *can't* wait at all, then check out the other novels in the series.

Or not. Time is precious, and anyone who spends their time reading my writing … well, I so deeply appreciate that. It's a dream I never thought would come to fruition, and yet, here we are. That people want to read my books is something that still staggers me, but I think my favourite quote from a poem by Alfred, Lord Tennison is apt here: *Theirs not to reason why, Theirs but to do and die.* I take it to mean that sometimes, we don't need to think, we just need to do. And writing is that for me; something I just feel I need to do. I often recite this quote to myself when life seems beyond my control. Just get the old head down and keep moving forward. Charge, Light Brigade.

Who knows what the future holds? Beyond the pursuit of this continued dream, I don't know. And sometimes, that's better, right? I don't know where I'll be in five or ten years, but I hope that might be here, reading more of my ramblings at the end of my books. The Author's Notes are a way for me to unpack each writing stint, obsessive and intense as they are; reflect on everything that's happened during the write, and really just take a moment to breathe and acknowledge you, the reader, and humble myself a little. Because sometimes it's easy to get caught up in what's happening on my side of things, and forget that writing is a complicit act that is given meaning by the presence of someone to read the dang thing.

So, once again, thanks for joining me on this adventure. I'll leave you with the poem in its entirety, in the hope that perhaps it'll give you a little inspiration or courage to carry on when things get tough. If not, heck, it's still a great poem!

THE CHARGE OF THE LIGHT BRIGADE

By Alfred, Lord Tennison

I

Half a league, half a league,
Half a league onward,
All in the valley of Death
　Rode the six hundred.

"Forward, the Light Brigade!
Charge for the guns!" he said.
Into the valley of Death
  Rode the six hundred.

II
"Forward, the Light Brigade!"
Was there a man dismayed?
Not though the soldier knew
  Someone had blundered.
  Theirs not to make reply,
  Theirs not to reason why,
  Theirs but to do and die.
  Into the valley of Death
  Rode the six hundred.

III
Cannon to right of them,
Cannon to left of them,
Cannon in front of them
  Volleyed and thundered;
Stormed at with shot and shell,
Boldly they rode and well,
Into the jaws of Death,
Into the mouth of hell
  Rode the six hundred.

IV
Flashed all their sabres bare,

Flashed as they turned in air
Sabring the gunners there,
Charging an army, while
   All the world wondered.
Plunged in the battery-smoke
Right through the line they broke;
Cossack and Russian
Reeled from the sabre stroke
   Shattered and sundered.
Then they rode back, but not
   Not the six hundred.

V

Cannon to right of them,
Cannon to left of them,
Cannon behind them
   Volleyed and thundered;
Stormed at with shot and shell,
While horse and hero fell.
They that had fought so well
Came through the jaws of Death,
Back from the mouth of hell,
All that was left of them,
   Left of six hundred.

VI

When can their glory fade?
O the wild charge they made!
   All the world wondered.

Honour the charge they made!
Honour the Light Brigade,
   Noble six hundred!

See you on the other side.

Morgan

Read on to discover the opening chapters of *The Mark Of The Dead*, the follow-up to *The Last Light Of Day*.

Find me on Facebook as Morgan Greene Author to stay up to date with the latest news, or join my mailing list on my website at morgangreene.co.uk to receive news of new releases.

ALSO BY MORGAN GREENE

Bare Skin (DS Jamie Johansson 1)
Fresh Meat (DS Jamie Johansson 2)
Idle Hands (DS Jamie Johansson 3)

Angel Maker (DI Jamie Johansson 1)
Rising Tide (DI Jamie Johansson 2)
Old Blood (DI Jamie Johansson 3)
Death Chorus (DI Jamie Johansson 4)
Quiet Wolf (DI Jamie Johansson 5)
Ice Queen (DI Jamie Johansson 6)
Black Heart (DI Jamie Johansson 7)

The Last Light Of Day (The Jamie Johansson Files 1)
The Mark Of The Dead (The Jamie Johansson Files 2)

WHAT'S NEXT FOR JAMIE?

Read on to discover the first three chapters of *The Mark Of The Dead*, the next thrilling instalment in the Jamie Johansson Files!

THE MARK OF THE DEAD

The Mark Of The Dead is the second novel in The Jamie Johansson Files series, and the sequel to *The Last Light Of Day*. With Aram Petrosyan's trafficking operation cut off at the knees, Jamie and Alina are their top target. Retribution must be had, and Petrosyan unleashes upon them a man like no other. The Nhang moves without being seen and kills without mercy. And he's coming for them both.

Can Jamie stay one step ahead of this deadly new adversary? She'll have to use all of the skills at her disposal if she hopes to survive. And with help from old friends and new, she'll once again rise to face the people that want her dead, and stand for those who can't defend themselves.

Evil may never rest, but Jamie Johansson doesn't either. And when they come, she'll be waiting.

Read on to experience the first few chapters of *The Mark Of The Dead*, the nail-biting, rollercoaster second instalment in The Jamie Johansson Files.

CHAPTER
ONE

She stepped from the darkness of the doorway, the sand cold beneath her feet, screwing her eyes up against the bright lights.

The girl knew that this was a fight day. They had given her meat – gristly beef or lamb or who knew what else. Boiled until it was as hard as leather, left bone-in and served in the juices. A cheap cut, given with a stale bread roll.

They only gave her meat on the days she was to fight.

She wanted to refuse it, to push it away, to throw it into the corner of the room they'd been keeping her in. It was maybe five by six feet, no more than a storeroom. She knew that by the holes in the concrete where screws had been, where the outline of shelves still remained, by the stains on the floor left by various cleaning chemicals, and the smells that still lingered.

They gave her a mattress to sleep on, thankfully. A few inches thick. But it kept the sting of the cold earth from her skin when she slept.

When she needed to use the bathroom, a bucket in the corner was her only option. A small sink provided metallic-tasting water, and a means to dispose of her own urine. Thankfully, they took her solid waste away when she banged on the door hard enough. Though it was always without a word, and if she was on her feet when the door opened, they'd shove her back onto her mattress and spit on her. So she learned to stay down. Where they wanted her.

The only time they seemed to want her on her feet at all, was when they wanted her to fight. Was on the days they gave her meat to strengthen her.

She would listen to the din of the crowd build beyond the steel door, her heart growing with it until they both thundered in time.

When the floor was vibrating from the sheer number of bodies in the place, she knew that it was time. That the door was about to open, a man would walk in and slip a noose over her neck, drag her to her feet by it, and then lead her into the blinding sea of lights.

The door opened.

It was time.

When she could finally see again, she was greeted by the familiar sight – a steel cage. Faces beyond it. Laughing, cheering, betting on her life. They drank booze and stuffed their faces with food.

The girl's stomach knotted, first in hunger, then in sickness. These people: they sickened her.

She closed her eyes, not able to look at them as their cheers grew. She knew what that meant, too.

That they were bringing down her opponent. No, not her opponent. The girl they wanted to die. The girl they wanted her to kill.

A girl like her. One stolen and brought to this place.

She swallowed, clenching her fists at her sides. The bandages wrapped around them to stop her knuckles breaking tightened and creaked, stained with blood. Tears came the first few times. But no longer. Now, she knew what she needed to do. She needed to kill. Kill to live.

She had learned how to make it quick. How to make it easy. She had taught herself. But when she did that, they beat her. The men with the noose, the ones that brought her here. They dragged her back into her cell and they threw her down and they beat her. Masters of violence. They knew how hard to hit so that it hurt. So that it hurt for days. But never so badly that she couldn't fight again.

Who this girl was, the one she was supposed to kill, she didn't know.

The girl was just brought down the stairs from the room where they kept them, and shoved under the lights, the cage door closing behind them. She was short. Older. Maybe eighteen or nineteen, even. She had narrow-set eyes and short, thick, black hair, a frightened look on her face.

The girl with the bandages around her knuckles looked away. This was no time for weakness. Weakness meant death. And she was determined to survive.

The cheers kicked up around them, people screaming. Screaming for blood.

The short girl with the black hair cried out, sobbing, mewling, for mercy. For help.

But no help was coming.

And all the girl with the bandaged hands could grant her was a good death.

And so, with the crowd howling like wolves around her, she opened her eyes, lifted her hands, and gave the girl that they had brought her just that.

CHAPTER
TWO

I t was the middle of the night when Alina woke, tangled in clean white cotton bedsheets, the memory-foam cradling her sweat-soaked back. She sucked in a hard breath and sat upright, heart beating hard, hands on her chest, the flicker of those bright, awful lights still dancing in her vision. The ache in her knuckles and the taste of blood in her mouth fading as reality set in and she once again remembered where she was.

There was a thud outside the door and her head whipped around to look at it, just in time to see a dark figure advancing quickly across the room.

Alina gasped as the figure climbed onto the bed and reached for her.

She recoiled instinctively.

'Shh, shh,' the woman said. 'It's okay, it's okay. Just another bad dream. I'm here. You're safe.'

And then Jamie Johansson took the girl in her arms and pulled her in, holding her tightly.

She felt Alina stiff in her grasp, and then melt into her embrace, breathing softly, her olive skin moist with sweat.

They'd been staying in hotels for more than six weeks now, their beds separated by just a few feet of space, but a chasm of separation. Alina's nightmares came every night. And every night she woke. And every night Jamie came to her, and held her.

She didn't know how long it would go on, or if it would ever go away. Jamie's nightmares didn't. She just got less afraid of them. Less afraid of going to sleep. Less afraid of not sleeping.

'I heard something,' Alina whispered then, keeping her cheek pressed to Jamie's ribs. 'Outside the door.'

Jamie turned her head to look at it. 'I'm sure it's nothing,' she said. 'Just the guards.' She stroked her hair gently.

There'd been two private security contractors outside their door twenty-four seven since the night that Jamie and her partner Hassan had broken up that underground fighting ring. Since the Armenians – Aram Petrosyan and his men – had slipped through Interpol's fingers and disappeared into the night.

Interpol were hunting them, but they weren't the type to just turn tail and run. And nor were they the type to get slighted and live with it. What Jamie had done, disrupting their operation ... Julia Hallberg,

Jamie's friend and point of contact at Interpol ... she hadn't minced her words: the Armenians would want retribution. In blood. They'd want Jamie's blood. And they'd want the girl's blood.

They'd tried and failed to get her back twice, and Jamie had killed their men. Now it was a matter of principal. Of vengeance. And of their own brand of justice.

Jamie held Alina tighter. Wishing she could take her away from all this. But Alina was a material witness. She'd experienced their horrors first-hand. And when the time came, she'd have to relive it all, giving statements and legal testimonies. And it was up to Jamie to keep her safe until then.

'I really did hear something,' Alina said, pulling away and looking at Jamie. She glanced at the door then, eyes large, lips quivering, her forehead sheened with sweat.

Jamie ran her fingers through the girl's hair, gently brushing the curled strands from her forehead.

'Alright,' she said, standing up. 'I'll go check.' Though she knew she'd only find her two bodyguards standing there, as always. Hell, one of them probably stamped their foot or dropped their phone or something.

Jamie approached the door and laid a hand on it, twisting the handle.

The lock clicked and light came into the room, but as she did, the door was pulled from her grasp, swinging inwards under the weight of the body slumped against it.

Jamie danced backwards as it flopped onto the floor, the lifeless corpse of one of her security detail, throat opened from ear to ear, eyes staring vacantly at the ceiling.

Alina gasped and leapt from the bed, hiding behind it.

Jamie's pistol was already in her hand, ripped from her holster at her bedside and at the ready.

She steadied herself, listening for any signs of movement, and then peeked, stepping quickly from the shelter of the room and into the corridor.

Her watch glowed on her wrist – three-twelve in the morning.

The hallway was empty except for the second guard, face down about ten feet in front of her, a wide pool of blood spreading from under his body.

'Fuck,' Jamie breathed, turning back and running to the room.

She dragged the body at the threshold into the corridor and then stepped over him, noticing then the strange mark on her door – painted in blood, a smeared and twisted 'S' shape with a split at the top that looked like the maw of a serpent.

But she only let herself get sidetracked for a moment before she darted inside and closed the door, double locking it.

She looked over at Alina, still hiding behind the bed,

and beckoned her from there. 'Come away from the window,' she said, her tone hard enough that she didn't have to say it twice.

Alina rushed towards her, putting an arm around her back as Jamie went to her bedside table and snatched up the two-way radio that the security team had given her. 'This is Primary, come in,' she said, holding the talk button.

A second later, a response came. 'This is Unit Two.' The second pair of close protection officers sitting in an SUV outside. 'Everything okay?'

Jamie resisted the urge to scoff. 'No,' she said, letting out a soft breath. 'Uh, Unit One is … They're down. They're both down.'

'Repeat that?' The alarm in the man's voice was apparent.

'They're both down.' Jamie felt Alina squeeze her tighter. 'They're both fucking dead.'

CHAPTER
THREE

Jamie kept her gun trained on the door until the Unit Two arrived, using their pre-agreed knock, and announced themselves.

Jamie let them in and they held the room until the police, the coroner, forensics, and then Interpol managed to get there.

Jamie didn't know what she expected – a squad of Armenians clad in military gear bursting in to take or kill them? Something like that. But whoever had dispensed with the two armed close protection officers outside the door – ex-military and highly trained themselves – had done so, firstly without waking Jamie and Alina, who were sleeping just through the door. And in such efficient fashion that the two men never managed to get a scream out before they were dealt with – never managed to even lift their radios and call for help.

Jamie played it over and over again in her mind –

how someone could have done that. No shots fired. Just a blade. And then, to draw that ... *thing* on the door? What did it mean?

Nothing good, Jamie thought. Anything drawn on your bedroom door in the blood of your dead bodyguards wasn't going to be good.

But why hadn't they just burst in the room and finished the job?

As Jamie watched Julia Hallberg pause at the threshold to inspect the strange symbol, holding her hand up to trace the swooping lines of the serpent drawn on the wood, it's all she could think about.

Why were she and Alina still alive?

Hallberg lowered her fingers, then hung her head a little. She pushed her hands into the pockets of her slacks, and stepped into the room.

It was gone five in the morning now and light was permeating the sky.

'Jesus,' Hallberg muttered, approaching Jamie. The professional thing to do was a handshake. But they were way past professionality. So Hallberg hugged her.

Jamie returned it.

'You okay?' Hallberg asked, holding her by the shoulders as she pulled away.

Jamie nodded, dipping her head towards Alina, who was standing at her side, staring at the door.

'And how are you holding up?' Hallberg asked her.

Alina looked up at her, and then nodded. 'I'm good.'

It had only been six weeks, but Jamie had been

teaching her English fiercely. There wasn't a whole lot else to do, and Alina was clearly smart. They'd been practicing English, reading together, and watching TV. Jamie had never watched some much TV in her life as she had the last six weeks.

Jamie thought that it gave Alina something to occupy her mind, something to focus on that wasn't what she'd been through. An outlet for her mind.

But Jamie also knew that an outlet for the mind was one thing, but practicing prepositions would never cure the anger she felt. Though Jamie knew a good way of channelling that too.

So, Jamie was teaching her to fight. Not to brawl, or to hurt, or to kill, as she had before. But to control herself, to discipline herself. Jamie's martial art of choice was Tae Kwon Do, but she knew how to box, too, knew some Aikido. It was worth its weight a hundred times over to know how to defend yourself in this world. It had served Jamie well, and though she truly hoped Alina would never need to use the skills Jamie was teaching her, they were important to have.

And she seemed to be learning them even quicker than English. She had a deep-seated desire to do so. To be able to protect herself.

No wonder, Jamie thought. And suddenly, she wanted to hold her.

'Your English is really coming along,' Hallberg said, smiling at her.

'Thank you,' Alina said back. 'I am learning … good.'

'Well,' Jamie corrected her. 'You're learning well.'

'I am learning well,' Alina said.

'Impressive.'

'Im-pressive?' Alina parroted back, then looked at Jamie, not understanding the word.

'It means she thinks you're really smart.'

Alina blushed a little, then looked away.

Hallberg motioned Jamie into the hallway so they could talk, and Jamie followed, gesturing to Alina that she'd be right back. She stepped out over the body now covered by a white sheet, and walked a few steps away from their room.

'You really didn't hear anything?' Hallberg asked as the SOCOs in the hallway documented the scene behind them.

Jamie shook her head. 'No. And I sleep light. Alina woke me up. She has … dreams,' Jamie said, holding her fingers at her temple, 'nightmares. About what happened to her. Every night. She wakes up, sometimes screaming. Other times just sits bolt upright in bed. Scared the hell out of me to begin with.' Jamie sighed.

'Shit,' Hallberg replied. 'I didn't know. Did you get in touch with that psychologist I recommended?'

'Yeah, left a message,' Jamie lied. 'But right now, she just needs … stability. She needs to feel safe. Not someone poking around in her brain.'

Hallberg narrowed her eyes a little, but didn't say

anything. She knew Jamie wasn't fond of the psychic arts. Mystical or practical. 'So that woke you up? Alina's bad dream?'

'Yeah. I went to her. She said she heard a noise outside, but I didn't hear anything.'

'A noise?'

'A thud. A body hitting the ground, I guess.'

'But nothing else? No groans, shouting, footsteps, nothing?'

Jamie just shook her head. 'Whoever did this was a damn ghost.'

Hallberg looked apprehensive. 'I don't like that mark on the door.'

'You recognise it?'

'No, but we'll find out what it is. Though I think it's pretty clear what it means. This is the Armenians, and they did this as a way to show us what they're capable of. That they can get to you wherever, whenever. That thing on the door, a snake or whatever it is – that's a mark of death. You're marked.'

Jamie let out a long breath. 'Brilliant.'

'Mm. Not ideal.'

'No, you're right. It's not ideal. So, what do we do now? We can't stay here, obviously,' Jamie said, tsking and folding her arms.

'No, no …' Hallberg agreed, though she didn't seem to have a better answer.

'What are we supposed to do then?'

Hallberg just met that one with silence.

'Are you any closer to tracking down Aram Petrosyan?'

'We're working on it.'

'I've been a detective longer than you have,' Jamie reminded her. 'Don't feed me lines.'

'Then no. We aren't.'

'Do you know if he's in the country, even?'

'His private plane left a small airfield in Shropshire the morning after the bust at the fighting ring,' Hallberg said. 'But we don't know if he was on it.'

'Great. So then we just sit on our hands, wait for Interpol to *not* catch Petrosyan, and for the ninja-assassin that murdered two CPOs last night to come back for Alina and me? Is there any point even locking the fucking doors?'

'I can tell you're frustrated,' Hallberg said.

'Something like that. I'm sorry, I'm not trying to take it out on you. I just ... I'm tired. And I hate running.'

Hallberg seemed deep in thought then. 'Have you stopped to consider just why Alina is so important?'

'Because she can identify Petrosyan,' Jamie answered swiftly.

Hallberg sort of shrugged. 'Maybe,' she said. 'But what would that matter? She wouldn't know his name. And they kept the fights going, didn't they, even after she had escaped and she was in custody.'

'What's your point?'

'I don't know,' Hallberg said, sighing a little. 'I just ... We managed to find the families of the other girls, managed to contact people through their embassies, got them home ... for the most part. But Alina ...'

'What are you getting at?' Jamie asked her, a little defensive now.

'I'm not getting at anything. Just that we don't know anything about Alina. That her name didn't come up with any matches anywhere. The name of the village she gave us ... we can't find that, either. There's no record of any epidemic sickness or death like she described ...'

'You think she's lying about that? Lying about her parents dying, her grandfather being killed? About being abducted and trafficked?'

'I can see you're tired,' Hallberg said bluntly then, 'so I won't read into your tone too much.'

Jamie collected herself. 'Sorry, just ... a sore spot. I've killed and almost died for this girl and I've been with her for six weeks straight. I think I know her pretty well by now.'

Hallberg smiled just a little. 'Yeah, no, it's probably nothing. Just my brain. Doesn't like things remaining ... unproven. Comes with the job, you know? Georgia is still rural in places. Really rural. It's not surprising that she could have slipped through the net.'

But the seed was planted, and whether Hallberg rationalised it away or not, Jamie knew that was going to niggle at her.

'There's no point you and Alina staying here, now. Why don't you go back and ask her to pack up her things. You can come with me. We'll get some breakfast, look for another place for you.'

'More protective custody?'

'It's pretty much all we can do until we have a case that we can prosecute.'

Jamie nodded slowly.

'We'll close the circle even further. No one will know where you are this time.'

'You said that last time,' Jamie muttered, turning back to the room.

'Hey,' Hallberg called. 'We'll get them. I promise.'

Jamie didn't acknowledge the words just went into the room and told Alina to pack up her things.

As she loaded socks into her duffle bag, she glanced up, seeing Hallberg inspecting the serpent drawn in blood on their door once more. And as much as the symbol scared Jamie, the look of apprehension and worry on Hallberg's face … that scared her more.

ENJOYING SO FAR?

The Mark Of The Dead is out in October 2023.

Thank you so much for joining Jamie and I on this adventure. I sincerely hope you've enjoyed it, and are looking forward to the next one. But if you can't wait, or you want to see how the story all began, there are ten Jamie Johansson novels out already, chronicling her story from her first murder case while working for the London Met, through to some truly harrowing cases set in the heart of a wild and brutal Sweden.

You can find them on Amazon, available in paperback and on Kindle.

If you'd like to stay up to date with everything Jamie and the other novels I've written, you can find me on Facebook as Morgan Greene Author, or you can visit my website at morgangreene.co.uk and join my mailing list.

Printed in Great Britain
by Amazon